DEFINITELY (MAYBE) DATING

LAUGH OUT LOUD OPPOSITES ATTRACT ROMANTIC COMEDY

MARINA ADAIR

THE ADAIR GROUP

ALSO BY MARINA ADAIR

The Eastons

Chasing I Do

Definitely, Maybe Love

Summer Affair

Single Girl in the City

(coming 2022)

Faux Beau

(coming 2022)

Romcom Novels

Situationship

(coming 2022)

RomeAntically Challenged

Hopeless Romantic

Romance on Tap (novella)

Sweet Plains, Texas series

Tucker's Crossing

Blame it on the Mistletoe (novella)

Nashville Heights series

Promise Me You

Sequoia Lake series

It Started with A Kiss

Every Little Kiss

Destiny Bay series
Last Kiss of Summer

Like the First Time

Heroes of St. Helena series
Need You for Keeps

Need You for Always

Need You for Mine

St. Helena Vineyard series
Kissing Under the Mistletoe

Summer in Napa

Autumn in the Vineyard

Be Mine Forever

From the Moment We Met

Sugar, Georgia series
Sugar's Twice as Sweet

Sugar on Top

A Taste of Sugar

This is a work of fiction. Names, characters, organizations, places, events, and incidents are either products of the author's imagination or are used fictitiously.

Text copyright © 2021 Marina Adair

Excerpt from *Faux Beau* copyright © 2021 by Marina Adair

Excerpt from *Summer Affair* copyright © 2021 by Marina Adair

Excerpt from *Chasing I Do* copyright © 2016 by Marina Adair

All rights reserved.

No part of this book may be reproduced, or stored in a retrieval system, or transmitted in any form or by any means, electronic, mechanical, photocopying, recording, or otherwise, without express written permission of the author and copyright owner of this book.

ISBNs: 978-1-947591-17-2

978-1-947591-16-5

Cover design by Lucy Rhodes of Render Compose

http://www.rendercompose.com

Headshot by Tosh Tanaka

1

Piper Campagna knew better than to tempt Fate.

Acting as the Ansel Adams of love for even a single wedding was as risky as blow-drying her hair in the shower. It wasn't that she didn't love the idea of love or even dream about seeing something so beautiful aimed in her direction. Once upon a time, Piper had given up everything in her quest for unconditional love only to wind up broke, homeless, and completely alone.

Nope, as far as she was concerned, happily ever after was about as realistic as Prince Charming riding in on a Pegasus.

She'd been to exactly five weddings in her lifetime. All her mother's. And all but one ended before the photos were developed. Making Piper the last person on the planet to take a resident photographer position at one of Portland's up-and-coming wedding venues.

Yet there she was, about to shoot a highly publicized engagement party for a local celebrity family—pretending to be the right person for the job. As if she truly believed in something as laughable as forever. She wasn't sure what that said about her, other than she was willing to do anything to land this job, even if it meant faking it.

Piper pressed the palm of her hand to her forehead and groaned loudly. She hated fakes.

Apparently, Fate agreed because just as the fairy tale of a wedding venue started to come into view through her cracked windshield, a guttural groan rattled the car. POSH—her Piece of Shit Honda—was telling anyone who'd listen that she needed more than duct tape and prayer to handle the steep hill and hairpin turns.

"Come on, girl, don't fail me now." Piper lovingly rubbed the dashboard.

The engine gave a low hum as it downshifted, pulling through the worst of the bend, handling the tight curve like a pro. POSH might have a junkyard past, but she was scrappy as hell and had an aftermarket gear-shift knob that was shaped like brass knuckles. When shit got real, POSH rallied. Breakups, breakdowns, letdowns, broken promises, and even a handful of impulsive decisions that nearly broke the bank, yet that car was the most reliable thing in Piper's life. Over 150,000 miles of shared history.

That's 150,000 miles of survival.

When Piper spotted the minefield of potholes ahead, her first reaction was to slam on the brakes. As a former rebel, she might do a little roaring and rumbling when cornered, but she knew when to push forward and when to concede. Yet as the steering tightened beneath her hands—jerking the wheel hard to the left with a force equal to Goliath playing the Hulk in a game of tug-of-war, with POSH acting as the rope—Piper's stubborn side kicked in.

"Not today, Fate. Not today!" Pulse accelerating, hands slick with perspiration, Piper slammed on the brakes and tried to strong-arm the steering into submission. She'd had plenty of experience with strong-arming, which was likely why she was still single.

"Shit!" Her hot-headed impulse backfired, and instead of braking on a dime, POSH, with her bare-tread spare and duct-taped chassis, broke traction. The back tires lost grip, spinning and kicking up gravel and dust, the car fishtailing into the oncoming lane.

Thankfully, there were no other cars on the road. Just narrow and windy with nothing but dirt and gravel to slow her down. And trees. Lots and lots of trees. Big ones, little ones, enormous ones with trunks the size of water towers.

She skidded off the road onto the shoulder and on a direct course with a pothole the size of the Death Star. There was a large white oak, its gnarled lurk swaying in the wind with the force of a batter swinging for a home run.

Ignoring her rising panic, Piper reached beside her for the e-brake and, channeling the tough-girl attitude that had helped her survive her teen years, she lifted the lever, smooth and steady. POSH released a loud pop, followed by some rhythmic thumping that beat hard in tempo with her heart. The car slowly decelerated, rolling off the road, finally coming to a stop inches from the oak tree, so close the leaves scratched back and forth across the hood.

She closed her eyes and dropped her forehead against the steering wheel, no longer judging Snow White for her hysterical reaction to trees. Allowing exactly one minute to collect herself, she took in a deep breath.

It took an additional three for her hands to stop shaking, but that was from frustration. At least, that was the story she was sticking to.

Ignoring the stench of singed rubber and desperation filling the cab, she popped the hood, then opened the door. Even before she got out of the car, she knew the power steering was shot. Confirming her suspicions, she let out an impatient sigh and made her way to the car's trunk. She grabbed the tire iron, because the belt was the least of her problems. POSH was sporting a blown back tire and, while she could technically drive the last mile uphill without power steering, no amount of tenacity could make up for a flat tire.

As if her day wasn't challenging enough, Fate sent in her official RSVP to the party, by way of a streak of lightning which cut through the inky dusk sky.

One Mississippi. Two Mississip—

The ground rumbled under the boom of thunder. The wind picked up, plastering her dress against her legs and whipping her hair around.

"Is that all you got?" Piper hollered, waving the tire iron at the sky, which was turning different shades of fury and brimstone.

Suddenly, it stopped, and an eerie stillness moved in, surrounding her as static crackled in the evening air. Thunder and lightning she could handle. It was the quiet before the storm that was the most unsettling. Knowing it was only a matter of time before the drops began to fall, she grabbed the tire iron and went to work on the lug nuts.

Ten minutes, three grease stains, and a few choice words later, she succeeded in loosening half. The other half were stubborn little assholes that wouldn't budge.

"I'm small, but I'm scrappy," she said, shucking her impractical shoes to stand on the tire iron. She gave a few bounces, willing it to budge, when another streak of lightning reached across the darkening sky, exploding so close to her car that every hair on her body became electrified.

"Lightning doesn't scare me!" she shouted over the rustling trees.

Neither did Fate. Piper had taken on tougher opponents and

survived to tell the story. Plus, fear clashed with the ballbuster vibe she'd worked so hard to perfect. Not to mention, too much was riding on tonight for anything to go awry.

Not only was the beautiful bride Piper's new boss, but her fiancé was also an agent to the stars. So the guest list read like a Who's Who in Portland—the exact kind of people Piper usually went out of her way to avoid.

However, circumstances had changed, and Piper need to adapt, so she went back to work on the flat. Within minutes, stray strands of hair clung to her skin, and smudges of brake fluid covered the hem of her dress.

She was an utter mess. And no closer to changing her tire.

Refusing to give up, she removed her blazer and placed it gently inside the car, then propped her knee against the fender and shoved. Up and down, and back and forth. She worked the tire iron as if more than just her pride depended on it. And she was making headway, creating a good rhythm for herself, when she heard a loud sound rip through the air.

"Shit!" She shot up, her hands going to cover her backside, her mouth gaping open.

She didn't need to look to know that she had blown out the back of her fitted "wedding photographer approved" work dress. Praying the draft made it seem worse than it actually was, she glanced behind her.

"Shit, shit, shit!"

It was bad. Pink silk with black hearts bad. And the zipper looked like it had jumped the track and split from her lower back to right below the lace waistband of her panties.

She reached behind her to unzip the dress, hoping she could somehow fix the rip, but the zipper was stuck. She tugged. And when that didn't work, she tugged while hopping around.

"I get it!" she yelled at the sky. "Message received. Now go away so I can make my own destiny."

Destiny. She snorted. Yet another thing she didn't believe in. Every decision she'd made up to that point had been hers and hers alone. Something she normally prided herself on. But today, it left her feeling vulnerable and alone. And as she took in the grease stains on her hands and bare feet, Piper knew she needed help.

Admission was the hardest part.

But with three months' rent on the line, Piper was willing to do just about anything. Even if it meant phoning in a favor.

She dialed Jillian Conner, wedding cake–designer extraordinaire, the person who helped Piper land this job, and the only soul she knew at the party besides the bride.

Jillian answered on the first ring.

"Piper, oh my god, where are you?" Jillian's voice came through the phone in a hushed whisper. "The mother of the groom has been asking for you."

"I'm almost there." Piper peered over the hood of her car to the historic mansion perched on the hill in front of her.

Located in the prestigious West Hills, Belle Mont House was three stories of Portland royalty, with extensive grounds and five large entertaining rooms, including a grand salon and conservatory which captured some of the most captivating views of the city and Mount Hood. It was a premiere destination for weddings, corporate parties, and highbrow events.

No family was quite as highbrow as the Eastons. Groom Gage Easton and Bride Darcy Kincaid were the couple of the night.

"Like at the door almost?"

Piper hadn't known Jillian all that long, but she could tell the woman was beyond stressed. "Like my tire blew out at the bottom of Belle Mont Drive."

"This is bad. So, so incredibly bad. Most of the family has

already arrived, and Margo is demanding to know when pictures are going to begin."

"The party doesn't start for another hour," Piper stated, but a bad feeling began to grow in the pit of her belly. She had met the matriarchal dictator of the Easton family once, at her initial interview. Getting struck by lightning would be less painful that going head-to-head with Margo Easton.

"The guests arrive in another hour, but most of the family is already here."

"You've got to be kidding me!" Piper looked up at the sky and squinted at the tiny molecules of rain flittering down. A drop landed on the tip of her nose.

She gave Fate a little wave of the finger—her middle one.

"Not even one bit." Jillian lowered her voice to barely a whisper. "Margo went over Darcy's head and told the family to get here an hour early. Darcy wasn't even dressed when Margo busted in with her closest friends in tow looking for tea. Now the woman is ranting about taking a picture of the entire family in the rose garden to use for this year's Christmas card."

Rain dotted the windshield and ground, and that bad feeling grew until Piper could feel it pressing against her ribs. "She does know that a storm is coming, right?"

Jillian laughed. "I don't think Zeus himself could take on Margo when she's like this. So please tell me you're going to arrive before she begins aiming her death glare my direction," Jillian begged. "With everything Darcy and Gage went through to get here, today has to be perfect. And that means keeping Margo appeased and away from Darcy. And since Darcy's my bestie, that task apparently falls to me. When I volunteered to be Margo's keeper, I had forgotten what nightmares are truly made of."

Piper had firsthand experience with nightmares who walked

in the daylight. She wasn't scared of a five-foot-nothing sourpuss in pearls. "She isn't that bad."

"She is. Which reminds me, are you wearing the dress?" she asked, as if Piper had a choice in the matter. Which she most definitely did not.

She looked down at the designer dress Jillian had made her try on—then buy. It was a little dustier—and a whole lot draftier—than it had been earlier, but with a few safety pins, a wet wipe, and lint roller, it would do. "I'm wearing the dress."

"Thank God. Margo told me everyone needs to be in appropriate attire, even the staff."

"My closet was filled with appropriate photographer attire. Some of it is even press-corps approved. Yet, I'm dressed like I'm going to high tea." She tugged at the neckline and signed. "Or the Queen's funeral."

"Yeah, well, if it goes with pearls, it's Margo approved," Jillian said. "She's driving me crazy. So when I say I need you here now, I need you here *now*."

Piper took in the tire iron extending from a lug nut, then the tempest on the horizon. She calculated that she had less than fifteen minutes before the late summer drizzle turned into a Portland downpour. "I can fix the tire, but it will take time. Can you come get me? I'm just at the bottom of the hill."

There was a long pause, long enough that perspiration beaded down her spine.

"God, I wish I could. But today, of all days, my son, who I had to bring along, decided he's suddenly scared of dogs and one of the brothers brought his wife's dog, who peed in my purse. Not on it—in it. Then there's the hundred-and-twenty-six mini cakes I have to frost before Margo decides my dessert isn't quite right and does it herself."

Piper eyed the distance from her car to the top of the hill. It was like being stuck in the middle of the ocean in a life raft with only a whisk to paddle to shore.

Suck it up, buttercup.

"I'll figure it out. I promise."

"Before the storm hits. God, Piper, please tell me you'll get here before the storm hits."

It would be close, but she could make the hike.

"Fate herself couldn't stop me." Especially if it meant disappointing Jillian.

The two had met at the community park over the summer, during team pictures for the local Tiny Tykes football league. Piper had been conned into taking the team photo, and Jillian had volunteered enough cake pops to feed a small army. They'd bonded over the coach being a ginormous prick, which led them to the conclusion that all men were ginormous pricks, and—several cake pops and a juice box later—they'd cemented a budding friendship.

A friendship Piper had come to treasure. She hadn't had many friends growing up. Especially ones like Jillian, who not only had her life together but also cared enough about Piper to stand in her corner if the need arose.

That's because you're difficult, a little voice said from deep inside. A voice that sounded a whole lot like her mother.

Driven, Piper corrected. *Okay, stubborn.* Two qualities that had saved her life more than once.

With an unpredictable alcoholic for a mother and a chaotic childhood, Piper was weary of people's intentions. Moving from town to town, her mom burning through husbands like most people went through chips—you can't just have one—it made it hard to cement connections. Even harder to trust that the relationship could go the distance. So, she built walls. Big, impenetrable walls that were nearly impossible to scale.

But while she might be afraid to let people in, a little

thunder and lightning didn't even rank on her list of things to run screaming from. If she had to trudge up that hill to get to the party on time, then trudging she'd do.

Piper opened the back door and pulled a pair of black combat boots off the floorboard and slipped them on. She grabbed her blazer—back-up clothes just in case the dress didn't make it—and was reaching for her camera bag when Jillian squealed. "Oh wait! I forgot. One of the brothers took an Uber from the airport and the driver just left. I can have him double back to pick you up."

Piper dropped her coat back in the car and climbed inside to avoid the rain. "You are a goddess. Tell him if he gets to me before the ground turns to mud, I'll double his tip. And Jillian, thank you. I so owe you."

"Friday night is girls' night. No excuses this time, and the first round is on you."

"Done and done." Piper disconnected.

Minutes ticked by with no sign of the hired car.

"Depending on a friend is not the same as being dependent," Piper said aloud, then pulled out a tub of emergency peanut butter from her purse. Because if there was ever an emergency, pink silk with black hearts was it.

And—*ah*, man—just the crinkling of the cellophane wrapper was enough to send all kinds of good feels to the brain. And then, because a jar of emergency peanut butter deserved some chocolate, she dusted off her hands and grabbed a fist of candy kisses from her camera bag.

The savory smell of peanuts and salt filled the car as she dipped the first kiss in and popped it in her mouth.

"Oh my gawd!" She sighed, closing her eyes to savor the momentary bliss. She hadn't eaten since breakfast, and it was fast approaching dinnertime. With the setback of the flat and the lack of an assistant, her next meal would likely be well after midnight.

When she ran out of kisses, she dipped her finger in the jar and scooped out a mouthful, then licked it off.

She was on her third pass when the sound of gravel crunching under tires came up behind her. Piper turned to find a sleek black car headed her way.

"Thank you, Jillian," she whispered, because help had finally arrived—and in Piper's world, that wasn't always the case.

With one last dip of the finger, she hopped out of the car and into the rain. Raising the jar in greeting, she gave an embarrassed little wave. The car got closer, and she sucked the remaining gooey goodness off her finger and stepped toward the road when—

"Holy shit!"

The sedan roared right past her with all four hundred of its horses powering at full tilt and nearly taking her out in the process. The car was so close it created a wind tunnel intense enough to rip the jar right from her hands. And cover her from head to toe in a fine speckling of mud.

"What the hell?" Piper yelled as the brake lights blared a steady red and the car skidded to a stop a few yards ahead in the middle of the road.

Piper grabbed her blazer and tied it around her waist, then ran to the car. She'd barely reached the driver's side when the window slowly rolled down, exposing the driver within.

He was big and muscled, his body filling all the space in the car. Under the dome lights she could see that his suit was freshly pressed, his dark wavy hair carefully manicured. He had the look of a man who controlled his world.

And he was gorgeous. The kind of gorgeous that made people want to stop and stare. Not that Piper was staring. Nope.

She didn't do gorgeous. And she most certainly did not do suits who nearly ran her over.

"Are you okay?" he asked, his voice low and gravelly.

"Do I look okay?" she asked, because he looked as if he was about to climb out of the car and see for himself.

"You look like someone who was standing in the middle of the road during a storm, at dusk, wearing black," he said. "What? Were you playing chicken or staging a car heist?"

"No, I was waiting for you."

This seemed to amuse him. He looked at her through the rolled down window and grinned—a big, smug grin that pissed her off. "You were waiting for me?"

"Don't flatter yourself," she said, wondering how he'd managed, in sixty seconds, to get under her skin. "Just looking for a ride."

"Well, hop in."

She glanced down at her mud and rain-soaked dress, then back to his expensive leather interior. "I'll ruin your seats."

"I did nearly run you over."

"You might not want to admit that," she advised. "Some people are jerks and would use it against you."

"Are you one of those people?"

"A jerk? Usually." She made a big show of dusting off her dress, which only made a bigger mess. "But life is too short to deal with lawyers."

His lips twitched. Not quite a smile, but enough to let Piper know it was at her expense. "Noted." His voice went soft. "But seriously, are you okay?"

His genuine concern deflated any hostility she'd been clinging to. She held her arms out to the side and when she looked down, she nearly laughed. "Well, my dress is ruined."

He looked at her over the half-rolled window and—sweet Mary, mother of God—his eyes were the exact color of the sky, a deep stormy blue with bright specks, like the lightning moments ago. Then there was the carefully crafted five-o'clock shadow.

"And yet, you're smiling," he said.

"My usual MO would be to swing the tire iron in your direction."

That twitch was back, and this time it exposed two double-barreled dimples that sparked all kinds of tingles. Their eyes held for a long moment, as if he was trying to figure out what to do with her. It was a look she was used to.

"I guess today's my lucky day."

"Mine is looking up," she said. "If you hadn't stopped, I never would have made it to the party on time."

"You also wouldn't show up looking like your dress fell victim to a finger-painting drive-by."

"Who doesn't love a good finger painting?" She lifted a single, sexy brow.

"I guess it depends on who's the canvas."

Not sure how she felt about that or the growing tingles, she said, "I'm Piper. And I'm late."

"I'm Josh, and I guess I'm your driver." He opened the door and stepped out into the rain, reaching out his hand.

"You're going to get soaked." When he just shrugged, she tried to hold one of her bags over his head, but she was too short.

"I'll hop in when you do."

She considered this, gauged his level of seriousness, and when he didn't budge—not even when the rain pebbled his button-down she gave in. "Do you have a towel or something in the truck, even a garbage bag to protect your seats?"

"If I said yes, would you climb in the car?"

"As soon as you produce the towel."

He walked right past her and popped his truck. He came out

of the trunk with a wool throw that had been protecting his spare. "Voilà." He handed it to her. "You headed to the party?"

"I'm shooting it." She lifted the camera bag, then looked at his still outstretched hand. "I would shake, but my hands are covered with—"

"Peanut butter," he said, and something playful lit his voice. "I saw."

Well, wasn't that embarrassing. She wondered what else he'd seen. The way his eyes held steadfast, almost as if he was fighting the urge to veer south, told her he'd most likely seen some pink and black silk.

Oh, lucky day!

"I'd offer you some but..." She pointed over her shoulder to the peanut butter–sized roadkill on the ground.

"You're mourning the peanut butter but not the dress?"

"I have other clothes in my bag. But that was my emergency peanut butter," she said.

"That would make me the jerk." He moved to open the passenger door when she reached for the back door. This seemed to amuse him, because he smiled. At her. As if their meeting was serendipitous. "How can I make it up to you?"

"How good are you with zippers?"

2

"Beg your pardon?"

Josh Easton was rarely, if ever, caught off guard. His ability to anticipate a person's every move was what made him so effective in the courtroom. But nothing about this woman was expected.

After the past few moments, Josh found it somehow refreshing.

And sexy, he had decided. Did he mention curvy? Even beneath the conservative black dress, he could tell she had one hell of a body. But it was her mouth that drew him in. Full and lush with a whole lot of 'tude. Josh didn't normally do 'tude, but this woman wore it well.

Then there were those eyes, more green than brown, and as close to bedroom eyes as he'd ever seen. Making the part of Josh which had felt suffocated since the day his dad had passed want to answer that he was a zipper grandmaster. Especially if she was referring to the zipper that started below the hint of partially hidden ink on the back of her neck and ran the length of her.

But the other part, the one that knew all actions had consequences, caused him to hesitate. Because while Josh prided himself on satisfying a lady's needs, the last thing *he* needed was to accidentally undress Darcy's photographer.

"My dress is a disaster and has to go, but the zipper is stuck." She reached behind her back and tugged at the zipper, which did amazing things to her front. It also sent her bags tumbling around her. "See my problem?"

Oh, he saw all right. Just like he saw a flash of neon pink lace.

"I got a little overzealous trying to change my tire and, well, *whoops*."

A pretty spectacular whoops if you asked him. In fact, one well-timed tug of that zipper and the entire dress would fall off her shoulders, showing him if she liked to match her bra to her panties.

"I know I'm late, but I can't stroll in late *and* looking like I slept in the gutter," she said. "Not that I'm late. I guess people started showing up early. So even though I'm technically on time, I'm the one somehow arriving late."

With a smile, she climbed in and closed the back door. Sighing, Josh got back into the driver's seat. There was flurry of bags and fabric rustling behind him, and the next time she spoke she was in the back seat—of his car. Making herself right at home.

"And don't get any ideas. I wouldn't ask for your help, much less get in your car, but I hate being late and Jillian vouched for you. So we'll have to make this fast." She scooted herself to the middle of the seat and twisted until her back was facing him. Long, soft brown waves with chunky dark-blue streaks spilled down past her waist. She glanced over her shoulder, and those light-hazel pools hit his and he caught a flash of something. The teensiest of diamonds pierced her nose. "So about those zipper skills?"

Right.

Josh cleared his throat. "You're going to change here?"

"I can change outside, but with my luck today, Satan's Keeper would somehow see," she said, reaching back to slide her hair over one shoulder. The zipper started at the base of her neck and ran well past her rear.

"Satan's Keeper?" he asked, his laugh a bit strangled.

"The mother of the groom. God, she's a head case. You know, one of those holier-than-thou types who can't help but stick their nose in other people's business."

Oh, he knew. Knew the woman intimately. Although Josh should be offended about the nickname for his mother, he couldn't help but laugh.

"Zipper," she repeated. In case that wasn't clear enough, she turned all the way around with her feet tucked under, her back completely facing him.

Josh moved a stray lock of hair out of the way and reached for the zipper. It was ridiculously small compared to his hands, and he moved it less than an inch when he fumbled. Big time.

WTF? Seeing the tip of her tattoo, which was seductively inked at the base of her neck, turned his hands to meat cleavers. Granted, with his recent workload, he hadn't had a whole lot of time to date. But he hadn't been out of the game *that* long.

He wiggled it some more, adding some pressure, until he heard a tiny tear. "I'm afraid I'll rip the dress if I pull any harder."

One slim shoulder rose and fell casually, showing a bit more of that tattoo he was suddenly desperate to unveil. "I don't care. I'm never wearing it again. Not really my style, you know?"

No, he didn't. But he'd like to.

"When I'm working, I'm more function over fashion, and there is nothing functional about silk and heels. But I was told there was a"—she tossed up some air quotes—"*specific* attire for today's event."

"Let me guess, Satan's Keeper?" he asked, but he already knew the answer. Which meant she really hadn't a clue as to who he was. Jillian may have vouched for him, but he had a feeling whomever Jillian vouched for, it wasn't an Easton.

Everything about her was a contradiction. From her designer dress and combat boots to her collection of mismatched Mary Poppins bags. Then there was that mysteriously delicate diamond that kept flashing his way.

"I actually don't think she's all that bad," she admitted. "More bark than bite. Did you have to deal with her today?"

"Not yet."

"Some might call you lucky then."

Lucky wasn't exactly how he felt right now. Tempted was more like it. And Josh was rarely, if ever, tempted by trouble. And this girl had trouble written all over her.

He tugged again, his knuckles brushing against her soft skin, but the zipper wouldn't budge. So he slipped his fingers beneath the hem of the fabric, and when they made contact, she shivered.

He held still, and so did she.

"Are you cold?" he asked.

"I'll be fine as soon as I get out of this dress."

Josh could count on a single hand the number of times he'd helped a woman out of her dress and didn't sleep with her.

"How long have you been doing this?" she asked, giving an impatient little wiggle, and Josh began to doubt he'd be okay after this. But follow-through had been ingrained in him since he was a kid, and because he took pride in being a hands-on kind of guy, he pushed forward.

"Undressing women?" he teased, sliding the zipper back to the top. He gave it another jiggle and—*look at that*—the teeth threaded back into place. Maybe he hadn't lost his touch after all.

"No." She laughed right as the zipper gave way, sliding effortlessly beneath her first vertebrae, then the second. Before he could help himself, it went past being helpful and turned into more of an exploratory effort, exposing enough silky skin until finally—the tattoo. Which was incredibly hot.

Strange, because Josh wasn't generally a tattoo kind of guy, but this one on this woman was all kinds of perfection. It was simply the letter F, but nothing about it was simple. Swirly and feminine lines circled it, making the letter look more like a bold work of art than a part of the alphabet.

"Nice tattoo."

"Thanks." One word. Short and sweet.

"What does it stand for?" His brother Owen had a dozen tattoos, and each had a unique meaning. They represented everything from a stage in his life to the death of their father. Some people are like Owen, while others get tattoos on a spring-break trip to Cabo with their sorority sisters. Tattoo Girl didn't look the sorority type, which made him think it had a deeper meaning. "Francesca?"

"What?"

"The F. Does it stand for Francesca?"

She glanced over, clearly offended. "Do I look like a Francesca? Plus, I told you my name. Piper."

"I once dated a Francesca. Senior year of college. She was an Italian exchange student."

"Lucky you."

He laughed. "Okay, not Italian then. And if not Francesca, maybe Frenchie?"

"If I told you it stood for *none of your effing business*, would you kick me out of your car?"

He burst out laughing. It wasn't often that people put him in his place instead of kissing his ass. The title Assistant District Attorney commanded respect and his last name made him an instant celebrity in most people's eyes. She didn't know either, but he didn't think it would matter. She didn't seem to be easily impressed by accolades.

"Well played," he said.

"Easy target."

"Thanks for the honest feedback."

"How long have you been a chauffeur?"

"What?" Josh's fingers stilled because, suddenly, so much of the past few minutes started to make sense. Piper had made an assumption—a very logical assumption—when he'd pulled over that he was her driver, likely sent by Jillian. That assumption gave her the security to climb into his car.

Making him the ass in this situation.

He needed to clarify some things before her real driver pulled up and she discovered Josh was, in fact, the eldest offspring of Satan's Keeper. Even worse, he was one of those lawyers she loathed so much.

"To be honest, you're my first ride," he began.

"It's my first day too," she interrupted. Hands pressed to her sternum to hold the dress in place, she twisted to look at him over her shoulder. "Never in a million years would I have imagined seeing the title 'wedding photographer' and my name in the same bio, but if tonight goes smoothly, I'll have to order new business cards. And maybe a bottle of champagne to celebrate some long overdue steady work. God, I could really use some steady right now."

"It's not all that it's cracked up to be," he said, because his world was steady all the time. In fact, driving strangers around seemed like a hell of a lot more fun than being another cog in a machine that was severely damaged. Especially if his fares looked even half as good as this one.

Piper shifted, the movement causing the fabric to do some shifting of its own.

Eyes up, eyes up, eyes up...

Except his eyes drifted down with the dress, lower and lower until he caught a glimpse of bright-pink lace with black hearts. That answered that.

"You done?" One brow rose in reprimand. "Or am I back to wielding the tire iron?"

He removed his hands. "Done."

"Then, eyes forward or lose them."

He laughed. "You're the one stripping in my back seat."

"It's called looking professional. And every time your gaze strays, there goes ten bucks off your tip." She snapped her fingers to demonstrate just how fast his money would disappear. Without another word, she ducked down to retrieve something from her bags on the floorboard.

"So you're a professional?" he asked, pulling onto the road amid the rustling coming from his back seat. "Maybe I should be tipping you."

Her head popped up. "You couldn't afford me. Plus, I'm already late, I can't show up late *and* covered in mud."

Her dress flew over the passenger seat, landing on his shoulder and partially covering his head.

"What the hell?" He glanced in the rearview mirror and caught a flash of skin before she squeaked.

"There goes another ten."

"Another ten? I thought the first one was a warning. More of a stating of the rules."

"Who says, 'a stating of the rules'?" she asked in her best Josh impression, making him sound like one of the many pompous Neanderthals he worked with at the courthouse.

"A lot of people," he pointed out. "And I don't sound like that."

Her face appeared from between the seats, and she gifted him a smart-ass smile. "If you say so, Jeeves."

"How do you know Jillian?" he asked to the flurry of material behind him.

"We met at her son's football practice. I was taking the team photos," she said. The sound of rustling and squeaking leather made his attention return to the rearview mirror. Her arms were sticking out of a vintage rock T-shirt, and her head had yet to surface. "When she heard the owner of Belle Mont House was looking for a resident photographer, she recommended me. By the way, that's another ten."

"How do you know I looked?" His eyes had been dutifully back on the road long before she had come up for air.

"You just told me," she said as one of her legs poked through the center console. A very long and shapely leg, with sparkly, pink-tipped toes that peeked out the foot hole of her black jeans.

Her foot moved this way and that as she tugged on the pants, her toes tickling his arm one moment, then kicking him in the rib, giving Josh a clear picture of exactly how much navigating was going on in his back seat. He told himself not to look, that whatever was going on in the back seat was none of his business. Her current state of dress—or undress as it may be—no longer required his attention. And wasn't that a damn shame.

"Seriously?" She laughed. "At this rate you're going to owe me money."

"What? My eyes were firmly on the..." He paused because, *damn,* they had been on the rearview mirror, watching the way the letters on her vintage rock T-shirt curved around her chest. "I like 4 Non Blondes, so sue me."

"Really?" she said, her innocent gasp making it clear she knew that he was full of shit. Then she was in motion, spinning around in his back seat looking for something when—*would you look at that*—his rearview mirror had an incredible view of her rear.

It was either a case of *'Objects in the mirror are closer than they appear*' or those black jeans hugged her in all the right places. Tough Girl had one of those completely cuppable, heart-shaped asses that Josh wouldn't mind swaying in his direction.

"Found it!" She plopped back down and blew her hair out of her eyes. "I took you as more of a Michael Bublé fan."

"What's wrong with Bublé? My mom listens to Bublé, so when we go to dance lessons on Wednesdays, I listen to Bublé."

"That's sweet." Her foot reappeared between the seats, propped up on the console while she laced those steel-toed boots, which went over the hip-hugging jeans and all the way up past her calves. "You still lost ten bucks for checking out my ass when I was looking for my car keys, but you sound like a good son."

"There was *literally* no place else to look."

"How about the road?" she suggested. "Or watching your tip float away?"

Josh couldn't care less about the fifty bucks. He was more interested in the sexy stripper in the back seat wearing a pair of black jeans fashionably shredded in strategic places, giving him a peek of silky skin every time she moved, an equally black T-shirt, and matching boots that were just about the sexiest thing he'd ever seen. She slipped a black blazer over the T-shirt, hiding the band's name and logo, and adding some buttons to her otherwise tough-girl vibe.

Damn, she was hot. Not like the buttoned-up women he usually dated. Not that he was even considering dating her, because if she was the photographer, that meant she worked for his sister-in-law, and he liked his boys where they were—not lodged in his throat.

"I like that outfit better." He put the car in Park and turned off the ignition.

"Even if it cost you your last ten bucks?"

"Even then." Meeting her gaze in the rearview mirror, he

gave her a wink before climbing out of the car. He reached for the door and held it open, though he could tell it irritated her.

"Now you're just trying to sweet-talk me into giving you your whole tip back."

"Or maybe I'm a full-service kind of driver. Did you think of that?"

She rolled her eyes, and as he reached for her bags, she swatted his hands away. "Seriously, I got this." She straightened, with all her thousand-and-one bags slung over various limbs. But he just stood there, blocking her way. She either had to shoulder past him or let him assist.

She did neither. She let an annoyed sigh slip through her lips before reaching into her bag and pulling out fifty dollars, which she sweetly wafted in his face. He gave the money a long, hard look, then stuffed his hands into his pockets.

"I'm more of a word than a number guy, but by my count, I was down to only ten bucks."

"Yeah, well, you got me out of a bind and probably saved my job. So, thank you," she said, looking everywhere but at him.

"Consider it on the house," he said, and if he ever needed to get her attention, he knew how.

Be nice.

One minute she was studying the eclectic collection of state-shaped stickers covering her camera bag—Alabama to Wyoming and every state in between—and the next her gaze was locked on his. He took note of every emotion that crossed her face, uncertainty and cautious surprise fighting for dominance, which made him wonder what kind of assholes she'd been exposed to. Then the shutters dropped, and it was all Tough Girl, all the time.

"Yeah, that's not happening." Once again, she thrust it his way. And once again, he didn't take it. "Take the money, then we're even. You helped me, I paid you—no substitutes, exchanges, or fine-print favors to come back and haunt me."

"No favor, no haunting. You needed a ride. I had a car." He shrugged. "Simple."

"You performed a service. I paid you. Doesn't get simpler than that." She shoved the money into his shirt pocket and gave it a little pat.

He looked at the bills sticking out of his pocket, then at Piper. "You and I know what kind of service I provided, but if my brothers see me with a beautiful lady who's stuffing bills into my clothes, they're going to ask where my G-string is."

"Not my problem. Now scoot." She even gave a cute little flick of the wrist as if she was used to people moving aside for her.

He scooted, right up the steps to the back door where, with a grand sweeping gesture befitting of Jeeves, he opened the back door for her. "Ladies first."

She moved in behind him and, looking around as if about to impart secrets of national security, whispered, "What are you doing?"

"Getting the door."

She stepped inside, then faced him. "Thank you. Now you can close it and leave."

When he didn't move, she crossed her arms and gave him a frosty glare to emphasize the level of irritation, which, based on the daggers she was shooting his way, ranked somewhere between a cool disdain and cryogenically freezing his nuts. "Seriously, you did me a solid, but I'm already late and I can't be distracted by you hanging around."

"I distract you?"

"You're missing the point."

"The point that I distract you was not missed but catalogued to discuss at a later date."

"There won't be any date." She wiggled her fingers. "Bye."

"We can talk about that at our second date." Before she could close the door on him, he stuck his foot out. "And did you think that maybe I'm going to the party as well?"

"Oh." Her cheeks flushed. "Do you have another client?"

"Nope."

Jillian appeared in the doorway, her hair spilling from her ponytail, her blouse covered in frosting—looking about one Margo-moment from losing it.

"Thank God you're here. Margo has too much time on her hands. She's already rearranged the flowers and put out a poll to see if anyone has food sensitivities, even though I explained that I have gluten-free *and* vegan options. Now she's watching YouTube videos on how to shoot a wedding using only a smartphone," Jillian said in one long breath.

"I can be set up and ready to shoot in two minutes," Piper said, feeling all kinds of confused when Jillian bypassed her to get to Josh.

"Josh," Jillian placed a pleading hand on his arm, "please go soothe the beast before she turns what's supposed to be Darcy's night into some kind of reality show. Because if your mom's in charge, I will be the first kicked off the island."

"Your mom?" Piper asked, and Josh smiled.

"Well, this is awkward," he said. "Usually, I know a woman's full name before I help her out of her dress. Then again, nothing about today has been normal." He stuck out his hand. "I'm Josh Easton. The best man. Nice to meet you."

3

After the disastrous start to an already disastrous first day on the job, Piper had gone out of her way to avoid Josh. She'd scouted two locations for the happy couple—neither of which Mother Nature or Margo signed off on—and was staging a third when Josh walked in.

Even with fifteen thousand feet and a ladder to separate them, he'd managed to track her down as if she were wearing a homing beacon. Now he watched her with growing amusement. Piper did her best to block him out—which was difficult since Josh was the kind of guy whose sheer size and energy expanded to fill whatever space he entered.

Piper focused on setting up her equipment in the atrium. Located on the west side of the Belle Mont House, the fifteen-foot-tall dome-shaped room was original to the manor and constructed from sourced quarry tiles and copper tresses, which had a century's worth of patina, and was situated high enough to overlook the Willamette River and downtown Portland. Divided into several intimate sitting areas and greenhouse, the massive room was separated by interior columns and several water features. With bright-fuchsia vines hanging against a background of palm and maple trees, and thousands of lavender goblet-shaped autumn flowers, there wasn't a more romantic setting inside the manor.

Still, Piper was having a hard time channeling any feelings of love and ever after.

Or maybe it was more that Josh was standing too close, which had her questioning the logic behind marriage ideology. Piper never understood why someone would be willing to open themselves up so fully and readily with a nearly fifty percent chance of getting their heart ripped out and trampled on.

People lie. It's what they do. People hurt other people. Innocently or not, disappointment was part of life. At least, that had been Piper's experience. Case in point, the man who'd led her to believe he was something he was not—and who'd just walked into the room.

"Hi, I'm *Josh*?" Piper asked, lowering her voice and sounding more like Meathead Josh than the Josh in question. "Seriously, just 'hi, I'm Josh' with no further explanation. Not cool."

"You didn't tell me your last name," he said, not seeming all that apologetic over the evening's unfortunate misunderstanding. Which really pissed her off.

"My last name wasn't significant," she said. "Yours? Had I known you're an Easton, our ride would have gone a lot differently."

"Wouldn't that have been a shame?" His voice caused all kinds of shameful and exciting things to happen south of her border.

Ignoring this, and him, Piper went up on her tiptoes, stretching as far as her vertically challenged body could handle, hoping to jerry-rig one of her hanging lights to a mature maple tree. If she could only get it high enough, it would bounce through the vintage leaded glass, causing the light to cast a warm and pinkish glow as if there were a setting sun in the background instead of a storm.

"I didn't want to make things uncomfortable," he continued. "You know, being the Son of Satan and all."

"I believe you'd be Satan's Keeper's offspring." Ignoring the tiny ping of guilt over that comment—and the Keep Off sign stationed near a stone water fountain—Piper climbed on and up the stones until she was high enough to reach the top of one of the columns. "And I'm sorry about what I said to you."

"I noticed you apologized for saying it to me without actually apologizing for saying it at all."

"Kind of like introducing yourself without actually *introducing* yourself." With a smile, she turned to hammer the point home, but nearly lost her balance.

"Let me help with some of your . . . how many cameras do you have?"

"This one is for portraits." She held up her new EOS camera. "And this one, well, she goes with me everywhere." Leica might look battered and old, but the 1972 German-made camera was a work of art. She was also the first camera Piper had ever owned. Given to her by her mentor, this hand-me-down had become an extension of herself.

"You're saying if I were to ask you out on a date, I'd be the third wheel?"

Josh now stood directly behind her. His feet were on the ground while hers were still perched on the stone wall, bringing them eye to eye in one of those reach-out-and-touch-someone distances that had her fingers tingling. One manly hand cupped her hip, steadying her, the other reaching up, up and over her head to secure the clamp—giving her an impressive view of his bulging bicep.

Josh laughed. It was soft and sexy.

Piper glared. Refusing to go mushy for a pretty boy with an

even prettier face, she kept her expression purposefully expressionless when she poked his arm. Her finger bounced back. "You're totally flexing."

"You're totally looking." His expression was smug and annoying, a fitting one since he was annoyingly smug.

"There you are," a motherly voice cooed from behind, and Piper felt her stomach hollow out.

Piper didn't have to guess who had entered the room. She could feel the flames of hell burning a hole through her back.

"Hey, Mom," Josh said. His hands vanished, his eyes refocused, and that cocky know-it-all vibe morphed into something softer, warmer even, as he went to greet his mom.

In her gray slacks, lavender blouse—which matched the surrounding flora—and reading glasses, Margo looked more like a couture Mrs. Claus than her usual abominable snowman self. And when she walked into Josh's embrace, Piper was shocked at how benign Margo appeared. Maybe it was the effect of being engulfed in her son's larger frame or maybe she had a nicer, friendlier twin, but Piper almost didn't recognize the pleasant person in front of her.

She looked even motherly as she took incredible care when straightening Josh's tie and giving his face a loving pat. It was all too much, the gentle way Josh held Margo and the soft, melodic tone she used with him. Inside Piper was making barfing noises while Outside Piper, who needed this job more than Luke needed the Force, busied herself with light checks.

To be fair, it was a sweet and emotional moment between mother and child. But Piper was allergic to sweet and emotional —and she wasn't all that experienced with mother-child moments.

The few times her mom had reached sobriety, she'd step up as a parent—not a good one, but she tried—and it gave Piper hope. Eventually, she'd meet husband number next, and Piper would be placed on the back burner again and left to raise herself. Then the relationship would end, leaving her happiness in the bottom of a bottle, and Piper became completely invisible—something that followed her into adulthood and made for a lonely life. The scars from that time left her wary of others to the point that she would rather be alone than trust the wrong person.

So what little mother-daughter experience she did have made situations like this uncomfortable. Left her feeling like she was crashing a party where all the guests had a similar set of genes and characteristics, except her. Piper's genes were nothing to write home about, and her characteristics were said to be an acquired taste. Which was why she was scratching her hand like she'd been exposed to a contagion rather than a healthy show of love. It was as inspiring as it was isolating, and Piper wondered, not for the first time, how Darcy competed with a lifetime's worth of shared memories and that unbreakable bond some families were lucky enough to have.

"Don't you look handsome?" Margo said to Josh. "Every time I see you, you look more and more like your father."

"And you look more and more like a happy grandmother," Josh said.

"Kylie and I had our first outing. Just the two of us," Margo said, and there was a wistfulness there that spoke to Piper. "We had a picnic at Pittock Mansion like I used to do with you boys, but Kylie didn't get mud all over her dress or chase after the geese."

"Give her time," Josh joked. "Beneath the ballerina slippers is an Easton waiting to break free."

"Is this where we're having the pictures taken?" Margo asked innocently, as if she hadn't vetoed all Piper's other ideas—or picked out her blouse—for such a backdrop. "I love the colors in here."

"It's as though the flowers bloomed just for you," Piper said, and Margo eyed her as if trying to figure out if she were being sweet or saucy. For anyone who really knew Piper, there wouldn't be all that much to figure out.

Piper smiled innocently, and Margo's eyes narrowed into two irritated slits of censure. "Shouldn't you be taking pictures instead of flapping your lips?"

Ah, there was the Margo that Piper knew and avoided.

"I'm almost done," Piper explained. "Just testing the lighting, and then we'll be ready for the whole family to join."

"Which is remarkable since she had car trouble and was still able to get this set up so quickly," Josh said, and Piper glared at him. Then, he surprised her for the third time that day, because instead of disappearing or placating his mom, he said, "Actually, we're lucky she agreed to shoot the party on such short notice. Think of how incredible the engagement pictures will turn out."

And just like that, Margo was back to looking more like a mom than a mafia boss. "You're right." Then to Piper, she said, "Thank you, dear. Give a ring when you're ready." And with a smile—an actual smile—the older woman disappeared.

"I don't think I've ever seen her smile," Piper whispered.

"What can I say? I have a way with women."

Piper laughed. "Is that what you want me to put on your Yelp review? *He has a way with women?* I think your career as a driver for hire will come to an abrupt end."

"My muddy seats and floorboards thank you."

"Also, if you call saying my photos are incredible as 'having a way with women,' you need to up your game."

He grinned. "Until a half hour ago, I didn't even know your name, yet I already know what color lace you prefer. I think my game is pretty solid." He leaned down and whispered, "But if you want to know about my dating status, you only have to ask."

She snorted. "Don't need to. Not interested."

"If you change your mind—"

"I won't."

His grin said he didn't believe her. But then he spoke, and that oh-so-sure-of-himself vibe vanished into something more sincere that made her heart go *boom-boom*. "About the pictures—it wasn't a line."

"I've got to get back to work," she said. Because *boom-boom*s—no matter how small—over a guy who'd left out something as simple as his relation to her boss, meant she needed to devote her attention to the task at hand.

"Aren't you curious about how I know they'll be incredible?" he asked.

Yes. It irritated her almost as much as the way her skin tingled where he'd touched it earlier. She'd learned early on that other people's opinions of her were none of her business. People saw what they chose to see, and when it came to her, it was rarely flattering or easy on the ego. But for some reason—maybe it was the sound of the rain tapping against the windows or that he'd taken on his mom for her—Piper wanted to know.

Only she was feeling too vulnerable to ask, so she shrugged.

"You would rather be honest than amiable," he said gently. "And in my experience, people who approach the world that way see the real moments others often overlook."

4

"You are so full of shit," Rhett said, leaning over the bar to fill his mug from the beer tap.

All four of Josh's brothers were in The Cave, one of the last remaining speakeasys left from Prohibition, which was located behind a secret panel at Belle Mont House. It had an underlit, dark mahogany bar top, with a floor-to-ceiling Marlborough brick backwall, and three columns of sunken shelves. It was easily the biggest draw for corporate suits looking to impress out of town clients.

So far tonight it was just the Eastons huddled around the original 1920s bar, watching the party proceedings from a safe distance, while the second eldest Easton, Owen, was pouring a beer for the brothers.

"Just because I didn't come with a date doesn't mean I won't leave with one," Owen bragged. Then again, when it came to Owen, he wasn't bragging.

"That was more directed at Josh."

"Me? Why the hell are you coming at me?"

"Between the Beast, the baller, and the two of us with brides, you're the last pick," Gage said, and the rest of the guys laughed.

After the day he'd had, Josh left work wanting nothing more than to go home, grab a hot shower and a cold beer. Which was ironic because his unexpected back-seat driver moved the first two into the delete file. Leaving only the cold beer still in play. And a hot woman who looked a hell of a lot younger than him —mid-twenties tops. A woman who had distraction written all over her. And if there was one thing Josh didn't need right now, it was a distraction. He'd worked too hard to get to this point in his career, and he wasn't about to lose sight of the prize.

"When was the last time you had a woman screaming something in your ear other than 'Objection, Your Honor!'?" said Owen, the closest to Josh in age and, up until a moment ago, his favorite brother.

"Screw you."

"Sorry, whiny event planners aren't my thing," Owen said. "But they have services who can hook you up with that."

Josh might not be famous like his brothers, but he never had a hard time finding company of the female variety. In fact, with his insane caseload at work, he'd chosen to come to the party stag.

"Since when did you become so interested in my sex life?"

"Since it's clear you aren't getting any on the regular. The constipated look around your eyes"—Rhett made eye-sized circles with his fingers—"is a dead giveaway."

Josh might be uptight, but after his dad passed, he had to let go of some of the parts of him that didn't benefit his new life direction—the impulsive, fun-seeking fraternity guy who wanted nothing more than to enjoy the college life, then work his way into a venture capitalist firm.

Then his dad passed and, in an instant, his life went from fun in the California sun to being the head of the family. He'd let go of his dream of working in a tech start-up and enrolled in Stanford Law School. Unlike his brothers, Josh didn't allow himself the luxury of time to grow up, instead finishing up law school with an offer from Portland's district attorney's office.

The DA's office had been his top choice, landing him on the exact route he'd envisioned for his new career path. Now that he was this close to becoming the next district attorney, a new dream was forming and within arm's length.

Josh wanted to make a difference, and the DA's office seemed like the best place to start. Now he was on the fast track to really being able to invoke change. While his Boy Scout attitude and diplomatic ways drove his brothers nuts, it served him well as an elected law official.

"I'm not the only bachelor tonight," Josh pointed out. He thought back to his unexpected fare and her pink silk with black hearts and smiled. Maybe everything had worked out for a reason. "I go to trial tomorrow. What's your excuse?" he asked Rhett.

Owen filled Clay's mug with a local craft amber-ale beer. "Yeah, where's Stephanie?"

Rhett's grin vanished, and he ran a hand down his jaw. "She had some paid appearance she couldn't get out of."

"I haven't seen her since your wedding," Owen said.

"Feels like I haven't either," Rhett said, and Josh noticed, not for the first time, that his brother didn't seem as happy as a newlywed should be. "Between her schedule and mine, I think we've spent more nights apart than together since the honeymoon."

"Sorry, bro," Clay said. His quiet, contemplative tone was in direct contrast with his broken nose and cracked rib, courtesy of some New York Giants punk and his unsportsmanlike tackle.

There might be a twelve-year age gap between them, making Clay the baby of the family, but he was the easygoing one of the brothers. Always had been. His level head and laser focus had made him a Super Bowl MVP.

"Me too. I figured when I got married," Rhett, his middle brother, said, "I'd have one woman in my bed for the rest of my life. Now I'm sleeping next to a damn furball."

Rhett and his new wife, Stephanie, had had a mountain of problems from the very beginning. Conflicting schedules, differing goals, private problems in the public eye. Josh felt they had rushed into the marriage, but love made people do stupid things.

Rhett was a guitar prodigy on the brink of stardom, and Stephanie was an influencer with millions of Instagram followers and events booked up through the next year. If you asked Josh, their lifestyle wasn't conducive to a stable and solid relationship. Bummer, since Rhett had spoken nonstop about trying for kids the moment they were married. The only baby Stephanie wanted was their fur-baby, a Maltipoo named Fancy, who preferred to go on the road with his rock-star dad than his jet-setting mom.

"Have you thought about meeting her halfway?" Gage, the man of the hour, asked. "Surprising her? Maybe being at the airport in Milan or wherever she's flying to next."

"Yeah," Owen added. "Bring her a bracelet, take her to some fancy dinner."

"Or," said a sex-soaked voice. Josh looked up to find a bombshell holding a camera. Owen's mouth dropped open, and Josh was sure his brother had stopped breathing. "Pick her up, bring her back to an Airbnb, cook her a nice dinner, and stay in."

"What the lady said," Owen added, then leaned across the bar. "What can I get you, sugar? No, wait, let me figure this out. It's my talent."

"Pouring drinks? Isn't that what a bartender does?" she asked. She looked unintimidated and unimpressed, making Josh liked her more.

"Which means, I make a mean . . ." Owen snapped his

fingers, studying her as if correctly guessing her drink of choice would unlock all Piper's hidden secrets. Josh had seen his brother do it before—and with alarming accuracy—but somehow he felt that Piper was a little out of Owen's league. One final snap. "A Negroni. It's made with gin, Campari, and sweet vermouth." His hands were moving quickly and precisely around the bar, mixing and shaking, pouring it into a martini glass. "An Italian refresher for an Italian lady."

"Like the rest of the world who watched Stanley Tucci's tutorial, I know what a Negroni is. Plus, I'm Greek and before you say Ouzo, I'm not a stemmed-glass kind of girl. Nor am I an alcohol kind of girl." Owen wasn't fazed, his gaze falling right to that sexy little nose ring.

"Bartender, can you pour five pints and make the head frothy." She lifted a single brow, challenging even one of them to comment on the word *head*. Wisely, they all kept their mouth shut except Owen.

"So, you're a beer girl? I should have guessed that right off."

"I'm more of a 'can you each grab a beer and get your asses closer together so I can do my job?' girl," she said. "Darcy wants a photo with all the brothers, and since no one wants a bridezilla crushing each of your nuts, I suggest you listen and move where I tell you."

She waved Owen to stand in front of the tap and he moved willingly like a lovesick puppy. She took each man by the shoulders, strong-arming them into position, some of them on bar stools, others standing casually around the bar. And none of his brothers' fame or fortune warranted a second look. Nope, Piper was a no-nonsense style of photographer. And that turned him on.

Which became interesting when she came to Josh. She didn't touch him—not once. In fact, it appeared she went out of her way to avoid touching him at all. Oh, he'd caught her watching him throughout the night, her camera lens pointed his direction. Only fair, since he couldn't take his eyes off her. He knew she was shooting him because when he winked, she'd pretend she was fiddling with her camera, then quickly turn her focus the other way, but not before he caught the look of *oh shit* in her expression.

Not that it deterred her. Five minutes later and she had her camera aimed at him again.

"There we go. Now smile." No one smiled. She shot them a look over the top of her camera that could cryogenically freeze their collective nuts. "This isn't a mug shot. It's an engagement party," she said cheerfully, then got close and lowered her voice. "Smile or so help me God, I will..."

"What?" Rhett said. "Get Darcy? Gage will have her smiling in no time."

Josh knew the moment Piper was done playing. "You are one in a long list of photos that I have to capture before I can go home. So unless you want to hear about just how bad my day was, and we're talking bad, like Satan's Keeper and Zeus coming at me bad, then I'd suggest you show some teeth. Otherwise, I'll be forced to jerk you around by the family jewels and drag you to Margo, who will learn that her sons are actively trying to sabotage her Christmas card photo."

"You can't, ma'am. I accidentally closed my eyes last year," Rhett said.

"And I forgot my socks," Clay added. "But she still hung it over the fireplace for the sole purpose of showing her friends the fiasco."

"Have you ever forgotten your jockstrap?" she asked, and Clay looked horrified at the idea. "Your strap is as important to you as your mom's stories about her sons are to her. Do you really want to send her, unarmed, into a group of one-upping old biddies? I wouldn't."

"If someone wanted to see your last Christmas card, where would your mom keep it?" Owen asked, his overt flirting rubbing Josh the wrong way.

"That information is classified." The group laughed, but he could have sworn there was something uncertain and almost defensive beneath her tone. The way she glanced away told him she was nervous. And that's when he got it. She didn't dress like one giant *screw you* to the world—she dressed to keep people away.

"Let's get smiling, fellas," Josh said, relieved he wouldn't have to kick some serious ass, because his brothers, even Rhett, sat upright, arms slung around each as if at a ballgame.

"On three. One." *Click. Click. Click. Click, click. Click.*

"Whoa!" Rhett said. "What happened to three? Every good photographer goes on three."

Trouble leveled Rhett with a look. "A good photographer knows when her subjects are a few too many beers in and might stumble over if I waited too long. Plus, I didn't want to run the risk of your blinking, Rhett." She blew them a kiss with her middle finger. "It's been real, boys."

"Well, shit, she told you," Clay said.

"What, Jockstrap Kid? You do know that today's socks were black."

"I was told dark gray—" Clay checked to find black.

As Piper was walking away, she looked over her shoulder at Josh. Those lips were slightly tilted into a mischievous grin; her eyes said *neener-neener*, but it was that smart aleck, take-shit-from-nobody vibe that had him sending a wink her way. To his surprise, she winked back, then disappeared down the hallway.

"Gentleman, I have found my date," Owen informed the group. "Nose ring, and did you see that tattoo on her neck? All I needed was a few more minutes, and she'd have been mine."

"Or you could let her do her job," Josh advised, because

Owen had a specific type: smart-assed, hot-ass, and a little crazy. Not to mention brunette, stacked, and tattooed. He also knew that Owen could be relentless when issued a challenge.

Too bad for Owen, Josh was already formulating a plan. A plan that did not include Owen, but rather Josh engaging in a night of flirting and fun with the sexy photographer. While she might be nothing like his usual type, his usual type seemed to be in crisis—adapting as new information developed.

"Darcy does have incredible taste in photographers," Clay said, throwing his hat in the ring. "I think she was flirting with me during the pictures."

"No way," Owen said. "She was definitely checking me out."

"Only because she knows I'm off the market," Rhett said.

"She wasn't flirting with any of you. She was being professional and trying to help you idiots get in the right places," Josh said, and the other brothers exchanged looks.

"How would you know?" Owen asked. "You were so busy undressing Pretty Picture Girl, you wouldn't have noticed if zombies crashed the party."

"I wasn't undressing—" Josh stopped right there. "Her name isn't Pretty Picture Girl. And don't you guys have something better to do than objectify her?"

"You going to tell us her name?" Owen asked.

"Nope," Josh said, and handed Rhett his empty pint glass.

"Where's he going?" Clay asked.

"To objectify her from up close," Rhett teased.

Josh gave his brothers the finger.

5

"I can't believe you got them to all stand still at the same time in the same five square feet," the bride, Darcy Kincaid, said.

"It's my job," Piper said, smoothing down her hair and hoping to control some of the frizz.

In addition to renovating Belle Mont House from the ground up, Darcy helped plan weddings for happy couples all over Portland—making her a real-life cupid. She was petite, patient, and as fierce as a lioness when it came to her family. She also seemed to be the mother hen of anyone lucky enough to be in her life.

Tonight, she was dressed in a fitted-to-perfection pearl-white dress which hit just below the knee. With a matching chiffon sheath offset with inlaid pearls, Darcy would give Jackie O a run for her money.

"I actually got some more candid shots, which I think you'll like better. But I snapped a posed one just in case." *Liar, liar.* She had taken that picture so she could stare Josh in the eye—tell him she wasn't afraid to look or even get caught. Touching, that was off limits, or at least on her terms. "I knew it was an important picture for you, so I made sure to give you choices."

"It's going to be my mother-of-the-bride present to Margo. The last professional photo she had of the guys together was Kyle's funeral."

From what Piper had gathered, Kyle, Gage's twin brother, had died in a car accident after being left standing at the altar. He'd been intoxicated and gotten behind the wheel, and the worst possible thing happened. For years, the family blamed his death on the runaway bride until it was revealed that Kyle wasn't particularly skilled in the loyalty department. His bride found out about his mistress on the day of their wedding and gave him a choice: the girlfriend or the fiancée.

Kyle hesitated, and she walked.

The bride had, surprisingly, been Darcy. Piper wasn't sure how Darcy went from Kyle's ex to his twin brother's fiancée, but she'd never seen a couple more in love. Gage even stepped in to be daddy to Kyle and Darcy's four-year-old daughter, Kylie. From what Jillian said, Gage had been forced to choose between the love of his life and his family—he'd chosen Darcy.

Eventually, his family had come around, but Gage had made his priorities clear. Piper wondered where Josh had stood on that decision.

She didn't know the happy couple back when this all went down, so it was hard for her to imagine a situation where a man would choose an outsider over his family. Then again, Piper had never been chosen—not once in her life.

"Is Margo coming around?"

"She doesn't really have a choice," Darcy said. "If she wants to be a part of Kylie's life, then she needs to make the effort. She needs to find peace with the past and realize that being Kylie's grandmother is more important than the anger over losing her son."

"You're a braver woman than I." Piper didn't scare easily but marrying into a family where the matriarch was Margo would be a hard sell.

"I know what you're thinking, but she has her moments," Darcy said. "Yes, she's stubborn and prideful and judgy as hell, but you should see her with Kylie. What she lacks in her public persona, she more than makes up for as a grandmother."

Both women looked into the Grand Salon where people were toasting with champagne and eating cake, but her gaze caught on a guy.

Josh, to be exact.

Under the fairy lights, in the center of the room, was Josh and his niece. The girl stood on his feet, her little hands in his and her head tilted all the way back so she could smile up at her uncle. They were swaying, twirling around in circles. This was not a dancing kind of event. There was no dance floor, no DJ—only quiet music in the background for ambiance. But Josh had created a moment for his little niece.

Piper's heart tugged hard. She had seen this kind of moment on Hallmark movies, but none of them affected her quite like this.

"What a perfect picture," Darcy said, her voice rough with emotion.

Piper's throat was a little tight as well. Watching Josh in such a pure and innocent moment was doing crazy things to her chest. Darcy was right. It was picture perfect.

Picture!

So caught up in the romance of it all, Piper nearly missed the moment entirely.

Romance?

Where had that come from? She was there to watch from the sidelines, not get emotional about something that didn't concern her. She was there as a professional, and it was time to go back to professional.

Cradling the camera, she looked through the lens and moved the center of focus to get the desired composition. A tingle radiated in her belly, her gut telling her she had the shot, then she pressed the button. The shutter snapped and when it opened, Josh was looking directly at her.

Unlike before, he didn't send her a flirty wink, and she didn't move. It was as if they were frozen and the moment had spun a spell around them, making it impossible to look away.

"You okay?" Darcy asked.

"What? Oh. I'm good." Piper lowered the camera and composed herself. "I was waiting for the right moment to, you know, s*nap*."

"Did you feel the *snap*?" Darcy looked amused, like she knew exactly what had Piper rambling.

"For the picture?" Piper pulled up the photo on her screen. "Tell me what you think."

"It's beautiful." Darcy met Piper's gaze and held. "You're really talented. Your pictures tell a surprising story."

She knew Darcy was talking about Josh and the way he was looking into the camera as if he were looking right at Piper—which he had been. But what had her heart pumping hard was *how* he was looking at her.

Like he wanted to eat her up whole.

Oh boy. "That's my job. To capture everything."

Before Darcy could comment further, Piper lifted her camera and snapped a close-up of the bride. Darcy put her hand in front of her face, and the two women laughed.

"I know we talked about photographing my party, but if you're interested, I heard from the Ladies of Portland, and they're considering hosting their annual Bid for the Cause here. It's a dinner and auction that raises money for local charities."

"That's amazing. Seriously, congratulations."

"It's not a sure thing yet, but Margo is on the planning

committee and really pushing for Belle Mont to be the venue. If, and it's a big if, I land the account, would you be open to shooting the event? It doesn't pay a lot, but it would be great exposure."

Piper gasped. "Are you kidding? Even if I gained one client, it would be more than worth it. But why me? You have a dozen photographers on speed dial."

"Because you're talented."

Uncomfortable with the praise, Piper lifted her camera, pretending to scan the room for another candid. This time when she looked through the lens, the entire Easton clan was dancing to nothing but background music coming from a lone speaker hidden behind a large potted tree. Each man had taken one of the elderly aunts for a fun spin around the room. They weren't Fred Astaire by any means, but the sentiment was touching.

Piper had taken a few photos when Darcy's face filled the frame. Once again, she noticed that Darcy's makeup was flawless, her blonde hair pulled up into a sophisticated twist with seeded tiny pearls that matched the ones that ran the height of her knee-length cape-like wrap. She was the kind of classy that made elegance look easy.

"So, is that a yes?" she asked.

Piper lowered the camera once again. "It's a hell yes."

To Piper's surprise, Darcy pulled her into an embrace.

Piper didn't have many girlfriends, nor was she a warm and touchy kind of person—PDA, even between friends, was so foreign to her she always felt awkward, like the too-tall teen who'd grown four inches in one summer. So when Darcy held on, as if waiting for Piper to return some kind of girl gesture, Piper gave her boss an awkward pat on the back.

Darcy laughed. "We'll have to work on that."

Piper had a list of things she wanted to work on. Making friends with her new boss wasn't on it. Mixing business and friendship had never worked out for her. She was a bona fide, tried-and-true relationship-phobe.

"Thanks for the chance. You're totally doing me a solid." Unsure how to end the conversation—another thing she found challenging: conversations—she waved Darcy off. "Enough about that. You shouldn't be out here talking business with me. Get back inside and have some fun with your family and friends."

"You can have a little fun too."

Piper glanced at the impromptu dance floor and a hive broke out on her right hand. "Thanks, but I don't think fun is a Margo-approved activity for the help."

"I not only hired you because you're the best photographer I interviewed, I also hired you because you're a friend," Darcy said, and Piper scratched her wrist. "I don't just let anyone around my family."

Not sure how to handle the comment or the feeling it created in her chest, Piper made another little *shoo* motion.

She hadn't had many girlfriends growing up, and the ones she did have would run screaming from a party like this. Given the choice, Piper would have been at the front of the pack.

It wasn't that she didn't appreciate Darcy and Jillian's generosity. Five minutes around them, and it was clear that their warm and welcoming ways were genuine. They seemed to be the kind of friends who could weather any storm—past and present. It made Piper wonder if it would be so bad to open herself up, to take a chance on making new connections.

Then again, not many people had a past like Piper. Even fewer knew what to do with it. As a young girl, Piper knew her family was different. The alcohol, the drugs, the revolving door of "daddies." The idea of giving her classmates an up close and personal show of the crazy was a nonstarter. Except for Faith, who'd empathized with Piper's situation and had foolishly trusted Piper.

In the end, it had been Piper who had failed her.

"You better go dance. Your mother-in-law is shooting me the evil eye."

"Bite your tongue. I still have six months before that title is a reality. And she's going to have to earn every precious thing that comes with it."

Piper hoped so because Darcy was quite possibly the most genuine person Piper had ever met. And her little girl was as sweet as they came. It would be a shame if Margo took advantage of their giving nature. Piper had seen it happen before, and the results were heartbreaking.

"Can you make her start by forgiving the photographer for being late on account of Fate being a raging asshole?" Piper grimaced.

"My fiancé represents athletes. I've heard worse," she said. "And speaking of Gage, he's waving me over. I promised him a stealth exit before his great-aunts cornered him about babies. When Aunt Alberta gets sauced, she tends to explain, in great detail, the best methods for ensuring fertilization."

They both looked at Gage, who was barricaded by a bunch of old biddies, with Aunt Alberta leading the force.

"I better go rescue my man."

Darcy turned to leave, and Piper gently touched the other woman's shoulder. "Thanks again for giving me a shot as your photographer."

"You've more than earned everything that comes with the title."

Piper wasn't sure about that, but she'd take the win. She'd also take the charity job.

Darcy headed back into the party, and Piper took the opportunity to slip away into the crowd. But it wasn't enough. The conversation had rattled her. Even more, the whole night had left her off balance. She worked hard to blend in. Her safe place was behind the camera, where observing was all that was expected.

She was a ninja people-watcher. It was what made her such a great photographer. Dark corners and hard-to-find nooks were where she felt the most comfortable. Over the years, she'd learned that most people want to be seen.

Not Piper. She worked hard to be invisible. But the Eastons kept pulling her out of her hidey-hole and into the light.

The only person in Piper's life who'd ever come close to what had been happening inside her house was Faith, Piper's best friend, who'd run away with her to Portland. They'd been fifteen, and neither of them had a stable home, a family who cared, or a safe way out. But they had each other. And most of the time, that had been enough.

Piper noticed Margo glaring at her, so when the older woman started Piper's way, Piper put the cover on her lens and slipped out onto the terrace.

She moved deeper into the shadows, praying her black clothes would help her blend into the night. The night was working against her with a full moon, a bazillion-and-one stars, and drizzle. Lots of drizzle.

Then there was the cold evening breeze, which cut through her function-over-fashion blazer. With a shiver, she considered heading back in. Until she saw Margo, still scanning the room. There was no way she was going in now. She'd rather turn into a popsicle than accidentally say the wrong thing to Margo and cost herself the auction gig.

"Raging assholes unite," she grumbled.

"Raging assholes, huh?" someone said from behind her. "And who would that other asshole be?"

Piper slowly spun around, ready to add him to her list of

raging assholes, when she stopped. One look at Josh, and everything inside her went warm and gooey.

He was leaning back against the railing, under a twinkle-lit awning that had been set up for the event. One arm was resting leisurely on the railing, the other holding a glass of champagne, looking sophisticated and safe and like a million bucks. He wore a dark suit, gray button-up with a bold silver tie, and that sexy grin which she was coming to realize made her stomach do these silly little flips. The man looked so at home in his own skin, it ticked her off even more.

Sexy with an edge, she decided. She'd long given up on sexy with an edge, as they always seemed to come with an expiration date set to "not looking for anything serious." And that date was the morning after.

No, sexy with an edge was most definitely not on her list of amiable traits.

Lifting her camera, she laughed when Josh gave one of those smiles with zero teeth, zero expression, and zero interest in being filmed.

"I'm willing to add another name to the list," she said.

Telling herself the shot was for Darcy, she held strong. Over the years, she'd learned that silence and patience were as important as lighting when it came to photography.

It wasn't about the first shot. It was the unexpected shot she waited for. And she didn't have to wait long. Looking straight through the lens, his eyes warmed, his expression was one of *challenge accepted,* and her belly did that same annoying little flip thingy.

He picked up two plates from a nearby table, balancing them in a single hand. His shoes clicked on the terra-cotta tile as he moved toward her, not stopping until he was standing so close she could smell the rain on his skin.

Not comfortable with him all up in her space, she walked backward, but he followed. "What are you doing?"

"Making sure my name isn't on the list, Florence," he teased.

"Oh, it's at the top and Florence says, '*Eff* off and leave the tattoo meaning alone.'" She looked up, surprised to find that she was under an umbrella and out of the rain. She waited for him to ruin the chivalrous moment with some kind of meathead move, like checking out her boobs or caging her in for a kiss.

"Hungry?" He held out the plate.

She took a step back as if the offering were from Ted Bundy. "What's this?"

"Since peanut butter and chocolate isn't a meal, I thought you might need something heartier."

Again, she waited for the big come-on. Instead, he said nothing more.

"Peanuts are protein, and chocolate is a heart-healthy antioxidant. Look it up, it's a super food."

"Chocolate kisses don't count, and there's enough sugar in your peanut butter to make Charlie and his Chocolate Factory look weak." He held out the plates, urging her to take her pick.

She looked at the assortment of things. Things with skewers and tapenade and names someone would have to be fluent in French to pronounce. "Do you have anything that comes in a to-go bag?"

He laughed. "Turns out there's a thing called UberEats. With my newly cemented career, I bet I could get you a discount."

"Actually, I'm really not that hungry—is that cake?!"

On the bottom plate was a slice of cake. Not just any cake. Limoncello cake with raspberry filling and mascarpone buttercream that she'd watched Jillian ice in the kitchen before the party.

Jillian's cake company might be in its fledgling stage, but she was already gaining a reputation in Portland for being the Cake

Goddess. And if her four-layer cake was as good as her cake pops, Josh just might work his way off her asshole list.

She licked her lips, and her stomach growled. "You're really working hard for that tip, aren't you?"

"I'll take a dance instead."

"There is a room full of women who'd be more than happy to dance with you."

"And yet, here I am. A boy, standing in front of a girl, asking her to dance with him."

Piper might have rolled her eyes, but her chest tightened, and her stomach gave a little flutter. Would it be so bad to lean forward and disappear into his big, warm arms, to know for a minute what it was like to be one of those people inside— laughing and sharing memories.

Only, she wasn't looking to make the kind of memories that followed stripping in the back of the best man's car. She knew how she must have come across. *Knew* how it would appear if she accepted the dance. She saw the way he'd looked at her, and he was a smart guy, so he knew how she'd been looking at him.

She wasn't an idiot. Guys like Josh, upper crust, upper class, and uptight—a loafers and tassel guy—took one look at her nose ring, army boots, and blue-streaked hair and saw a wild night with a wild girl. When, in fact, Piper was the furthest thing from wild. Her early teen years had been one wild ride after another, followed by three more years of uncertainty. So when she aged out of the system at eighteen and her life became her own, she made a conscious decision to be better than her upbringing.

And even though he'd been a perfect gentleman, as a rule she didn't trust gentlemen. Perfect or otherwise.

She ordered her hormones to cool their jets and squared her shoulders. "Do you think I'd come into your work and ask you to dance?"

"My office isn't really big enough to dance. Well, maybe a middle-school sway. But to really show off my moves?" He grinned, shrugging out of his coat and stepping forward.

Again, she took a big step back and held out a halting hand. "Look, I get it. I asked for help with the zipper and then we were flirting, so I can see how that could come across." She hated that her throat caught on the last few words.

His smile faded. "My mind wasn't even going there."

"Then why did you follow me out here?"

"Because you looked . . ." He faded off, and suddenly she wanted to know exactly how she looked.

"Go on," she challenged. It had never mattered to her before, but for some reason, with him, it mattered. She looked down at her clothes, at the scuffs in her boots and the mud splatters on her blazer—she could even feel her hair frizz from the humidity in the air. She scratched the inside of her wrist.

"Cold," he whispered, and she could tell that wasn't what he was going to say. And just when she thought it couldn't get any worse, she felt a warm coat slide over her shoulders. She opened her mouth to tell him she was fine when she realized she was shivering.

Only, not in the way he thought. It was a head-to-toe shiver that had everything in between going toasty warm.

"I'm fine, really," she said.

"Humor me." He tugged the edges of his coat and pulled it closed. "Think of it as a perk of hiring a professional chauffeur."

She sank deeper into his coat, which was still warm from his body and smelled like cool summer nights and a dependable man.

She lifted her camera and Josh gave a large, playful grin which she snapped, but instead of lowering it, she waited until the cocky driver faded into something real.

"My answer is still no," she said. "Even if I wanted to say yes, you're in the wedding party; it would be unprofessional."

He thought about that. "If I were just your driver and you weren't on the clock, would you want to say yes?"

"Why me?" she heard herself asking for the second time that night.

"I was inside alone, watching everyone dance, and I saw you out here alone watching them too, so I thought maybe we could be alone together. But if you want to tell me to fuck off, I'll go."

Fuck off was her modus operandi. Never in a million years would Piper ever agree to dance with a guest at one of her jobs. But being surrounded by all the bliss and happily ever after had left her feeling lost.

She shrugged. "It doesn't matter."

"It matters to me." He didn't step closer, didn't crowd her, and his gaze never left hers to wander. A real Prince Charming for a girl whose car was more a POS pumpkin than a carriage.

"You're a man, the rules are different."

He considered that, actually considered what she'd said, his earnest blue gaze going serious when he finally answered. "They shouldn't be." He moved back, ever so slightly. "Since I discovered I had a niece, I've started looking at the world differently. Seeing things I never noticed before."

His answer was as surprising as he was fascinating. Most men discounted or ignored the different rules of play. He'd not only acknowledged them, he also seemed to have grown from them. "Like how it could be perceived if I dance with you."

"Know that I didn't mean it in any way other than wanting to share a dance with a beautiful woman and I'm sorry." His apology had her stumbling. Piper had apologized for a million things over the years, but she'd seldom been on the receiving end of an apology. People with her background rarely were.

"Maybe when I'm not working, you can ask again?"

"Maybe works." His grin popped those double-barreled dimples, then he handed her a business card.

She flipped it over a few times. "What's this?"

"In case maybe turns into a yes and you want to try being alone together over dinner sometime."

She read the card and snorted. "You're a lawyer?" Of course he was a lawyer. "You really are Satan's spawn."

"I prefer Satan's Keeper's offspring. And being a lawyer means I know how to argue my case."

"What case are you going to argue?"

"That is a debate for another night. And before you toss the card in the trash with every other card you probably get at these things, you never know when knowing an ADA might come in handy."

She studied his card. "District attorney, huh?"

"*Assistant* district attorney."

Still impressive as hell. He couldn't be more than five years older than her, and he'd climbed a whole lot of rungs in the public servant's ladder. She'd climbed from stock-image photographer to exactly one engagement party, and possibly a charity event—which was why she should give him back his jacket and walk away.

This was the highest paying job of her artistic career. She couldn't afford to be sucked in by a charming assistant district attorney.

"What's your stance on filing claims against deities and demi-gods?"

"Depends on their offense."

"Oh, they're so offensive they're—"

"Raging assholes?" he finished, and she actually felt a smile threatening. "If I represent you, do you solemnly swear to remove my name off the raging asshole list?"

"You aren't on it," she admitted, and at his smug grin added, "yet."

Piper's phone buzzed. She fished it out and glanced at the screen. "The happy couple has successfully escaped the clutches of a, uh, *mothering* mother-in-law."

He laughed. "You are a terrible liar. Plus, I know Darcy well enough to know you swapped out some adjectives. Are we engaged in a game of Engagement Party Mad Libs?"

They were engaged in something, all right. Piper just wasn't sure she had a playbook for this game.

"The bride has *verb* the *noun*'s clutches of her *adjective* and *adjective* mother-in-law." Even as he said it, Piper knew he was kidding. He wasn't ignorant of his mother's shortcomings, but he still clearly loved her in that protective way sons on mobster shows loved their mob boss mothers.

"I plead the fifth."

"Smart woman." He winked and, *sweet baby Jesus,* was he one delicious snack. Piper had to look away so as not to keep staring at his lips. He glanced over his shoulder and followed her gaze into the salon, which was quickly emptying out. "I didn't mean to keep you."

"It's okay. The bride and groom are gone, so I'm off the clock." The minute the words slipped out, she tried to shove them back in, but it was too late.

Josh lifted a single brow. She was sure he'd call her on it, but in the end all he said was, "You have my card. I hope you use it."

6

Piper was in the middle of a mid-day crisis.

She'd been summoned to Skye's the Limit, a safe haven for homeless girls in Portland. Its founder, Skye Arlo, was having a bit of an emergency.

In Skye's world an emergency could range from a doughnut shortage to blowing up her oven. Piper never knew what she was going to walk into. Not that it mattered. She'd walk through fire for Skye. The woman who had pulled Piper off the street and embraced a screwed up, troubled teen, no questions asked. She was the closest thing to a parent figure Piper had, so if Skye needed cronuts at two in the morning, then Piper would bring her as many cronuts as POSH could carry.

Piper pulled up to the pink and yellow Queen Anne Victorian, and a rush of emotions surfaced. They always did. She'd lived there only two years, but they were the best two years of her childhood.

Skye stood on the front porch in a tie-dyed tunic dress, Tevas, and enough turquoise bracelets to open a jewelry store.

"Thank the Universe you're here," Skye said, enveloping Piper in an all-encompassing hug. Even though Piper tensed up like she always did, the scent of incense and mothballs smelled like home.

"What's going on?"

"I don't like to emote negative energy into the Universe, but I'm so screwed, and I don't know what to do."

"You aren't screwed, because there's always a way out of things." Piper had gotten herself out of so many scrapes by wit alone, including the time she was arrested for shoplifting a pair of rain boots. "How can I help?"

"I never wanted to bring you into this."

"You're not bringing me into anything. I'm walking in of my own free will."

"Free will is important, dear." It was one of the many things most people took for granted and one of the gifts Skye gave back to each of her girls. "Tea. We need some dandelion root tea. All this worry has my chakras out of balance."

Piper helped the older woman inside and put the teapot on the stove. "Now, what's going on?"

"It's the house. The bank put a lien on it."

"Under what authority?" Skye had paid off her house in the eighties.

"Under the authority of the United States government," she whispered as if Homeland Security was about to kick down her door at any moment. "You know how I'm not good with numbers. Well, I accidentally overextended myself, and I've fallen behind a few years on my property taxes."

"A few *years*? How is that possible? We set up a payment plan to avoid this exact situation."

"I may have used that money to pay for college tuition."

Not for herself. Nope, Skye had a big heart and a generous nature. Her business model centered around a "give you the shirt off my back" business plan. While it was touching, it also landed her in financial trouble. Often.

Skye promised every girl who maintained above a 3.0 GPA while in her program a free first year of junior college. It was how Piper had been able to kickstart her journey into higher learning.

Piper had paid back her loan by her second year of art school. Other girls struggled to pay rent let alone pay Skye back. Skye didn't care. For her, it was all about bringing balance to the Universe. And even though Skye didn't have that kind of money, she never went back on her word to further educate her girls.

"You can't help everyone," Piper said quietly.

"I know, but a few of my girls were accepted into top-notch art schools. How could I say no?"

Piper's heart did something rare—it rolled over and exposed its soft underbelly because there was no situation on earth where Skye would turn her back on someone in need. Especially a teenage girl. Helping those less fortunate was stamped into Skye's genetic makeup.

"How many girls?"

"Three." Okay, so that wasn't so bad. She'd been expecting an outrageous, have to sell the house kind of number. "I feel so stupid. I can't lose this house."

Skye's house had been handed down from her mother, who had taken in single women looking to escape abusive relationships. It was one of the original safe houses in the underground railroad for abused women and children in the fifties. Skye had carried on her family's tradition, focusing on runaway teen girls who were escaping unhealthy family situations.

"You're not stupid, Skye. You're a guardian angel to so many girls. Including me."

Piper's eyes stung, and her throat swelled with emotion. Skye hadn't only been Piper's guardian angel; she'd been the first person to show Piper what healthy love looked like.

Piper still had a hard time believing in such things as unconditional love, but she believed that Skye believed, and most days that was enough.

She took the stack of papers off the table and flipped through them. "We're going to fix this, and I'm going to help." Piper didn't have a lot of money, but whatever she had she'd give to Skye, no questions asked. Had it not been for Skye, Piper would be in jail or dead by now. "How much are we talking?"

"Six times four years is . . ." Skye's fingers moved at lightning speed as if working an abacus. "Twenty-four thousand dollars."

Piper choked. That was a lot of photoshoots. "Okay, not what I was expecting, but not impossible."

"I'm relieved to hear you say that because the auditor said that if I don't pay my back taxes, the bank will foreclose."

She patted Skye's hand. "We'll figure something out." Piper might be cash poor, but she was rich in the get-shit-done currency. If she co-signed a loan, they could cover part of it, then figure out later how to pay off the balance. "How long do we have?"

"Till the end of the year."

"That's only four months! Why didn't you tell me sooner?"

"I didn't want to worry you."

"Well, now I'm worried."

"Then, dear, we need to unworry you. The auditor said I could set up a payment plan. Does that make things better?"

"A little. But we need to find a way to get some cash now."

Piper thought back to the upcoming charity event, and an idea began to form. "What about doing that art show we've always talked about?"

"And pair up with Urban Soul?" Skye asked, referring to the non-profit fine arts program for kids the system forgot about. It was a combination of art therapy and exposing kids to a creative outlet. Through art, girls were able to express themselves in a positive way and have a permanent reminder that they mattered.

It was a charity that was near and dear to Piper's heart. She'd gone from student to volunteer to teacher.

"We'd need a venue that would give us a deal on rent. We'd set it up like a real gallery and showcase local teens from the program. We can invite the public in hopes that they buy some art." Piper's chest filled with excitement and a few nerves.

Skye thought for a moment, then clapped as if everything were kismet. "Oh, just think. The girls can earn money from their beautiful work." If this worked, Piper could help a lot of people who deserved to have someone in their corner. It might not bring in the tens of thousands that Bid for the Cause would, but it would impact a group of people who were often overlooked and would help local youth display and, hopefully, sell their work.

"Forty percent of the proceeds go to the artist's college fund and the other forty percent goes to Skye's the Limit, and what's left over will go to the venue. And if we hold it in November, we can cash in on the Christmas crowd."

Piper thought about all the people looking for a unique present for a loved one.

"We can charge admission," Skye suggested.

"I say we make it free. The whole point of the show is to get bodies in the room to look at the art. If we charged, we might lose a good percentage of shoppers."

"This all sounds wonderful, but the first payment is due by October fifteenth." Skye rattled off an insane number, and Piper's stomach churned. "Maybe they can move the date."

"How many times have they already moved it?" Skye went uncomfortably silent. "Okay, then we have to have it sooner than we'd hoped. That means we need to get moving."

Skye smiled as though she liked the plan. "We can have it here, like a block party. But with that many people coming and going, I'd have to get a permit, which the city won't give me on account of the time the police did an illegal search of my house."

"You bought ayahuasca from an undercover agent."

"He said he was a shaman from the rain forest," Skye said, as if that made it less of a felony. "Who lies about being a shaman?"

"A police officer trying to catch drug dealers."

"I'm not a dealer. It was for personal use, for the summer solstice."

Of course it was. "You're lucky they didn't press charges. I'm not looking to add a Thelma and Louise trip to my passport."

"Oh, but imagine having that sexy Brad Pitt in the back. Talk about a way to go."

Piper wasn't looking to "go" anywhere. She'd felt as though she'd only arrived at a life of her own choosing. Six years of art school—on the 'support as you go' payment plan—and another three apprenticing under one of the town's most acclaimed urban landscape photographers, she was at a place in her career she could be proud of. A struggling artist with a boatload of connections and experience, which she planned on using to help Skye help other girls like Piper.

"So you can't have it here. No biggie." Piper shrugged. "We can move it."

"How about one of those fancy ballrooms downtown?"

"I can check." But she was sure it was a big fat not going to happen. There were only so many venues in the greater Portland area that donated space for discounted rates. And with the limited time, they'd have to get more creative.

"There has to be a hundred parks or outdoor spaces we can use. Like Art in the Park."

Skye let out a strained sigh. "They still won't issue me a permit."

"I can put it in my name. Next problem."

"September in Portland?"

"So it has to be inside?"

"Maybe you can ask your friend with the big house on the hill."

Darcy was the first person Piper thought of too. She didn't want her new boss to think she was taking advantage of her generosity, so Piper would pay her a percentage of the proceeds. That was if she was on board—and that was a big if.

"I know she's booked solid, but maybe she has an afternoon open. As for the money, this is as much about saving your house as it is giving the girls a chance to shine. Next problem?"

Skye was too busy tearing up to go for problem number three. "You'd do that for me?"

"I'd do anything for you." Even hug, apparently, because when Skye pulled her in for a soul-to-soul embrace, Piper did more than endure it. She actually hugged Skye back.

"Thank the Universe," Skye whispered, still holding firm. "I thought I was going to need to bake some special cookies to calm down."

Piper pulled back. "Hold off on that, I've got an ADA to call about securing a permit, and he doesn't look like the special brownie type."

7

"Why does it look like a Vegas show and bachelorette party threw up in your office?" Rhett asked, stepping over a bronze peacock statue with real feathers.

"I was in a meeting with the mayor about a high-profile case when his wife came in and somehow drafted me into helping her plan this year's Ladies of Portland fundraiser."

His brothers burst out laughing, but it was Owen who was stupid enough to ask, "How the hell did that happen?"

Piper. That's how. He'd been so busy thinking about those big, haunting hazel eyes that said *maintain a safe distance* when Kitty Caldwell mentioned that Darcy's friend had volunteered to photograph the event. Before he knew what he was agreeing to, Josh was offering his help.

He meant to imply he'd help set up or do some heavy lifting the day of the event, creating a legitimate reason to see Piper again. The next thing he knew, it looked like Kitty had emptied her entire attic in his office.

"I was trying to convince her that Mom was right, and Belle Mont House was the perfect venue for the auction, and she took my interest as support that I wanted to plan the entire auction portion of the evening."

Clay walked under a hanging Swarovski chandelier, batting at one of the five-foot strands of crystals. "And here I thought Gage's bachelor party was going to be held in Elton John's house."

"Who let you guys in anyway?" he asked.

"I did," Sadie, Josh's college intern, explained. If pressed to describe her in a single word, it would be *nervous*. "I didn't think it would be a problem," she said, looking a little intimidated by Owen and a whole lot starstruck by Rhett.

"Don't worry about it, sugar," Rhett said, and Josh could almost hear the girl's heart sigh a giant *oh my*. Even before he hit the Billboard chart, the ladies always got tongue-tied around his middle brother.

"They're not staying long," Josh said as his three brothers took a seat, Owen practically blowing the armrests off with his sheer size. He might be the biggest of the brothers, and with his buzzed head and body art, he looked more like a bouncer than an upscale bar owner, but he was a mama's boy through and through.

Owen ran the family business, Stout. Started by their father as a place for locals to gather and share a drink, it had become a meeting place for businessmen and politicians, and an epicenter for the music scene. It was where Josh spent his summers working alongside his dad, and the place that Rhett got his big break. When their father passed, Owen walked away from a successful career as a tattoo artist to take over the family business. He'd not only pulled the bar out of the red, he'd turned it into one of the most successful gastropubs in town.

"Coffee, water, a soda?" Sadie asked Rhett—and only Rhett. "Anything at all?"

"Hot water would be great," Owen said.

"I'm good," Clay said.

Sadie blinked, as if realizing that there were other people in the room. "Hot water? Oh, for tea. Well, I have peppermint, green tea, chamomile, or I can always run downstairs to the coffee shop."

"No need for all that. Just hot water." Owen pulled out a silver canister that held a single tea bag. "And thanks."

"You carry your own tea leaves now?" Rhett asked when the door shut.

"Says the guy wearing women's shoes."

"Dude, these are one-of-a-kind sneakers," Rhett defended, then put his one-of-a-kind sneakers on Josh's desk.

"They're yellow. What kind of self-respecting man wears yellow shoes?" He also had on weathered jeans and a faded AC/DC T-shirt that probably cost a few hundred bucks. He looked like some overaged DJ who frequented the LA club scene.

"There's a couples' therapist across the street. I can get you two her name," Josh said.

And since Rhett and Owen liked to bicker like an old married couple, Owen asked, "What's up with the designer handbag?"

Josh peeked over his desk and snorted. Next to his brother's feet lay a small brown suitcase-looking bag that had little CGs all over it and a mesh front. There was a giant golden emblem that looked like someone had stolen a hood ornament and tied it to the handle.

"It's Littleshit's carrier," Rhett said, referring to his wife's pocket-dog. He lifted the bag and started to set it on Josh's desk when the little shit went ape shit. Josh shot him a death glare.

"Last time you brought the mutt here, he crapped under my desk. My office smelled for weeks."

"What can I say? He likes to establish his dominance," Rhett pointed out, like this was a legit reason for a dog to dump on another man's space.

A snarling came from inside the bag, followed by a loud thump as the beast threw itself against the bag, little needle teeth gnawing through the mesh like some kind of gremlin.

"You take that thing everywhere?" Owen asked.

"He has separation anxiety. We're making good progress with the animal behavior specialist."

"Your dog has a therapist?"

"Animal behaviorist. She's the real deal. Even has her own show on Animal Planet."

The brothers all stared in disbelief, speechless that their tough as nails brother was a fur-daddy to a five-pound accessory with whiskers and a bark that sounded like a squeaky chew toy.

Owen shook his head. "That's grounds to revoke your man-card."

"Me?" Rhett asked, clearly offended. "What about him?" He jerked his chin toward Josh. "He's the one planning a tea party."

"He's got a point," Owen agreed. "If the whole DA thing doesn't work out, Darcy's looking for an assistant planner. I can put in a good word for you." Owen nudged a box of decorations with his foot. "What is all this shit?"

"Items for the auction," he explained. "That over there is a self-portrait of Kitty Caldwell. And the framed plate over there? It's from Rosco's Chicken and Waffles. Justin Timberlake once ate off it."

All three brothers burst out laughing.

"You don't have time to help me plan Gage's bachelor party, but you're helping Mom's friends pick out china patterns?" Owen asked.

"No one in this office would tell Kitty Caldwell no. And if any one of you lets it slide to Mom that I'm helping out the woman who beat her out for Auction Chair, I will tell Mom that you've all RSVPed for the auction and you're also heading up the charity dinner portion of the evening."

Owen paled.

Rhett shook his head. "No way. You saw what she did to my wedding. One more mom-run event, and Steph will leave me and grant me permanent custody of Littleshit."

"Why aren't you scared?" Owen asked Clay.

"Mom loves me the best."

They all groaned, but no one argued. It was a widely known fact that Margo Easton doted on her youngest son.

"Well, when Kitty sweet-talked me into helping, the mayor took it as some personal favor for him. Now his wife thinks I'm her assistant." He held up a stack of messages and mail. "I've got decoration and flower people calling my private line, boxes with samples and auction items being delivered around the clock. There are so many sequins and tassels in here, I feel like I'm working out of a Vegas strip club."

"No wonder you've been MIA since the party," Clay said, picking up a crystal vase, then setting it on the other side of the chair.

"And here I thought you were avoiding me because I like to point out how badly you screwed up my bachelor party," Rhett said. "But really you were protecting me and Steph from Mom's meddling. Thanks for taking one for the team, man."

"Glad the slow death of my career benefits your sex life," Josh said. "And your bachelor party was epic."

"If that's what you call epic, then you need to get out more."

Rhett was probably right. Between his caseload and announcing his run for district attorney, Josh hadn't had much time for much of anything. It was a rinse and repeat cycle that fluctuated between work, home, sleep. The most fun he'd had was his little sparring session with a sexy, sharp-witted, and beautiful woman he couldn't stop thinking about. Which made no sense at all. He needed a relationship about as much as he needed another silent auction item. Plus, Josh went for blonde intellectual types who wore mile-high heels, frequented the Whiskey Depository, and loved to talk politics. Piper was none of those things, but talking with her had been the most stimulating conversation he'd had in months.

"Hello?" Owen snapped his fingers in Josh's face. "There you go, thinking about Pretty Photographer."

Josh shoved his brother's hand away. "I'm thinking about how I'm going to kick your ass if you don't get out of my office."

Owen ignored this and leaned all the way back in the chair, stretching out his legs and making himself right at home. He turned to Rhett. "When did Steph get in?"

"Last night. She felt bad about missing the party, so she flew in to take Darcy to the spa for a girls' day," Rhett said. "But tomorrow she flies to New York to attend some pop-up boutique. A shoe company hired her to go on behalf of the brand. Timing blows because I'm in the studio for the next two months and she's traveling pretty much every week. It's just me and Littleshit."

Littleshit barked with delight.

"All the responsibilities, none of the benefits," Owen said. "Welcome to how the rest of the world lives."

"Why are you guys still here?" Josh asked.

"Because we want to know why you didn't tell the mayor to shove it," Rhett said. "There's no way you can help his wife, run an effective campaign, and still keep up with your caseload without suffering massive burnout."

"I bet Russell Heinz is doing the Snoopy dance in his office," Owen said, referring to Josh's opponent in the upcoming election. "I thought the mayor was supposed to be endorsing you."

"He is."

"Then why, when everyone knows Heinz has a snowflake's

chance in hell of winning, is the mayor offering him a snow machine two months before the election?" Clay said.

Clay was more introspective than analytical. When he spoke, it was usually a conversation stopper. He wasn't introverted by any means, but he had a quiet strength about him, an elevated way of looking at things that made people want to listen. A trait he'd inherited from their dad.

And as always, Clay had a good point. The mayor had approached Josh about the election, not the other way around. Caldwell was looking for someone with a chance of beating Heinz, and Josh was the only one with the accolades to run a clean campaign and win. Unlike Heinz, Josh was already a prosecutor for the state of Oregon. But when it came to support, Josh felt as though he was in the fight alone.

Clay carefully studied him in the assessing way of his that always made Josh squirm in his seat. Clay might be the youngest, but he was the most emotionally mature one out of the bunch. "Whatever I can do to help, I've got your back."

"We all do," Rhett said earnestly.

"Great, take over the auction for me."

Clay's palms came up. "No can do. We're playing the San Francisco Forty-Niners this week and the Packers next. The only reason I'm here is because my old high school coach asked me to come and host a charity game to raise money for a new football stadium. After that, I head back to Seattle."

"What about family dinner? Mom's going to kill you if you miss it again."

Clay looked torn. "I know, but I'm already missing some publicity thing with the team today. I have to be back on a plane tonight."

All eyes went to Rhett.

"Hell no," Rhett said. "I meant making an appearance,

reaching out to my contacts. I know they're in the wrong industry, but politicians love celebrities."

Josh sent him a banal look. "Not all politicians."

"You have to get elected to be a politician," Owen pointed out, and Rhett laughed.

"Can you get to the point of this visit so you can leave?"

"We're having poker night at his place." Owen jabbed a thumb Rhett's way. "I've got the new manager covering for me tonight, so I thought we'd toss back a few and play cards."

"Why my house?"

"Because the last time you came over, your dog pissed all over my shoes."

"Women have been doing that for years. Why take it out on Littleshit?"

Josh looked at the stack of files on his desk and sighed. "Screw it, I need a break. I have an aggravated assault case that I need to prepare so it can be filed tomorrow, but I can get there around eight."

There was a knock at the door, and Sadie came in with Owen's hot water. "Your mom called again. She wanted to remind you that you have dance tonight at Partners in Time and if it isn't too much could you pick her up on the way."

"Hey, Fred Astaire, Mom's house is about as 'on the way' as San Francisco is to the Pearl District."

"You want to tell her that?" he asked Owen. "Better yet, why don't I call her and tell her that you're dying to be her plus-one to the charity gala since you don't have a date." Owen paled. "That's what I thought."

"Thanks," he said to Sadie, but instead of closing the door behind her, she stood frozen in the doorway, fixated on Rhett.

"Anything else?"

"Oh." She blinked. "There's someone to see you. She doesn't have an appointment, but she said to tell you that she has a problem and an ADA might come in handy. Want me to have her make an appointment?"

"No." A stupid grin slipped out before he could stop it. "They were just leaving. Tell her I can see her in a minute."

"What kind of handy are we talking?" Rhett asked.

"Does handy mean hands are involved?" Owen added, then stopped. "Is it Pretty Photographer?"

"Piper. Her name's Piper, and how would you feel if you were working, and a woman leaned over the bar and told you she liked your package?"

"I'd say it was my lucky night."

"Out." Josh stood. "Get out." When they didn't move, he went around the desk and forced them to stand, then ushered them to the side door that exited into the hallway.

"You should have said five minutes," Rhett suggested. "One minute makes you sound desperate."

8

Josh slammed the door in their faces. Laughter and kissy noises erupted from the other side. Josh ignored this and walked back to his desk, feeling ridiculously excited that Piper had changed her mind.

He straightened his tie and was organizing his piles when the door opened and she walked in.

Josh began to say "hey," but his tongue was stuck to the roof of his mouth. He hadn't prepared for a knockout brunette in a pretty, blue top and hip-hugging jeans. Their gazes locked and, *damn,* the air seemed to crackle around them.

Her mouth opened a little. Apparently, he wasn't the only one experiencing this crazy chemistry sparking between them.

"This is a surprise." The kind of surprise that had his heart racing. Piper, on the other hand, looked as if she was mapping out every exit for a quick escape. "Have a seat."

"Okay." She glanced over her shoulder, then sat. "I, uh." She looked at the stacks of files on his desk, the disaster of an office, then at the door and blew out a breath. "I hope I didn't interrupt anything. You look busy. Of course, you're busy. I should have called."

She started to stand, and this weird sensation, something similar to panic, filled his chest. "Actually, you caught me at a good time. I was thinking about heading out for lunch," he lied. The only way he'd make a big enough dent to go to dance and then to poker with the guys was if he ate at his desk. But Piper was a hell of a lot prettier than his brothers. "Have you eaten?"

"No," she said distractedly, and he was about to ask her if she wanted to grab a bite with him when she nervously bit her lip. "I need help."

"The kind of help that requires a lawyer?"

"What? No." She sounded pissed. "I don't do that kind of trouble."

He got the feeling there was a silent *not anymore* tagged on the end of that statement. The thought of Piper being a trouble-making teen made him smile. He imagined Teen Piper would have been hell on wheels, whereas Adult Piper was a complicated mix of badassery and understated sweetness. Being around her was like walking a tightrope—one wrong step and he'd hang himself. "Never said you were."

His answer seemed to please her. "I need help with a permit," she began. "I spent the whole morning arguing with the head of the Department of Parks and Rec," she explained. "A friend and I are planning a fundraiser with a local art program that benefits at-risk teens. We hope to have it in South Park or Chapman Square or maybe somewhere inside in case of rain. The girls are so excited, but I may have jumped the gun a little because I'm not sure if I can secure a permit."

"What kind of event were you thinking?"

"Well, Urban Soul is a non-profit organization that gives kids who fell through the cracks a safe place to go after school. They get free art classes in a variety of mediums. I teach photography three days a week. I've even gotten some cameras donated from some of my contacts. It might not seem like a big deal to someone on the outside, but to those of us who went through the program, it's everything."

Her wording let him know that she'd been one of the kids who'd fallen through the cracks and had found a sanctuary in the art program. It would explain her love of art and photography—and the haunted and heartbreaking smile that never quite reached her eyes.

"Is that where you learned photography?" he asked quietly.

"It's where I learned a lot of things, which is why I need this event to happen. It will not only raise money for Urban Soul, but it will help a safe house for young women remain open."

"How many people would attend?" Because that would determine what kind of permit and special services they'd need.

"That's the problem. I don't know. Fifty? Five hundred? Five? It's our first stab at this, so it's kind of a guessing game at this point. We considered having it at the home, like a block party, but the artists have worked so hard I really want this moment to be special for them."

Josh wanted to know more. About the event, the place she loved enough to call home, and the passionate, tough as steel woman who worked her ass off for a group of girls she seemed to care a great deal for.

"Have you thought of asking Darcy to use Belle Mont House?"

She slumped in the chair. "That would require favor number two."

Josh got the distinct impression she didn't like favors and that, at some point in her life, Piper's world consisted of people offering assistance and demanding something in return. Which would explain why she was slow to trust.

She didn't want his sympathy, and she didn't want a handout. She didn't particularly want his help either. He knew this. Yet there she was, sitting across from him, studying him and clearly expecting him to tell her all the reasons why he couldn't help.

"Don't think of this as a favor; think of it as me doing my job as a civil servant."

She seemed to like this answer because she held up a form. "They told me to fill this out. But the lady didn't look hopeful."

She squirmed in her seat, looking uncomfortable and a little crazed. She also looked at his door, as if coming up with a backup exit strategy for when he said no. But she was here, asking for his help. He never knew he had a thing for crazy cuties with permit problems.

His day had suddenly turned around.

"I know you probably get requests for favors all the time, so I understand if you can't do it. Oh . . ." She reached into her pocket and pulled out a check-sized piece of paper. "Since I understand your time is valuable, here."

He looked at the check, shocked that she thought he'd take her money, then he saw it was an IOU. For pictures.

"I don't know if you want new headshots for your campaign posters or maybe bus benches."

"Do I look like a bus bench kind of guy?"

She bit back a smile. "I don't know, Loafers. Lawyers and bus bench ads seem to go hand in hand."

"They're dress shoes," he clarified even though he knew she was teasing. "And I'm not an ambulance chaser, so bus benches are a hard pass, Trouble."

He wasn't sure what he'd said, but her walls slammed shut and her smile vanished. "Trouble?"

He got the distinct feeling that she'd been called that before, but not in the playful way he'd intended. "I was playing off the Loafers dig."

She nodded, but he could tell she didn't believe him. "Good to know," she said quietly. "Anyway, if you want, I can take them maybe this weekend or whenever our schedules match up. You know, a favor for a favor."

He couldn't tell if she was averse to the concept of favors or the idea that she owed someone something. That's not how favors worked in his world. When he did someone a favor, it was given with zero expectations attached. But the embarrassment in her pretty eyes told him that her world played by different rules.

"I have head shots."

"I know."

"You don't like them?"

She flashed him an amused grin. "They look like an ad for some kind of laxative commercial."

"You're saying I look constipated."

She shrugged.

He took the gift card and form. "Deal. But I'm going to have to pull some serious strings to get this emergency permit through." Serious strings that would include bringing Annette over at city hall a box of pastries from her favorite bakery. "Why don't we talk about it over lunch?"

"Now? I can't. I promised I'd take Kylie's cheer team's photos."

And he couldn't because he had back-to-back meetings, a call with his campaign strategist, and zero time to take a woman on a date. Especially a woman who was a living, breathing distraction personified. Still, he found himself saying, "Maybe another time."

"Maybe." She looked at her watch and groaned. "I'm going to be late."

He noticed that she didn't stand or even look at the door this time. Her gaze was locked on his, and there went that crackle. Her eyes widened with surprise.

Right back at ya.

"I wouldn't want to be the reason you're late."

"I'm the one who came here." She bit into that soft curve of her lower lip. "And you're the one doing me a favor. Which, I will, of course, pay back with a favor of my own. Headshots," she clarified as if she still wasn't sure what kind of man he was. Which made him wonder what kind of assholes she'd been exposed to.

Raging assholes, he remembered, and something new unfurled in his gut as the pieces began to click together. She was tough as nails but startled easily. Fiercely independent but prepared for disappointment, and hands down, she didn't trust anything with the wrong appendages.

Her past wasn't his business, but a part of him deep down wanted to show her that there were other kinds of men out there. Men who respected and appreciated her humor and candor, found her below the surface shyness intriguing. Men like him.

"Headshots and a dance," he said with zero pressure in his tone, giving her the out if she needed it. "If that's a fair deal."

"A dance? Here?" She looked around at the boxes and boxes of crap and grinned, but wisely didn't comment on the contents.

"No. Somewhere date-like."

"You want to take me on a date?" she asked, as if he were speaking ancient Hebrew.

"Why should that surprise you?" It surprised the hell out of him.

"I don't know. I guess I didn't think I was your type."

He rested his elbows on the desk and leaned forward. "I find you fascinating."

She did not seem to like that answer. Her eyes narrowed, her lips pressed into one tight line. "Fascinating? Like, she's a wild one who gets into *trouble* fascinating? Because I'm really pretty boring and I don't date suits, Suit."

"Like funny, captivating, a real kind of fascinating, and let me make a note." He pulled out a pen and paper, then made a list. "No loafers. No suits. No lawyer speak. Anything else, Fairy Princess Piper?" He dragged out the F, and she laughed.

"For the last time, drop it."

"No *F* jokes." He set the pen down and looked into her warm, whiskey eyes, which were sparkling with amusement. "So what do you say? You, me, dinner . . . a date?"

"With a dance?" Her gaze darkened with the same thing that had kept him up every night since Gage and Darcy's party.

"And a dance," he said quietly. "I'm talking a dress, heels, and I pick you up kind of dance. It doesn't have to be anything more than you want it to be."

That wasn't completely true. He wanted her naked. But first he wanted her to trust him, so he'd put the ball in her court and see if she sent it back over the net.

She considered it so long he knew she was going to turn him down, which would be new. He hadn't been turned down since freshman year, when he asked Colleen Snow, a twenty-year-old pre-law student who was a server at his dad's bar, to the homecoming dance.

"No dress, I drive myself, and no funny business."

"Does that mean the heels are a go?"

9

By the time Piper finished the school photos, her jeans were grass stained, her shirt had a smudge of glitter, and she was dead on her feet. She'd also landed two new customers, both wanting family photos.

Being a portrait photographer wasn't exactly living the dream, but it kept her and the power company on good terms.

"Thank you so much for stepping in to do the school pictures at the last minute," Darcy said, and Jillian nodded her head in agreement. "I know it's not your thing, but you saved the day."

"I don't know if I'd go that far."

Herding thirty-plus kids for a group photo was about as easy as trying to catch wind in a fishing net, but their energy was contagious. So contagious that being around that many pint-sized people all at once made her a little panicky. They were so small and squirmy.

Squirmy made her nervous. Made her break out in hives. It wasn't that she was allergic to kids, she just didn't know what to do with them. Being an only child, then a street kid, she hadn't had much experience in that department. And her mom certainly didn't pass along any nurturing genes.

"I was almost embarrassed to ask you. It felt like calling Tom Brady to coach a Tiny Tyke football team, but when the other photographer called in sick, Jillian had the brilliant idea to give you a call."

"I'm glad I could help," Piper said.

Jillian snorted. "You hated every minute of it."

"Hate is a strong word."

"Next time, I promise girl time will include a kid-free location with enough mommy juice to require a rideshare home," Darcy said and, at the memory of her last rideshare, Piper's lips started to tingle.

And wasn't that concerning.

"Watching the kids race around like little gremlins who'd been fed sugar after naptime was a little crazy."

"I blame Susan for bringing cotton candy. Every mom knows that red-dye number five causes compulsive laughing, mass hysteria, and, in most cases, temper tantrums."

Piper's mom didn't know that. She'd practically been raised on Pop Tarts, red licorice, and Kool-Aid.

"The cheer moms were kind of intense," she admitted, hoping that she didn't insult Cheer Mom Darcy.

"That was only a local youth league. I can't imagine what it will be like when Kylie's in high school."

"Who knows, maybe she'll decide she wants to play softball instead." Piper credited her middle school softball team for her mad bat skills.

"Somehow I can't imagine her trading in her dance shoes and pom poms for a mitt," Darcy said. "Anyway, you saved the day."

Piper took a deep breath and centered herself. Here she went, about ready to blow up any kind of relationship between her and her new boss. "I may need some saving myself." To her utter surprise, the two women looked at each other, then smiled Piper's way. Big and bright. "I need help figuring out where to throw a non-profit art event for at-risk teens."

At-risk always seemed like a benign word for how risky it was for girls living on the streets. Every day, every night, every time they camped out in front of a store or walked into a coffee shop for a dry place to hang out, they ran the risk of someone calling the cops—or worse.

Piper knew firsthand that there were a lot of things worse than the cops.

"Urban Soul," Jillian said to Darcy. "It's amazing. A few months back, Piper had me come in to teach some of the girls how to bake, and one of them is interning for me now."

"We're throwing an art show as a way to raise money for the students and save a safe shelter that has been home to so many girls over the years." Piper looked at Darcy. This was the big moment. "I need a venue for the first Saturday or Sunday in October. I know it's a big ask, and I wouldn't even think about using Belle Mont House if I wasn't desperate."

"I'm glad you thought of me," Darcy said. "And I want to say yes, but the house is booked every weekend for the rest of the year."

"That's fantastic! Only a year, and already you're killing it," Piper said, feeling silly for even having asked. She should have known that Darcy's place wouldn't have any openings. Her wait list was eighteen months long, and that included weeknights.

"I said the house," Darcy corrected. "I have that large grassy area down by the rose garden that you can use. It has a winding brick walkway lined with cherry blossom trees and beds and beds of roses. It's beautiful and the perfect place to stroll while looking at local art. You'll need a permit because half of the property lies in city limits and the wedding guests will take up the house, veranda, and parking area."

"Already on it." She stuck her hands behind her back and crossed her fingers that Josh came through. "I can't pay you a lot, but I insist on paying you something."

Darcy waved her off. "Don't worry about that. It's available so I'm glad someone can use it. The only downside is the rain."

Piper had thought about that the moment she left Josh's office. Portland was home to Voodoo Doughnuts, the historic Pittock Mansion, and forty inches of rain per year.

"What about tents?" Jillian suggested. She was dressed in an adorable blue-and-white shirt, capris, and strappy sandals. She looked like an Ann Taylor ad went yachting. "You can rent some of those big white tents that they use at the farmer's market. Each tent could showcase one or two artists. That way the weather can't ruin your day."

"I have contacts with party rental businesses who I'm sure would love to help sponsor this kind of event. I can call them for you," Darcy offered.

Piper looked at her friends and found herself speechless. What did one even say in such a moment of friendship and generosity? She was used to being on the helping end of this kind of equation. She'd never experienced people offering to help her just because.

"I don't know what to say," she admitted.

"Five words," Jillian said. "All we need you to say is five words."

Piper racked her brain trying to come up with what that could possibly be.

"Girls' night is a go," Jillian said, sticking out her pinkie.

"Girls' night is a go," Darcy repeated, linking her pinkie with Jillian's like they were ten and making a blood pact. Then both looked expectantly at Piper.

"Girls' night is a go?" she said awkwardly, then linked pinkies. "The kids are going to freak when they see their art displayed in such a classy setting."

At the thought, a feeling of excitement vibrated through her.

She was still riding the high as she headed to her car after Darcy and Jillian forced her to run through the high-five tunnel, where she smacked dozens of sticky, sweaty, and kind of cute little hands. Even though her heart turned over, she decided anyone under four feet would remain a complete mystery to her.

Now, distrustful, angry-at-the-world teens? That was an age group she could relate to. Which was why when she pulled up to Skye's house and caught a teen kneeling down and spray-painting the garage door, she didn't call the cops. She didn't even raise her voice. She just said, "Mas Maxxx is a better paint. It sprays quicker and dries fast. Plus, the nozzle won't clog up and stain your fingers."

The girl leapt to her feet, her eyes wary. She was maybe sixteen and sporting black Converse, denim overalls, and her hair was a shade of red that didn't appear in nature. Everything was speckled in various colors of paint. People like Josh wore suits to the office; people like Piper sometimes wore paint stains and a chip on their shoulder.

"Unless you're paying, I'll stick to mine," the girl said with so much false bravado Piper's gut squeezed.

Arms casually at her sides, like approaching a feral cat, Piper walked over to study the girl's art. Spanning the entire height of the garage door was the image of a teenage girl in a well-worn jacket and red beanie with a robin sitting on her finger. The composition was outstanding, the shading impressive, and the signature woven into the robin's beak read: Bex.

The teen eyeballed her. "You going to call the cops?"

"Just looking at your work," she said. "I'm Piper, by the way."

"I'm Celeste, *by the way*," she said, and they both knew she was lying.

"What do you call it?"

"What do you mean?"

"A piece like this deserves a name," Piper explained. "All the street artists name their work."

This seemed to be new information to the teen. Piper stood quietly as the girl mulled it over in her head. Celeste took a step back, a shocked expression on her face, as if seeing her work for the first time as real art. "Cinderella's a Lie."

The title was as much a shield as the fake name. But who was Piper to call her on it? There was a time when she'd been a surly wiseass who'd say or do anything to keep people from getting too close.

"I like it. Not sure the color scheme matches the house, but the name fits."

Celeste's eyes flashed. "I knew you were going to call the cops!"

"Look, I'm as wary of the cops as you are."

This seemed to appease her. "Why? You got a record?"

"Yup."

"For vandalism?"

"And shoplifting, but the shoplifting wasn't really my fault since I was planning on paying for the boots when I had the money." Celeste looked impressed, as though that gave Piper street cred.

Piper picked up a can of paint and moved to slip it in the girl's bag.

"Hey!" Celeste snatched up her bag and scrambled back a few feet, holding the backpack close to her chest. "That's mine."

Appearing unbothered when the girl's distrusting expression actually bothered Piper a hell of a lot, she held out the paint can. "First rule of vandalism. Hide the vandalizing equipment. It's easier to deny when confronted."

"I knew that." She took the spray paint and put it in her backpack, which looked as if it held all her worldly possessions.

"Where do you live?"

"Around."

"I lived *around* once too," Piper said, taking a handful of emergency chocolate kisses out of her camera bag. She opened one and popped it in her mouth. "*Around* sucks."

Celeste shrugged. "Other places suck worse."

Piper's heart went out to her because she'd been exactly where Celeste was. Alone and scared with nowhere to go and no one to go to bat for her. Until she'd met Skye, who'd taken her in and showed her the world wasn't all bad. She'd not only gone to bat for Piper, but the older woman had also given her the tools to survive.

"Been there too." Piper held out the chocolate kisses, and the girl eyed them like they were laced with anthrax. "Can you hold these for a second?" Celeste took the chocolate, and Piper pulled out her camera. "I want to take a photo of this. Do you mind?"

The girl shook her head. "Chocolate for a picture?"

Piper stepped back until the high sun was squarely at her back, casting a long shadow of her body on the driveway, then snapped the shot. She checked the image on the camera's screen, then walked over to show it to Celeste.

"If you want, I can get a picture of you next to *Cinderella's a Lie*."

"Second rule of vandalism—don't take an incriminating photo."

"Good point." Piper slung the camera over her shoulder. "I can print you a copy if you want. I just have to go inside and use my friend's printer."

She tossed up her hands. "So you can rat me out? I knew you weren't cool."

"I'm cool as shit. And from the smell of it, my friend is probably at her neighbor's baking special brownies, and she has something against permits, so I doubt she'll bat an eye at a piece of street art on her garage."

With the girls in the house, Skye had a strict no drugs or alcohol on the premises rule. But that didn't mean she didn't bake goodies across the street at Ms. Whitmore's house. Twice a week, Skye and Ms. Whitmore delivered fresh-from-the-oven pharmaceutical-grade brownies and cookies to cancer patients in the neighborhood. They never charged, and they never missed a delivery.

"You going to tell her I'm out here?"

Piper shrugged. "Don't need to. She's right there."

They both looked toward the front porch to find Skye in her trademark tie-dyed muumuu with a matching sweatband and white running shoes.

"Well, isn't that amazing," Skye said, her hand to her chest, her expression one of pride. "It's even better than the last."

Piper eyed the girl, and that's when she noticed the tiny silver necklace linked together by an infinity symbol. It was the first thing Skye gave a girl when they came to live with her. "Wow, *around* is a lot closer than I thought."

Celeste shrugged. "I had to make sure you were *cool*."

"She's as cool as your aura is red," Skye said, then looked at Piper. "Rebecca has a strong and passionate energy force. She's going places, this one. Reminds me of you."

"How long have you been at Skye's, *Rebecca*?"

"Oh, Rebecca's here on a trial basis," Skye said, walking down the steps and resting a loving hand on Rebecca's shoulders. "She's testing to see if my 'come and go as you need' policy is true. And I'm testing how many vegetables I can hide in her food."

"Be careful of the mashed potatoes. It's really cauliflower," Piper whispered and laughed when the girl grimaced. "Has Skye told you about the Urban Soul showcase?"

"She said that people who sell their art can make money."

Skye looked at Piper and gave a *keep her talking* gesture. "You should consider entering *Cinderella's a Lie* in the show."

Rebecca rolled her eyes. "I can't really enter a garage door."

"That's why the show is all photographs," Piper explained. "Some of the area's top photographers capture each piece of art on film and then blow up the photo. That's what goes on display and is sold. It's a way that everyone can participate regardless of their medium."

It was also a way to ensure that the pieces sold for serious money. A signed photograph from someone like Clive Kessler could go for thousands, and that was the kind of money they'd need to earn to save Skye's the Limit.

"Can I enter more than one?"

"You can enter as many pieces as you like."

Rebecca studied her shoes as if they were the most interesting thing in the world. "I'll think about it."

"Why don't we let her finish up her work, and you can help me make the cauliflower potatoes." With the intuition of a master chess player, Skye knew when to talk and when to let people process. She understood that after being on their own for months or even years, it was hard for some girls to hold eye contact or conversations for long periods of time. Piper still struggled with group settings, which made shooting events like Darcy's party exhausting.

Piper followed Skye inside where two mugs were already steeping with dandelion tea. "How did things go at city hall?"

"There was a small snafu with some paperwork, but I took care of it," Piper assured Skye—and herself.

"So we don't have to have it here at the house?"

God, she hoped not. She'd only managed to convince some of the photographers to donate their craft because of the pull of a venue like Belle Mont House, and while she'd gotten Darcy to move the date, there was still the small matter of the permit going through.

Piper was more of a do-it-yourself kind of woman. Especially when others were counting on her. But Josh said it wouldn't be a big deal, so she hoped Josh came through; otherwise, Skye might lose her house, which was the only place Piper considered home.

Not to mention, letting down a group of girls who'd had a lifetime of letdowns.

10

After a particularly difficult week involving a handful of bad guys who walked on technicalities, driving his mom to three different appointments, and logging over a hundred auction items, Josh found himself once again back at his desk. It was well past the dinner hour, the office staff had cleared out, and he still had a couple hours of work.

The charity dinner had taken on a life of its own. So had his campaign. Between signing for boxes of sequenced tablecloths and preparing for an upcoming case involving a real estate scam, Josh was averaging sixteen-hour days—and on the fast track to early career burnout. Unfortunate timing, since he had coffee with his campaign strategist the next morning and he hadn't had a spare moment to consider his next steps. At this point, he was beginning to think that maybe it was big goal, bad timing.

Deciding to go home, he gathered up his things and headed to his car. The weather was in a mood. A slight chill cut through his jacket as the fog, so thick it stuck to his lungs, made the air heavy. He took it as a sign that summer and fall were engaged in a battle of the fittest, and he'd put ten-to-one odds that fall was going to emerge the victor.

He shoved his hands in his pockets and was reaching for his keys when he spotted the mayor heading toward the Whiskey Depository, an upscale, membership-only bar and restaurant across the street that specialized in overpriced steaks and one of the largest collections of whiskey in the country.

The last thing Josh wanted was to shoot the shit with a guy who, as it turned out, dished out shit for a living. The mayor had been dodging his calls, making Josh question the man's intentions behind convincing Josh to run in the first place. As the incumbent who was leading twenty points in the latest polls, Mayor Caldwell was a shoo-in. While he had no control over who would be the next district attorney, his endorsement would go a long way. With the current DA retiring at the end of this term, the seat was up for grabs.

Prior to a few months ago, running for office hadn't even been on Josh's radar. It had been the mayor who had approached him, all but begged him to announce his candidacy, promising his full support. At first, Josh had politely declined. While running for the position was always in the back of his mind, he still had a lot of work he wanted to accomplish first. He'd gone to work for the district attorney's office to make a difference, to represent the state in prosecuting people who had zero remorse for their actions and ensuring that the people who went to court should be on trial to begin with.

His strength was as a trial lawyer, arguing cases in a courtroom, whereas the district attorney spent a good amount of time managing and assigning cases, which would give Josh a bigger say in which cases went to trial. Granted, the DA's workload made Josh's look like a book report, and the responsibility with the job was immense. But when Josh's nemesis, Russell Heinz—a high-paid ambulance chaser who had screwed Josh's family by filing a bogus suit against Josh's dad—announced his intentions to run, Josh knew what he had to do.

"Mayor Caldwell!" he called out, and it appeared the mayor's dodging extended to childish antics, such as pretending to be hard of hearing.

Dumping his briefcase in his car, Josh started across the street, managing to catch the mayor as he was about to enter the restaurant. "Let me get that." Josh opened the door and ushered Caldwell inside.

"I've been meaning to call you," the mayor began. "It's just been a crazy time, with the election and Kitty wanting to make the auction the event of the century. You know how busy it can get."

"Oh, I know." Josh halted his explanation of just how full his own plate had become when he noticed the older man's appearance.

The mayor didn't just look busy; he looked harried. His suit was wrinkled, his tie askew as if he'd slept in it, his gray hair was standing on end, and he looked thinner than usual. Then there were the thin lines of exhaustion under his eyes. His disappearing act might have less to do with dodging and more to do with burnout, which had Josh questioning the wisdom of his decision.

"Which is why I thought I could buy you a drink," Josh said, knowing he could use one himself. Being DA was his endgame, had been since he enrolled in law school. But days like today, it felt more like a life sentence than a life goal.

"As long as you're buying." The mayor clapped him on the back.

They took a seat in the bar area, choosing a table near the window, which looked out onto the gas-lamp lit Chapman Square. Lined with hundred-year-old elms and ginkgo trees, twinkle lights strung from lamppost to lamppost, the plaza was one of Josh's favorite places in the city.

"Kitty says you're doing a bang-up job helping with the fundraiser," Caldwell said. "I know you're swamped and planning a party isn't high on your list."

"Or even in my job description."

The mayor ran a hand through his hair, which only made it messier. "There will be a lot of movers and shakers there. Volunteering will go a long way toward gaining some local support." The mayor leaned in. "The kind of support that matters."

The support that mattered to Josh was the support of the everyday people. People like his old man, who deserved more from the justice system than what he had been dealt.

"In fact, I'm meeting Kent Spring for dinner. Have the two of you met?"

"A few times, casually."

Josh and Kent did not run in the same circles, but they had, on occasion, bumped into each other in court. Kent was the head of one of the largest family-owned logging companies in the region. He was known for wining and dining politicians and greasing hands. When that didn't work, he invested in a team of lawyers to find the loopholes in matters that Josh believed should be ironclad. The Spring family also invested their time, and money, into local politics.

The mayor was a stand-up guy, but it didn't matter how clean you played the game if you were watching from the stands. Josh understood how the game was played, how the support of legacy families could turn the tide. Didn't mean he had to like it—or give in to it.

"Maybe it's time you had an official meeting of the minds."

A few months back, when Josh announced to his family he was running, Clay had asked if he really thought someone could run a clean race and win. Josh's immediate answer had been a resounding yes. Lately he was beginning to have his doubts, beginning to question what kind of man he'd have to become in order to win. And if that man would make his father proud.

"Maybe," Josh said with a smile. "I can stay for drinks, but I don't want to intrude on your dinner."

"No intrusion at all." The mayor signaled for the server to bring them two drinks. When they were once again alone, he zeroed in on the reason he was drinking twenty-dollar-a-glass whiskey instead of crawling into bed to dream about a beautiful, curvy photographer in pink silk with black hearts.

"I've been talking with my campaign manager," Josh said, "and she said that now's the time to start solidifying endorsements. Make sure I know where people stand."

"Smart woman. And I've been brainstorming with my strategist, and he warned me not to make any public statements too soon. To wait until the right candidate emerges with support of some local unions and businesses."

"I thought I was the right candidate."

"You're a straight shooter, don't mind asking the hard questions to get the answers you need. I like that. And I want to help you, but finding the right moment is better than just any moment, don't you agree?"

Josh was as far from agreeing as the Easter Bunny was from the North Pole. That right moment? It had come and gone a dozen times over. "Any idea when that will be?"

"I see your brain churning, and don't worry—you're my front-runner. In fact, I was thinking the perfect place might be Kitty's charity auction. Some of the people attending are the people you need backing you. You work that charm throughout the night, get your family involved. A few famous faces will go a long way."

Josh knew his brothers would stand by him in a heartbeat, but he didn't want to leapfrog off their fame. Between agents and managers and obligations, they had enough people wanting a piece of them. Josh wanted them there, but not as pawns in a game. Someone as important as a state prosecutor should be elected on merit, not by who they had in their pocket.

"My brothers will be there to support my mom, but I don't—"

"Mayor Caldwell, I thought I saw you."

Wearing diamond cufflinks, a thirty-thousand-dollar watch and—*well, shit*—shoes with actual tassels, the last person Josh wanted to see approached the table, eyeing the empty seat. Had Josh not been so ticked that Russell Heinz was interrupting an important and private conversation, a long overdue conversation, he would have laughed because Heinz was a loafer. And that brought to mind Piper and their date-to-be-determined dance.

The mayor hadn't been the only one to dodge him this past week. After talking with Annette at the Parks and Rec department over in city hall, Josh had done enough dodging for an entire dodgeball team. Seemed getting a permit in such a short amount of time was near impossible. There were a lot of moving parts, like clearing roads and directing traffic for parking and thoroughfare.

He hadn't given up, but he was running out of ideas. Not that he'd tell Piper. Not yet, anyway. He wanted to make sure he'd exhausted all possibilities before delivering the news.

As a prosecutor, an important part of his job was looking at things from all sides and thinking through every possible outcome. Josh was known as a fixer in the DA's office. He knew how to finesse, where to go for answers, and when to ask for a second opinion. The permit wasn't a done deal, it just needed some finessing.

They'd shared a few texts over the past few days, nothing

special. Only him inquiring about their upcoming date and her inquiring the status on the permit.

She'd filled out the paperwork and refiled with the updated information. Josh had taken a box full of Parisian pastries to city hall to sweeten up Annette, who assured him she was working on it and would have an answer by the end of the week.

Josh hoped it was the kind of news that could be celebrated over dinner. The kind of news that would open a slot in Piper's schedule. He thought *he* was overworked. Between events, portraits, and her volunteer work, Piper was a workhorse.

According to the little recon he'd done at the last family dinner, and what he'd discovered from Darcy, Josh was starting to think her timetable for that date included never. Even the girls had struck out on a no-cameras-allowed night out. From the moment Piper had climbed in his car, he'd had the feeling she was more of a lone wolf. Unlike other women he'd dated, it didn't appear to be some ploy to appear mysterious. He didn't think going it alone was a preference—more of a necessity to avoid disappointment.

So while he didn't have a definitive yes or no on the permit, he did have some news and promised to keep her appraised at every turn. So, while Heinz launched into his typical brown-nosing, Josh pulled out his phone and looked up Piper's contact to tap out a fun text.

Josh: Checked Yelp today. Still no review. Beginning to wonder if I should have driven her home.

Piper: Having a hard time locating Just Josh to post review. Please advise.

Josh: He regrets the name decision immensely.

• • •

Piper: My pumpkin has yet to grow up into a big girl chariot, but she keeps rolling on.

Josh laughed aloud and both men looked at him oddly.

"We keeping you, Easton?" Heinz asked.

"I didn't mean to take over your night. I know you've been working extra hours for my Kitty. Is there somewhere else you need to be?" the mayor asked. "I'm sure Russell here will keep me company until my guest arrives."

Yes. Josh needed to be anywhere but there. Maybe somewhere nice and quiet, that served top-notch cake followed by dancing—with Piper.

"Just confirming a meeting," he said. "My apologies. It will only take a moment."

Josh: If she gets temperamental, remember temperamental is my specialty.

Piper: I thought your specialty was arguing for arguing's sake.

Josh: Actually, it's listening. I'm a master listener.

Piper: You're a peeker too. No one wants a nosy chauffeur.

Josh: A decision I do not regret.

Piper: Such honesty. And before you go on about how your mother raised you right, remember I know your mom.

• • •

Josh: Then it's even more imperative that you get to know me. I can't have you thinking I'm Satan's Keeper's Boy Spawn.

If his mom ever saw this text, she'd send him into time out. Margo was already sniffing around to see why he was sharing texts with Kitty Caldwell, the first woman in seven years to beat out Margo for Auction Chair. He didn't need to give his mom any more ammo, or he might wind up disowned.

Piper: . . .

In texting, three blinking dots were the equivalent of a thick silence between questions. Silence made people uneasy, inciting a need to fill it. Not Josh. It was in the silent moments that he won battles. Sure, he could push a little harder. Use some flirty technique to extract more information. But Cross Examination 101 warned against asking one question too many. When it's going well, the temptation to ask one more thing is strong. However, with some people, like Piper, the next question would allow her to reflect, realize she's giving away personal information, and retreat. So Josh decided to give her some additional information on himself.

Josh: Having drinks with Satan himself. Want to know how I know he's the legit fallen angel?

Piper: Horns?

Josh: No horns. Loafers. Tan leather. Side stitched. Mock toe shingle. Double tassel.

Piper: I don't know what's worse. Mock toe shingle or you knowing what a mock toe shingle is.

. . .

JOSH: It's the tassels. Trust me.

PIPER: So, you're grabbing drinks. A Tinder date? Let me guess, your shared love of loafers brought you together? What does Satan with Tassels order?

JOSH: A $400 bottle of scotch and is going to try to sneak it onto my tab.

PIPER: You need new friends.

JOSH: Working on it. Seriously though, I have an update on the permit. I have my best person on it.

PIPER: ...

This time the three dots seemed heavier, as if there were a significance behind them. It lingered on and on until they vanished. Connection dead. He read and reread his text, his heart pinching for the woman who was so gun-shy of being let down she'd rather be alone.

He waited for her to return, but she'd gone radio silent. So he was forced to listen to Heinz kiss ass and try to weasel his way into stealing the mayor's endorsement. Caldwell wasn't ignorant; he knew what was going on, but the old man loved to talk. And Heinz was a skilled talker.

"I'm just confirming with the photographer for the auction," Josh explained as he pocketed his phone.

"I thought I heard something about you being an event planner." Heinz laughed. Josh did not. "Seriously though, if you need to put on your party planner hat, the mayor is more than welcome to join me. I have a table reserved in the dining room."

"I'm waiting on Kent Spring," the mayor boasted as if Kent were the head of the United Nations.

"Kent and I go way back to our days at Stanford," Loafers said, his chest so puffed, he looked like the Stay-Puft Marshmallow Man. "I even represented him a few times over the years."

Of course he had. Josh had faced Heinz enough times in court to know exactly the type of clients he took on. Heinz started to preach about all the projects he and Spring had worked on over the years, and Josh went back to listening for his phone to vibrate.

"It would be great to catch up." Heinz sent Josh a Cheshire-like grin. "If you don't mind me crashing the party."

"The more the merrier," Caldwell said.

"Great."

Josh felt a headache blooming behind his right eye. He was starting to regret stalking the mayor instead of heading home when a pair of scuffed-looking boots appeared in his line of sight.

It was the exact person he needed to see in that moment.

Piper.

She looked softer than usual. Her long, dark, blue-streaked hair was pulled up in a messy ponytail with little pieces sticking up in the back, looking a little ruffled and a whole lot tempting. Her incredible face was all natural, and her top was black, off-the-shoulder, exposing a tiny little strap that was made to mess with a man's mind. The strap was too little to conceal a bra, which meant she was either going strapless or braless—both options gave him a hard on.

And—*would you look at that?*—she had on bright-red knee-high boots. Not suede, not leather, and no straps or eyehooks. Oh no, Piper had on rain boots. Red ladybug rain boots.

"Hi," she said to the table, her voice sounding shy, and he decided shy looked good on her. Sure, she was dressed like she'd been shooting wildlife in the park, and she had her usual collection of bags slung over her chest, but just looking at her made his stress drop ten decibels.

"Hey." He stood, unsure if he should hug her or shake her hand. She looked one wrong move away from bolting. So he went with professional. "What are you doing here?"

"You said you had news and when you mentioned loafers and whiskey, I put two and two together."

He wasn't sure how he felt about the comparison, but her assessment had been pretty damn accurate. In a five-square-mile city, she'd located him in under ten minutes. "Only that it's in progress and—"

The mayor cleared his throat.

"Excuse me, Mayor Caldwell," Josh said. "This is Piper Campagna."

Looking both embarrassed and uncertain, she took in the mayor and his overall snooty ambiance, then studied her own boots. When she met his gaze, it was resigned. "I didn't mean to interrupt. I saw you through the window and thought that . . ." She waved a dismissive hand, sending her million-and-one bags clattering together. She put a firm hand on them. "I should go."

"Don't," he said, and everyone looked at him.

"But you're in a meeting." She lowered her voice. "We can talk later."

"Nonsense," the mayor said. "We're finishing up with the business half and are about to enjoy a bite to eat. Join us."

"Yes, please," Heinz said. "Have a seat and tell us how you and Josh know each other."

She looked from Heinz to the mayor, and back to Josh, a

vulnerable plea for help to define their very undefinable relationship. "Piper is an up-and-coming Portland photographer who has generously offered to take some portraits for my campaign as well as shoot Bid for the Cause."

"Nice to meet you both," she said.

"It's very nice to meet you, Piper. Maybe I should give you my card. I might be in the market for some new headshots myself." Heinz didn't stand, didn't look her in the eyes, just held out his card and did a slow, insulting once-over. "Russell Heinz, candidate for district attorney."

Josh watched as every single wall locked into place, making a fortress around her. Her posture shifted to chin up and shoulders back—and, *damn*, she was pretty when she was riled. "Actually, I'm an urban landscape photographer by training and portrait photographer by circumstance. And as circumstance would have it, my schedule is pretty full, Russell."

That was the most personal information she'd ever offered up about herself, and Josh wanted to know more. All he knew about photography was that either he liked it or he didn't. But he did know about how circumstances could define the direction of someone's life.

"But really, Assistant District Attorney Easton, we can catch up later." She looked at her watch. "Actually, I'm late for a meeting." She scratched her wrist, something she did when nervous.

Or lying.

"It was nice to meet you," she said, and Josh noticed she only addressed the mayor.

Caldwell stood and shook her hand, and Josh realized that he hadn't sat back down. He was so enamored with Piper, he'd been standing the entire time. Or maybe it was because he didn't want to sit back down. Maybe he wanted to be in that meeting she so clearly lied about having.

She'd come here, to a place she clearly felt out of place in, just to find him. And he wanted to know why. More than he wanted to spend the rest of his night with a bunch of men who liked to hear themselves talk.

"Mayor. Heinz. Thanks for the drink, but I forgot Miss Campagna and I have something to discuss."

"Are you sure?" she whispered. "It isn't very important." And there was something about the way she said it, as if she were used to being unimportant, that didn't sit right with Josh.

"Actually, it is." He turned to the mayor. "I'm working with her on a fundraiser for Skye's the Limit, and there's a lot to get in place over the next few weeks."

Heinz scrunched his face like he'd caught a whiff of his overpowering cologne. "Wait, isn't that a shelter for wayward girls?"

"Do people say *wayward* anymore?" she asked, then looked at Heinz. "Nice shoes. Are those mock toe shielded? My minister has the same pair." Before Heinz could determine if it were a genuine compliment or not—it was most definitely not—she turned to the mayor. "I like to think of Skye's as a safe haven for young women. It's one of the best places in the city for homeless girls who deserve a second chance and have aged out of the system. They don't have anywhere to go or anyone to help them, so Skye provides a home and family. For some of them, it's their first real home. And we're fighting to save it."

There was a fierce protectiveness to her tone that made him wonder again what her connection was to the home. His gut told him this fundraiser was more personal for her than she was letting on.

"You're in good hands. Easton here has become quite the event planner." Heinz chuckled.

"He's big on giving back. I think it's one of the reasons he'll make a great DA." This time that fierceness was for his benefit, and it turned him on.

"I agree," the mayor said. "It was nice meeting you, Miss Campagna."

"It was nice meeting you." She turned to Josh. "I'll call you tomorrow about the permit."

She was halfway through the restaurant when suddenly Josh didn't give two shits about Heinz, Spring, or the dinner. Grabbing his coat off the hook, he said, "Mayor, I'll catch up with you next week."

The mayor stood, looking puzzled. "What about your drink?"

Josh picked it up, drained it, let the burn heat his chest, then set the tumbler down. "Thanks for the drink, Heinz. Mayor, see you first thing Monday."

If the mayor chose to back a guy like Heinz, he wasn't the right partner for Josh. Over the next couple months, there would be dozens of stuffy donors at suffocating dinners like this, at the Whiskey Depository or fundraisers. This might be his only chance to walk around with Piper and say... what?

That with her candid honesty and sweet smile, she could fix this crazy mess of a life he'd created. She represented a new direction he wanted to go in.

Jesus, what was he doing? He'd come to corner the mayor into coming through on his original promise, not leave him with his biggest opponent at a dinner that could dictate the outcome of the election.

Sure, Heinz had thrown him off guard and he wasn't his usual self, but if he were a smart man, he would give Piper the full update on her permit, then pack it up and go home. Alone.

Except that's what he'd be—totally and completely and pathetically alone. Clay and Rhett were back to doing what they loved. Owen was having dinner with Mom, and Gage was playing peewee golf with his family. And Josh? He was exactly where he'd been the day he'd moved home from Silicon Valley

—sprinting toward a finish line in a race he didn't even remember entering.

Somewhere between law school and announcing his candidacy, his focus had shifted, sometimes sacrificing the why for the win, knowing that without *why* the win doesn't matter. Which was the only reason he could come up with for why he burst through the front door.

"Boots!" he called out when he spotted her halfway down the block. Her bags flapping around her, she was making good time hurrying away from him. "Piper."

She stopped, her hand in front of her face and squinted. He gave a stupid little wave, and her eyes went wide. She looked behind her, at her car and back to him. Josh couldn't really say the moment he knew she wasn't going to run, but all that pent-up stress from the week vanished into something warmer.

They both began walking, his legs eating up the ground between them a little faster, but he wasn't the only one chasing in this scenario. Something had changed. It was all over her expression.

Her boots echoed off the pavement, not letting up until she was standing close enough to touch. Close enough to smell— which was freaking incredible. She looked up and let loose a killer smile—and he smiled back.

"What are you doing?" she asked over the sound of his workweek driving by. She set her camera bags on the hood of a nearby car, the motion causing that little strap to slip off and down her bare shoulder.

"Chasing you," he admitted. "And I think you were chasing me back."

11

Piper no longer believed in chasing—friends, men, even family members. In her experience, people ran for a reason—none of them good—so it was safer to avoid confrontation at all costs.

But if she wasn't chasing Josh, then why the sheer number of nerves pulsing through her body at the speed of light?

She looked back at POSH, her reliably unreliable speedy escape, then blew out a breath. "I thought I was running away, but I must have gotten turned around."

"Lucky me." He moved closer.

"Lucky you." She didn't move back.

He looked down and gently nudged her boot with his toe. "Nice boots."

"Nice loafers." He started to argue, and she held up a hand. "I will downgrade their offensiveness to somewhere between dress shoes and deck shoes." She was working hard not to grin. "Have you ever heard of Nike or Vans?"

"Your ladybugs are fitting in the drizzle. My Nikes are blue and clash with my slacks."

"I'd ditch the slacks then."

"Maybe that's an indoor request," he said, and this time his smile packed some serious punch.

"That would be the way you're looking at me," she said quietly, glancing down at her scuffed boots, stained jeans, and oversized sweater. "I thought you wanted the whole dinner, dance, dress trifecta?"

"I guess I just want you. The rest is negotiable," he said, and Piper decided this was the best conversation she'd had in years.

Her brain checked out. Just like that. One sweet comment, and she was a goner.

"Why did you come here tonight?"

"To ask about the permit." Last time she'd checked, the permit wasn't stuck to his lips, but she was powerless to look away.

"It's moving through the system, and I should know more next week." He reached out to fix her strap, only to cup her hip instead. She didn't shift away. She might have even swayed like they were in high school, and she was waiting for him to ask her to prom. "But you could have called me about that. Instead, you came and found me."

"I'm good at finding people." She picked up her camera and pointed it at his face.

He palmed the lens and lowered it. "Don't hide."

"That's another thing I'm good at."

Some people stayed in the shadows because they didn't want to be seen. Others hid because they wanted someone to care enough to look for them. Adult Piper knew that waiting to be found was like playing hide-and-seek in the Grand Canyon, but a small part of her, the scared and lost teenager, still held out hope someone would venture into the shadows for her.

There weren't many shadows tonight, not with Josh's light radiating around her.

"I know," he said, and he sounded sad, which was fitting

because it was hard to remain happy when being alone was her modus operandi.

Instead of handing her camera back, he asked, "May I?" He tapped her camera.

Her first instinct was to say no and grab the camera back, and he knew it. She reached for the strap and held tight. The look he gave her was one of gentle challenge. She was cryptic and closed off, this she knew. But her photos were beyond personal. They were a glance into all the things she hid behind her ironclad walls.

"You've seen my stuff," she said.

"Correction. I've seen the stuff you take because someone pays you. These are the ones you take because they spoke to you. I want to know what speaks to you, Boots."

"Boots?"

He looked down and grinned. "It seemed fitting.

That he was willing to ask, to take the time to get to know her through the lens she viewed the world, made a complicated knot of desire and vulnerability twist deep inside.

In the end, she let go of the strap.

He winked at her, then flipped through the images on the screen. She watched him watching her world unfold, and never in her life had she been so nervous about someone's opinion. She took photos for herself, captured the things that resonated with her, told the kind of stories she related to. Her photos weren't necessarily pretty; they were real and raw and complex, showing the complicated side of humanity most people try to ignore.

It was in the flaws that she found life's beauty, but she knew what he saw: a homeless man in the sea of suits, surrounded by dozens of concrete park tables and graffitied benches. The men were gathered around a table, watching a game of speed chess unfold.

"This is Pioneer Square," he said with a grin. "My dad and I used to have lunch there every Sunday. After going to the zoo or a long hike, we'd grab something from one of the food trucks on Fifth, then come sit in the plaza and people watch."

"Did you always want to be a lawyer?"

"God, no. I wanted to be a forest ranger. Then a cowboy. And finally, I wanted to work with tech start-ups."

"What happened?"

"Life." He slid her a glance. "Loafers are a side effect of necessity."

Piper knew all too well about the impact of curveballs and how they could permanently change the course of one's life. Not always for the better.

"What changed?"

"My parents found themselves trapped in a lawsuit that never should have gone as far as it did," he said, the pain in his voice sounded as if it had happened yesterday. "Watching what they went through, knowing my dad spent a good portion of his last years fighting to keep what was rightfully his, caused me to change majors and apply to law school."

She rested her palm against his chest—right above his heart. "I'm so sorry."

The gesture had been one of caring, but the innocent contact quickly changed, and the air zapped around them. Holding her gaze, he slowly moved his hand until it covered hers. He paused, giving her a chance to retreat, but instead she found herself frozen in the moment.

"What about you? What did you want to be?" he asked.

At first, she wasn't sure what to say. Then she decided to go with honest. "Safe," she whispered. "When I was little, I just wanted to be safe."

He watched her for a long moment, and she waited for the pity to shine in his eyes, for him to take a small step back like most people did when she opened up about her past. Instead, he laced his fingers with hers. "Is that why you came to Portland? To be safe?"

She shrugged. "I thought so, but then I realized that if I wanted to be safe, I'd have to work hard and get my own place, where no one could come in and no one could kick me out."

"It sounds lonely."

She tilted her head. "There are worse things than lonely." She could name a hundred off the top of her head.

He lifted her knuckles to his lips and kissed them. "You're pretty amazing, you know that?"

"For embracing loneliness?"

"For seeing the world the way you do and becoming the woman you are today."

"I didn't have many choices, and the ones I did have would have landed me in jail or worse." Like Faith.

Still holding her hand, they started walking. "When did you become interested in photography?"

"I didn't even hold a camera until I was a teenager. But looking back, I loved to stare at photos. I used to go to garage sales and buy old pictures. I know it sounds weird, but when things were bad, I would imagine I lived inside that one perfectly captured moment."

A moment like this.

Before she knew what she was doing, she lifted her special camera and turned the lens to bring his face into focus, blurring the background until the lights from the historic gas lamps created a soft glow around him. He didn't shy away or flash one of his charming smiles, instead looking right into the camera as if he were looking at her.

His usually assessing eyes were a warm sky-blue, his expression open, and there was a vulnerability that made her breath catch. The sound of traffic and glow of brake lights blurred around them, drizzle clung to his hair and lashes, and a sense of rightness began to grow.

She pressed the button, and the shutter opened and closed, and he still didn't look away. Feeling exposed, she lowered the camera and slung it over her shoulder.

"You still shoot with film?" he asked.

"I prefer film, but clients like options. Lots and lots of options. With film, there's no post edits or effects. Just thirty-five millimeters of life. And what you see is what you get."

"What did you see a moment ago?"

She saw someone who could break her heart if she wasn't careful. She stepped back and cleared her throat. "I can't imagine trying to keep track of all your brothers at the zoo."

Even though he didn't say anything, she could tell he wanted to ask her more about her past, but he let it go.

"Sundays were just me and my dad. With six boys, he made sure he did something different with each one of us. Mine was nature and shawarma. Rhett's was anything that had to do with music. He tailored everything he did with us."

Piper couldn't even begin to fathom what that kind of childhood would have been like. Her mom was an addict: alcohol and men. By the time Piper was ten, she'd had five different dads. None of them stuck around long, especially the nice ones, which made Piper gun-shy of commitment.

"I knew you had a lot of brothers but hearing the word *six* is terrifying to someone who was an only child."

"I can't imagine not having siblings. Was it lonely?" he asked.

She shrugged. "Sometimes, but I guess I didn't know any different." Piper had learned that lonely and being alone were vastly different states. She didn't mind being alone, but the lonely part was getting harder by the year. "What's it like with so many brothers?"

"Loud," he said, and they both laughed.

"Quiet can be overrated."

He looked at her so long, she began to squirm. It was as if he were seeing all the parts of her she did her best to hide. Piper knew she wasn't everyone's cup of tea, but some of her parts, her most challenging parts, were hard for people to accept or understand.

"So can all the noise."

"My friend would tell you to just turn down the volume," she said.

"Does this *friend* wear slacks and a tie?"

She snorted. "This *friend* wears tie-dye and the Universe's blessings. And in case you were angling to figure out if I'm single, the answer is yes."

"Good to know since I've been thinking about you nonstop since the party."

A thrill zinged through her. "What have you been thinking about?"

"Most recently, I've been obsessed with what's going on under that sweater." His hand slid around to her lower back, and he tugged her closer. "Lace or silk, Boots?"

She laughed. "A little of both."

That earned her a half-smile, which always managed to make her knees quiver. "Are we talking pink with black hearts?" He looked at her boots. "Please say they're red."

"You'll have to wait a lot longer than one date to find out the answer to that question."

"This is a date, then?"

"I'll let you know."

"While you're figuring it out..." He took her hand in his, and the most incredible thing happened. Instead of making up some excuse, Piper laced their fingers, and that was how they walked, side by side, silently holding each other's hands. It was a gentle and sweet gesture that reminded her of picture-frame photos she'd seen in drug stores.

No pretense, no games—just a simple act of connection that moved her.

"Do your parents live in Oregon?" he asked, and Piper's chest filled with a lethal combination of embarrassment and anger, like it always did whenever her mom was brought up in conversation.

"My dad left when I was little, and I don't know where my mom is."

"I lost my dad when I was in college, and it shattered my world. I can't imagine not growing up without him. Do you miss him?"

She never understood why people were always so fascinated with who one's parents were. Then again, she didn't really have parents. She had a family in Skye, but she didn't have parents. That always made people more uncomfortable than it did her. And since she was engaged in an actual adult conversation that didn't involve the word "cheese," she wanted to steer clear of pity topics.

"You can't miss what you don't remember. It was just me and my mom, that was all I knew." Until it was just Piper.

There were still days she wondered what would have been harder. Being alone on the street or being scared in her own house.

In a very Josh-like move, instead of asking her more questions, he took the spotlight off her and gave her a chance to catch her breath.

"I used to be so mad at the world. Then my dad died," he said. "Then a few years later, my brother Kyle died. He and Gage were twins, and I remember at his funeral being relieved that my dad was gone. Losing Kyle would have crushed him."

After watching how bonded the brothers were, she couldn't

even imagine how hard it must have been on them to lose a brother—for Gage to lose a twin. "I'm so sorry. That must have been hard. Especially on you."

He stopped, looking surprised. "Why me?"

She watched the emotions play in his deep-blue eyes and knew she was right. Knew that everyone likely gave Gage the wide berth and support he needed to grieve. But Josh had been the one giving the support, being strong for everyone else, burying his own pain to be there for his family.

"You love your family, and you take your role as eldest seriously. I saw you at the party, watched the way you kept your eye on your siblings, making sure they were okay." She gave his hand a gentle squeeze. "Then there was the way you were with your mom. Gentle, but stern when she crossed a line. It was clear that you love each other very much."

"She likes to cross lines, and at the party she crossed a few too many with you."

"Mothers of the groom can sometimes be more difficult than mothers of the bride. After a few weddings, I kind of expect it." And before he could make some grand gesture about protecting her from his big, bad mother, she said, "The way your family loves is pretty special."

"Sometimes it feels as if we're all in each other's business, but I know how lucky I am." They had been quiet for a long moment, just walking through the park, when he asked. "Do you play chess?"

She looked around and realized they were in the part of the park where the stone chess tables sat. A few homeless men were tucked tightly in sleeping bags or their overcoats, sleeping on the park benches.

"God, no. Do you?"

"Not really." He tightened his grip, then tucked their hands in his sports coat pocket and that was how they walked, fingers laced and cocooned in his warm embrace.

"Herman, he's the one in the photo, is a legend. He was a chess grandmaster. I mean he *is*. I don't think such an accomplishment can be taken back. Do you?"

He glanced down at her. "Do you?"

"I hope not," she finally said. "It would be cruel to take something away after working so hard to earn it. And he must have worked really hard. He once showed me a copy of *Chess Review*, and he was on the cover."

"Do you know what happened? How he ended up on the streets?"

"There's a lot of reasons people end up here, but Herman never shared that with me. I'm pretty sure he's bipolar and the meds take the edge off. It's kind of sad, when you think about it. Choosing between living a regular existence or engaging in an extraordinary love." She looked up at him. "What would you choose?"

"Don't you think you can have both?" he asked, his gaze full of consideration.

Reason enough to call it a night. Their worlds were so far apart, she could drive a Greyhound bus through the distance. Yet, she found herself answering. "Depends on the person, I guess."

He slowed to a stop. "Why did you come looking for me tonight?"

"You mentioned expensive whiskey and a sea of loafers. I saw your car was still in the lot and thought, *Self, where would Loafers go?* I looked across the street, and there you were."

"Now that you've seen a real loafer, you have to take that back."

"I'll think about it," she teased. "And I could lie and say it was because of the permit, but I think it was because I wanted to see you. I didn't mean to pull you away from a dinner. With the mayor, of all people. I really am sorry."

"Don't be. I have dinner with him once a week. I'll catch up with him on Monday," he said, but she got the feeling he was sugarcoating the situation. "In fact, you're kind of saving me. I haven't gotten out of my tie before midnight in weeks."

She stopped and turned to him until they were facing each other, then slowly loosened his tie. She watched him watching her, the heat in his gaze so explosive one carefully planned touch and they'd ignite in a giant ball of pent-up sexual tension.

Tie loosened, her fingers began to tingle, and she dropped her hands. "I don't want you to think I'm not grateful for all your help. It's just there are a lot of people counting on me, and I don't want to let them down."

"Monday, I promise."

That word gave her heartburn. "Didn't your mama tell you that you shouldn't make promises you don't know if you can keep?"

"Mama?" He lifted a brow. "Do I detect an accent? Piper Campagna, are you a southern belle under those ladybug boots?"

"I learned early on that when it rained it poured, and the only way to tackle life's mud puddles was with the right pair of boots." Or at least that's how she justified her obsession. "Some women love handbags. I take it your mom collects jewelry." His eye roll said she'd nailed it. "For me, it's all about the boots. Ankle, knee-high, thigh-high. Leather, suede, or steel-toed. Doesn't matter. If they were made for walking, I have to have them."

"Forget the heels and tell me, in great detail, about these thigh-high boots."

She laughed. "Thigh-high is definitely fifth date material."

"What are you doing tomorrow night?"

"Working. But I'm free next Sunday."

"Then, sadly, it would have to be a good pair of hiking boots." He took her hand and tucked it back in his pocket. "Do you like hiking?"

"I'm a photographer; I live outdoors." She was beyond touched that he was inviting her to be a part of a tradition that reminded him of his dad. "And I have an excellent pair of hiking boots."

"What started your boot habit?" he asked. "Unless your shoe fetish is off limits."

There was a lot about Piper that was off limits. But tonight, with him, she wanted to make a connection. "I was five and they were rubber. Army green and black camo."

"Birthday present?"

"Lost and Found. They were two sizes too big, but they'd looked tough." Something she'd desperately needed to feel at the time.

One look at the already-worn galoshes, and Piper was hooked. Lost and Found boots began a yearly back-to-school tradition, which lasted until Piper was fifteen and her mom's newest boyfriend became tired of looking without touching. Piper had snuck out the window, made her way to Portland, and celebrated her newfound freedom with her first pair of never-before-worn boots.

They were steel-toed for impact, jet black, and the kind of kick-ass that made her feel invincible when she'd slid them on. And they'd nearly cost her a night in juvie—since she'd neglected to pay for them on her way out. But the owner had cut her a deal, landing Piper with her first-ever job and her first-ever pair of ass-kicking boots.

A lot had changed in Piper's life since then, but she never left the house without a spare pair of boots.

"From the southern accent, I'd have thought cowgirl boots."

"I'm from Georgia, but my accent only slips when I'm tired. Most people don't even hear it."

"Georgia peach." He nudged her playfully. "Did you know peaches are my favorite fruit?"

"Again, you need to up your flirting game."

"Okay, so no funny business, but flirting is allowed?"

Indecision weighed heavily, nearly pulling her all the way under the water so that the oxygen deprivation made flirting with Josh seem like a good idea. She took her phone from her bag and dialed. His phone rang and his grin went into a full-fledged smile.

It rang a second time. "You might want to get that. It could be important."

Gaze locked on hers, he ever so slowly reached inside and pulled his phone from the pocket. "Josh Easton, assistant district attorney and professional chauffeur. What can I do for you?"

"You can ask me to dance."

"I'm a little busy right now, filing suit against Fate, Satan's Keeper, and raging assholes of all kinds."

"Actually, I'm calling to talk to Josh Easton, the guy who gave me his card."

"Hold, please." He handed her the phone, then went about unbuttoning the top button of his shirt and, Lordy, if Josh the ADA was hot, then Josh the laid-back single guy who wanted to dance was smoking. He took the phone back. "Hey, Piper. I was hoping you'd call."

"You're not even going to pretend it could be some other girl you met at the party?" she asked into the mouthpiece.

"Nope."

That was it. One word. But it was delivered with so much conviction Piper could scarcely breathe.

"Well, what I wanted to say is—" Actually, Piper didn't want to say a thing. She wanted to feel. "I don't want to talk right now."

"What do you want to do?"

She took an instinctual step back, because no matter how badly she wanted to kiss him, she knew it was a colossally stupid idea.

"Don't overthink," he said, stepping into her until she was flush against the trunk of a walnut tree, the soft glow of the moon spilling around them. "Just tell me what you want to do."

"Not talk."

He looked at her lips. "I got that. You need to be more specific." He studied her intensely, his expression dead serious as if trying to figure her out. "You're a contradiction."

"Is that a nice way of saying I'm confusing?"

He took her phone and pocketed them both. "It's a nice way of saying you drive me insane."

She closed her eyes. "That doesn't sound like a glowing review."

"People surprise me on a daily basis. Do you know how few of those surprises are good?"

She thought about what he did for a living, the kind of screwed-up situations he must be exposed to, and her heart went out to him. "Not a lot, I imagine."

He cupped her face. "But you? You are the kind of exciting, unexpected, breath of fresh air surprise."

She opened her eyes to find his unwavering and purposeful. "My life is one big question mark," she began. "Every day, personal and professional, I never know what's headed my way or how I'm supposed to react. Being around you"—she swallowed hard—"feels safe."

"In this example, is safe synonymous with sexy?"

"You talk too much," she said and suddenly she was feeling very . . . flirty. And sexy. And before she could stop herself, her arms were around his neck, her body pressed against his, and her teeth sank gently into his lower lip.

It took him a moment to respond. A moment so long she thought he'd changed his mind. Then with a low, guttural groan, he drew her up against him and covered her mouth with his.

She finally understood why he was such a great lawyer. His mouth should be licensed as an infinite law-making machine. One kiss, and he had all her checks and balances tilting toward a solid *oh my*.

He nipped at her lower lip, then her upper, starting off slow, then moving straight into confident demand. His fingers were confident, too. Teasing the edge of her sweater, tracing up, underneath the hem, to explore the bare skin beneath. Making her hotter and a little crazier every trip he took. His thumb slid around to trace her hip bone, across to her stomach, rubbing back and forth over the sliver of skin right beneath her belly button.

Someone moaned. Okay, she moaned. It was needy and desperate and—

"You taste like strawberry."

"It's my lip gloss."

He drew her lower lip into his mouth and let it go with a pop. "It's my new favorite. Morning smoothies will take on a whole new meaning."

His comments released a flutter of nerves. *New favorite* made her think of flavor of the month and while this was their first kiss, she wanted more. Wanted to be in his arms longer. Never one to shy away from anything, she slid her hands up his very defined chest to his undone tie and tugged him closer.

"Jesus," he groaned, his hands sliding around to grab her ass, then walking her backward until he was holding her in place with his mouth.

God, his mouth. He was a kissing master of the highest order

—teasing her lips. Which she parted, and when his tongue did a gentle sweep against hers, it obliterated every sane reason for why this was an unquestionably bad idea.

He didn't say anything else. Didn't need to. His very large pledge of allegiance was front and center, pressing into all her good parts, telling her he wanted this as badly as she.

She finished undoing his tie and went to work on the second button when a big rig drove by, rustling the leaves overhead, and that's when she remembered where she was. In a public park with her tongue down Josh's throat and his hands on her ass where any passerby could see.

Josh must have thought the same, because he pulled back enough that they could both suck in some much-needed air. Not that it helped. The night's air was thick and weighed heavily in her lungs.

"That was—"

"Yeah."

"What exactly was that?" she asked against his mouth.

"Chemistry."

"I've felt chemistry. That was—"

"Insane. I can't tell what's more shocking. That you kissed me or that I managed to wait that long for this kiss." He gave her a softer, shorter kiss.

"I believe you kissed me."

"However you want to play this, Boots." He held her between the hard tree trunk and his harder manly trunk.

"I'm not playing at anything," she whispered.

"Neither am I."

12

Josh spent the first part of the morning trying to fix the permit problem, and the last half trying to figure out how to tell Piper that no amount of pastries could get an emergency permit approved with only a month's notice.

"It's like you're not even trying," Owen said, pinning Josh to the mat.

Every Tuesday and Thursday whichever brothers were in town met at Lucky's Gym to beat the shit out of each other. Today, everyone was there except Clay, which meant they all had a fighting chance of coming out the victor. Even though Owen had three inches and thirty pounds on Josh, Josh was used to winning.

Not today.

Today, his mind was on Piper and that kiss they shared. It had been five days, but he could still taste her strawberry lip gloss. Remember the way she felt pushed up against him. All the years of wearing suits, he'd never dated a woman who used his tie as foreplay.

It was hot. And sexy. As were all the other scenarios of what could come after, that he'd played out in his head.

Josh was still thinking about how silky her skin felt beneath that sweater when he stood, and out of nowhere, Owen rushed him and took him to the floor—hard. They both groaned at the impact.

"What the hell was that?" Josh asked, rolling onto his side to get up.

"You, easily distracted by a girl," Gage said from outside the ring, his arms lazily resting on the ropes.

Josh paused. "What?"

Owen took the moment to go for a cheap shot, landing a boxing glove above Josh's right eye.

"Jesus, bro! I have court tomorrow."

"Better not bruise his pretty mug," Rhett said, and the guys laughed.

"Ha-ha, but the next time one of you needs a lawyer, remember this moment."

The brothers had been boxing since the day Josh, Rhett, and Owen had gotten into it over a Power Ranger action figure and their mom shoved them through the screen door and into the back yard, then locked the house and didn't let them back inside for an entire night. The next day, their dad signed them up for Aikido. When that didn't help—it just expanded their torture tools—their mom enrolled them in boxing.

Twenty years later, they still needed a way to blow off steam and work through problems.

"No wonder Heinz is gaining on you," Rhett said. "If Owen can take you, then a little prick like Heinz should have zero trouble."

"I could take you in my sleep, little man."

"If you miss another Friday-night family dinner, Darcy is going to kick my ass, then yours," Gage said.

"Since when are family dinners at your house?" he asked,

because family dinners had always been at his mom's or at the bar. Always.

"Since Mom started thinking that dinner on her turf justified verbal Krav Maga on Darcy. So we moved it. Three weeks ago," Gage lectured, and Josh realized why his mom had been bugging him about family dinner night. "Three weeks and you haven't come once."

"Tell Darcy I've been busy at work, but I'll make it up to her," Josh said.

"And deliver that pathetic apology? Hell no! I like my sex life just the way it is, thanks."

"Then tell her I owe her," Josh said, hoping to hell Darcy wasn't going to have one of her single friends at family dinner, brought for Josh. Darcy had set him up with three women, which was part of the reason he'd skipped a few dinners. Now, if she'd brought her sexy, single, photographer friend with the strawberry lip gloss, he'd be the first one at the door.

Gage leaned a hip against the ropes and grinned as if this was the strategy all along. "Great. I need help clearing out the attic at Belle Mont. Darcy wants to renovate it into a honeymoon suite, but first it needs to be cleaned out."

"There's a hundred years of crap up there and, with this sudden heat wave, it's got to be a hundred degrees up there."

"Which is why another hand would be great. Thanks for offering, man. Be there Friday at eight."

"Some of us work Fridays." He looked at Owen. "Ask him."

"I missed Kylie's recital, so I'll be there too."

Rhett laughed. "Tough situation, guys. That's why I went to the recital and all the dinners."

"I have court in the morning," Josh explained, and it wasn't like he could skip due to a personal health day. He'd be fired and maybe held in contempt. "I can be there by three."

Rhett let out a low whistle. "Trust me, you don't want an Easton woman on your ass."

"What did you do?" Gage shook his head in a very *tsk-tsk* way that had Rhett sighing.

"I didn't tell Steph the exact date of your bachelor party, and I guess it conflicts with fashion week in Milan."

"This trip has been planned for months, and we specifically booked it that far out to make sure it didn't conflict with anyone's schedule," Josh said, and *we* referred to him.

Even with everything on his plate, Josh had been tasked with planning Gage's bachelor party. Rhett would be in the studio, Owen was ramping up for Oktoberfest, and Clay would be neck deep into football season. And it wasn't like Gage could plan his own party. Which left Josh—responsible, reliable, unable to say no Josh. Who had as much on his plate, or maybe more, than any one of his brothers.

He'd gone over the family calendar, which was like deciphering German code without a cypher, searching for seven consecutive days that they were all free, or at least could move things around. After some negotiations and a lot of finagling, he'd managed to find one single solitary week that worked for all. And Rhett had screwed the pooch.

"Why didn't you just tell her?" Josh asked.

"Oh, I did. I just didn't write down the exact dates."

"She knows that with Grandpa here planning it there won't be any strippers or anything remotely exciting, right?" Owen said, and Josh flipped him off.

"She's not mad about the party. She's mad because I didn't tell her ahead of time, and now we don't have a dog sitter for Littleshit."

"That's it?" Josh asked. "Your life crisis is that you don't have a dog sitter?"

Josh ran a hand down his face, surprised at the amount of

stubble. God, he was tired. The kind of tired that went so bone deep, sleep didn't even touch it.

When had everything become so screwed up? Between spearheading the auction, attending strategy meetings, and managing his family's comings and goings, he didn't have time for a life.

He wasn't implying his brothers hadn't worked their asses off to get where they were. Josh was just the only nine-to-fiver who answered to someone other than himself. And his work was suffering because he was the steady one in the family.

"Recitals? Dog sitter? Peacock statues?" Owen looked disgusted. "I am calling the man card committee and deactivating everyone's membership."

Rhett ignored this. "She wants me to bring him on the trip."

"Not happening," Josh said as the other guys gave a resounding "Hell no."

Owen was the only one to laugh because he was the last one who hadn't yet been stuck Littleshit-sitting. He'd only been spared because he worked eighty-hour work weeks running their family bar, and the health department took issue with pocket-pets lifting their leg in commercial kitchens.

"Well, he can't go with Steph. And we can't board him, because he bit a mastiff last month and now we're banned from every good kennel in the city."

"Not my problem. Your mess. You clean it up," Gage said. "Don't you know the secret to a happy marriage? Transparency is the key to getting laid."

"Actually, it's being in the same time zone," Rhett mumbled.

"Actually, it's being a big boy and cleaning up after yourself," Josh said, taking off his gloves and tossing them into his gym bag.

"Or maybe cleaning up for someone else," Gage suggested. "You're so used to being the one chased, sometimes you have to be the one chasing. A relationship is as much of a job as your job is the job."

"I have people counting on me to be there," Rhett said.

Rhett had a private jet full of people counting on him. From roadies to band members and everyone in between, he was responsible for families being able to pay the bills and put food on the table. It was a responsibility that was hard to shoulder, and Josh felt for his middle brother.

Josh, too, shouldered a large burden. If he got it wrong, innocent people's lives were ruined. He'd seen the devastation an unjustified lawsuit had on his own family, which was why he was so diligent in doing his homework. When he filed, it was because he was certain it was the right thing to do.

Josh found his thoughts moving back to Piper and the fact that he'd known for three days there was a problem with the permit. She'd made it clear that a lot of people were counting on her, which meant she was counting on him—and he wasn't about to let her down. Not after he'd gained so much ground last week.

Especially not after learning about how much disappointment she'd suffered at the hands of others. He worked hard to school his emotions as she shared a little glimpse into her childhood, but it broke his chest. His niece had been without a dad until recently, but Darcy had loved her enough for ten parents.

It sounded as if Piper didn't even really have one parent, and that lit a fire inside him.

"This whole situation isn't all on me." Rhett pushed through the gym doors like a grown adult throwing a tantrum. "I invited Steph to come on the road with me, but she hates the road."

Josh thought back to that day in his office with Piper. She'd been slow to agree to a date, but he'd made it crystal clear where he stood on wanting to spend more time with her. "Make her a deal," he heard himself advising. "A 'you come on the road with me and I'll fly out to see you' kind of deal."

"Relationships aren't about *deals,*" Gage said as if Josh were completely female deficient. "They're about showing up."

"Steph won't even consider going on the road. She hates the roadies and isn't so hot on spending time with the band."

"Do you blame her?" Owen asked. "You've become that chick on the cover of *US Magazine*. Between the band and Mom, I'm surprised she hasn't dumped your ass."

Josh unraveled the tape on his hands, quietly taking in everything his brothers were saying.

"Mom can be . . . invasive," Gage said. "You need to set her straight, and now. Trust me, the longer you wait, the harder it will be. Mom knows that if she wants to spend time with my family, she needs to meet us on our terms. Steph should be number one, the one who you please, not anyone else. If you give Mom a hint of control, she'll take over your entire life."

"Mom's over-involved because she's still mourning Dad and Kyle," Josh pointed out. "So if being in control brings her a sense of peace, I don't see what's the big deal."

"Says the guy who chauffeured her to her lady doctor's appointment last week."

Instead of jabbing back, Josh reflected on how much time he spent, even on a weekly basis, driving her to appointments, doing handy work around the house, being guilted into staying for dinner—and now secretly handling peacock statues and decorations for his mom's charity events. And that was in addition to his eighty-hour week. He might not make it to family dinners regularly, but he broke bread with his mom at least three times a week—and usually during his work hours.

Rhett opened his locker and sat down on the bench. "So pretty much, you're saying I need to grow up and grow a pair?"

A seed of interest began to form in Josh's chest. He thought about what Gage had said as he showered and got dressed. Relationships didn't seem as hard as Rhett was making them out to be. Show up. Make her feel important and . . . What was the third thing?

Transparency will get you laid.

Josh had been thinking nonstop about getting laid. It had become his number one priority. But from where he was sitting, with a huge permit problem—that he'd kept from her—things didn't look like they'd swing in his favor.

His intentions were in the right place, but his timing had been off. He looked up to find his brothers looking at him. "What?"

"You coming to watch the game this week or you going to break your mom's heart?"

When the Seahawks played, everyone would gather at Stout to watch Clay kick ass and to spend time as a family. Josh had never missed game night until he'd decided to run for DA. He didn't want to miss another night.

"I'll be there." He wasn't sure how he was going to make it—he had piles of work on his desk—but he wasn't about to miss his baby brother play the former Super Bowl champs and smear their asses all over the field.

He was checking out his eye, which was already starting to purple, when, before he could stop it, he heard himself asking, "What happens if it's too late for transparency?"

His brothers stopped what they were doing to stare at Josh, then burst out laughing.

"You actually screwed something up," Rhett said. "And by that look, Mom's perfect prosecutor screwed up something bad."

Owen grinned. "Please tell me you blew it with Pretty Photographer. I've been dying to give her a call and ask her if she wants to come to my place for a little Netflix and chill."

"For the last time, her name is Piper, and don't bother. She's not interested," Josh said, which only made his brothers grin harder.

They were all looking at him with unholy glee. "You've got it bad," Gage said, and Rhett nodded in agreement. "Tell us, what did you do that's going to make Piper rip you a new one?"

"Nothing yet. I still have time to fix it." Which he did. Her event was three weeks away, and he could get approval through a different route; he was sure of it. At least he had been until the only brother in a serious, healthy relationship, who knew more about women than the other four brothers combined, gave him a *seriously?* look.

"If you think you can fix something with a woman by hiding it from her, you're never going to get laid again," Gage said. "Whatever you did, you need to be up-front with her and come clean."

"There's nothing to come clean about because I can fix this."

Gage laughed. "That right there is why you will remain single, my friend."

"That and the ugly eye," Rhett said, and Josh punched him in the face.

13

Josh had done it. He'd called Piper.

He hadn't actually spoken to her, but he'd left a message and they'd shared a few texts in which he said he had news, and she invited him to swing by her house tonight after work.

He hadn't said what kind of news, and she'd been in the middle of a shoot, which worked for him since he had one last trick up his sleeve.

He was packing up to leave his office when a giant basket arrived. It was a signature-required kind of basket, filled with a signed football and jersey, four neon-green foam fingers, matching totes and drink koozie, and four fifty-yard-line Seahawks tickets. Attached was a card:

> When your job is cool enough
> that you don't need to plan
> Mommy's party...
> ~ The Favorite

Josh sent Clay a picture of his middle finger, then quickly raced out of his office, calling Kitty Caldwell on his way home.

"I hope you're calling to tell me that someone donated a Fabergé egg for the auction," Kitty said by way of greeting.

"Better than that. I secured a Seahawks-themed basket with four fifty-yard-line season tickets. Compliments of my brother, Clay."

Clay's bank account, to be specific. A couple of tickets were nothing, but fifty-yard-line season tickets would cost in the tens of thousands. Good thing 'the favorite' made the big bucks.

"Not Fabergé, but it will be a big-ticket item." Kitty was downplaying her excitement. "How many lot numbers are there?"

"We're nearly at a hundred," he guessed, based on the clutter in his office.

"That's wonderful." Kitty paused, a pregnant, *I need a favor* pause. "I understand your mother is trying to steal you away to help the decorations committee."

If his mom knew he was working for Kitty, he'd be disowned. "You know how it is with sons and moms."

"I have all girls, but anytime your mother gets a chance to brag about her boys, she goes on and on. How successful you all are. How driven you all are. How handsome and sweet you all are." Kitty sounded not one iota impressed.

"Not as successful as your husband," Josh said, and the woman practically purred through the phone. "Nor as successful as this auction is going to be." And here was his pitch. "I know you've already announced that the proceeds are going to help Portland People Against Purebreds, but I have an idea that will make this year's charity auction the talk of the town."

Kitty was silent for a long moment. "Did your mom put you up to this?"

"No, she doesn't even know about it." He grimaced. His mom

might be a braggart and busybody, but it all stemmed from a place of love. Usually. After losing Kyle, her interest in her sons' lives may have gone a little overboard. Even if it meant burning bridges or driving her sons crazy in the process.

As Josh and his brothers grew up and started forging their own paths, Margo held on tighter, becoming more and more creative in her attempts to insert herself in their lives. Going as far as to nearly chase off both Gage's and Rhett's women. Josh was embarrassed to admit he'd been so focused on his mom's happiness, he sometimes overlooked the trouble her stubbornness brought. So Kitty had a right to be cautious.

"If this idea of yours is so brilliant, why not wait until Margo steals the board chair position from me next year?"

He wasn't touching that with a ten-foot pole. "I'm telling you because I feel as if we're co-chairs of sorts and I've really come to enjoy my contribution." That was a big, fat fib if he'd ever heard one. "Which is why I want this year to be the best it can."

"The mayor will be so happy to hear that," she said. "When I asked him the best person to help with my little time management problem, your name was the first one on his lips."

Another thing to talk to the mayor about. "I'll be sure to thank him next time I see him. In fact, he's part of the reason I'm calling. We had dinner the other night, and he met an up-and-coming photographer, Piper Campagna."

"Isn't she Margo's addition to the volunteer list?"

She had no idea how far from the truth that statement was. His mom would rather shoot herself than have Piper back. But thankfully, the decision was the board's, not just his mom's.

"Actually, she was Darcy's recommendation, and we're lucky to have her. In fact, she volunteers for a non-profit art school in Portland, called Urban Soul. She had the brilliant idea of throwing an auction of her own, where the girls can showcase their art," he said, knowing he was going to hell for this next part. "Then I thought that you, Kitty, after seeing your stunning self-portrait and learning that you are an artist yourself, would want to be a part of this."

"Well, I don't know how I feel about having two auctions in Portland scheduled for the same month."

"Of course not, which is why I think you should combine the events. A home that helps educate girls in the arts would be a great cause for the Ladies of Portland. Plus, it's an election year."

"How would it work?" she asked, but he knew he already had her. She loved being the mayor's wife and everything that came with the title. There wasn't much she wouldn't do to ensure her husband's reelection.

"We could display the art around Belle Mont during the dinner portion, then host a special segment of the auction where all the proceeds go to the artists and Skye's the Limit, the home where many of these girls live."

"We'd have to get the board's approval."

"Of course, but I know that the board will love your idea."

"My idea." Kitty let out a pleased sigh. "That sounds lovely. But a sponsor of some kind would go a long way in convincing the rest of the board."

"A sponsor as in Stout donating the beverages?" he asked, loving how much this would tick off Owen.

"Isn't that generous?" Kitty said. "Now, if I only had one more board member on my side to help push through next year's budget."

He closed his eyes. "I can talk to my mom." She was the main board member against Kitty's budget. Not only that, he had no idea how he was going to convince her to work alongside Piper and Kitty.

"You make this happen, and those girls will get the art show of their dreams."

Josh hung up and felt like he needed another shower. If this was what it was like to wheel and deal with local charities and influential families, maybe being an elected official wasn't for him.

Pocketing his phone, he headed across town to tell Piper the good news. Which was how he ended up outside her house, feeling like some teen about to pick up his prom date. Well, pick up his prom date after the winning touchdown at the state finals. He'd run by home, changed out of his suit and dress shoes, and applied an icepack to his swollen cheek—which he hoped gave him some street cred in her eyes. He stopped by the store to get her some flowers, then decided flowers might be overkill and put them in the trunk—and he was still twenty minutes early.

Her house was cute—homey. A small Craftsman on the southside of Portland, it was a quaint one-story bungalow with slate shingle siding, large front windows, and an even larger porch, supported by a massive, detached redwood beam. It was a mash-up of vintage meets modern—not surprising, considering its owner.

Realizing he was sitting in a dark car casing her house, he considered pulling around the corner and catching the last part of the game—the guys were going to kill him, but so what—when he noticed something move on Piper's porch.

With no porch light on, it was hard to tell. Adrenaline shot through his veins and into his hands. Located at the end of a cul-de-sac, two houses from a streetlamp, it would be the perfect place for someone to hide for a variety of reasons—none of them good.

Piper didn't live in a bad area, but it wasn't exactly Main Street, USA.

Turning off the dome light, Josh opened his door, got out, gently clicked it shut, then walked around the side of the yard. Back against the house, he crouched down and slowly made his way toward the porch. Taking a brief moment to ask himself what he was doing, he stepped out, ready to get physical if the situation required.

The porch was empty, but he heard footsteps running away.

He should have let it go, called the cops and reported the incident. Had it been his house, he would have. But this was Piper's place, and he didn't want to think of the million-and-one reasons someone would run, fleeing from her house after hiding in the shadows. Unless they were guilty of something.

"Stop!" he called out.

The dark hoodie and jeans did the exact opposite, sprinting toward the fence leading to the back yard and going up, up, up and over. Josh was surprised the kid could move so quickly with his jeans pulled down around his hips.

With a tired sigh, Josh took off after him. He vaulted the fence in one move and rounded the corner right as Dark Hoodie started climbing the back fence, which led to a wooded area. Josh grabbed the backpack and yanked down. The kid came crashing to the ground. He scrambled to his feet and started to run when Josh caught the back of the hoodie and tugged him to a stop.

"The cops are on their way," he said.

"Shit!" the prowler said, and that's when he realized that Hoodie wasn't a boy—she was a slight-sized girl in oversized clothes.

"Get off me!" she yelled, and Josh immediately let her loose.

She looked young and small, her baggy clothes making her body look like a coat hanger. Her hair was red and her eyes scared. She looked like a deer caught in a hunter's scope.

Josh took a big step backward. "You okay?"

"No. You tore my sweatshirt," she said.

"You ran."

"Because I saw you creeping in the shadows!" She kicked him in the shin and tried to run again.

"Damn it!" he grumbled. "And I wasn't the only one in the shadows. I was waiting on a friend and caught you standing in the dark, and I made an assumption."

She crossed her arms around her backpack, holding it to her chest as if it contained gold bullion. "What? Because I'm wearing a hoodie in a good neighborhood, I must be a bad person?"

Well, when she put it that way, he sounded like a jerk. Which, he could tell, was exactly how she wanted him to feel. He gave her a long look, which she returned.

"What's your name?"

"I don't have to tell you."

"No, you don't. But unless you really want me to call the cops, you'd better answer some questions." Not for Piper's safety, but for the girl's. Her sweatshirt was torn in several places, her pants dirty, and there was a small dark spot on her cheek—a bruise.

"Why is calling the cops like every adult's go-to?"

"Name?"

She rolled her eyes. "Fine, it's Brandi. With an I. No E."

"What happened to your face, Brandi?"

"What happened to yours?"

"My brother took a cheap shot."

"Does he hit you a lot?" she asked, like they were peers and sitting outside the CPS office.

"Does yours?"

"I knew you'd go there!" Her gaze darted away from his. "And no, I don't even have a brother."

She may not have a brother, but someone from her past had been rough with her. It was in the way she carried herself, the stubborn set of her chin, the way she kept looking for a way out. Kind of like someone else he knew.

"Can I go now?" she asked, but she was already walking. Backpack slung over her shoulder, she started toward the front gate. Josh jogged to catch up with her, unlatching the gate when it looked as if Brandi with an I, no E was going to scale it again.

"I thought you were waiting for a friend."

"I was, but you're ruining the vibe."

Two beams of light came from down the street, momentarily blinding him. He felt more than heard the girl turn to run. He reached out and grabbed the loop of her backpack and pulled her back to his side.

"Look, your friend is home," he said.

"She is my friend, and she said I could come here anytime I want." She looked at Josh, really looked at him and then her shoulders slumped. "Never mind, she's busy."

This time it wasn't Josh chasing her off. Nope, Brandi was leaving because she was certain that Piper would choose a guy over her. Which told him that Brandi didn't know Piper all that well, because if she did, there'd be no doubt that Piper would give the shirt off her back to someone in need—especially a rough-around-the-edges teenager.

"Rebecca?" Piper got out of the car even as it was slowing to a stop.

"Rebecca?" he mumbled to the girl.

"What? You never told me *your* name."

"What are you doing here?" Piper asked, coming over and putting herself between Josh and Rebecca. A purposeful and tactical move. There was an urgency to her voice and a sadness in her eyes that told Josh she knew exactly what kind of night, and what kind of life, Rebecca had endured. "Are you okay?"

She didn't reach out to touch Rebecca's cheek, and she didn't step toward her. In fact, she looked the girl square in the eye and curved her shoulders to make herself appear smaller.

"Heading to Skye's and wanted to tell you I can't do the art show thing."

"But you're so good." She turned to Josh. "She's so good. You should see the piece she spray-painted on Skye's garage door."

Josh wasn't sure how Skye felt about someone spray-painting her garage, but his mom would have freaked. And called the cops. Just like Josh had threatened to do. And he thought his mom was out of touch. So maybe the apple didn't fall very far from his paranoid, loveable, entitled mom's tree.

"I can imagine. She has a vivid imagination," Josh said, and Rebecca shot him a glare.

"I'll think about it," she said. "See ya."

"No way. I have like three pounds of pasta and garlic bread in the house, and I need someone to help me eat it." Josh opened his mouth, but Piper gave him a small head shake.

She handed Rebecca the keys and when the teen didn't immediately take them, Piper shoved them in her hand. "I'll be in in a second.

Rebecca evil-eyed Josh, then, to his utter surprise, went inside and shut the door behind her.

"I'm so sorry. I didn't know she was coming," she said. "I was going to cook you a homemade dinner to say thanks for everything." She paused. "I'm hoping it's thank-you news, but if it's not, then tell me. Not right now." She covered her ears. "I just asked that poor girl to enter into a show that won't happen if that permit didn't come through . . ." She looked at him, her eyes a little too glassy for his liking. "Did it? Come through?" she whispered.

Transparency will get you laid.

Not tonight. Not after the five-foot-tall date-block with a mean kick. But Josh was playing the long game.

"There was an issue with the permit," he began. "We'd need off-duty cops, traffic direction, and that all takes more time than a few weeks."

Her whole body seemed to cave in on itself. "I figured," she said, then plastered on a big, bright smile. "But thank you for trying. Not many people would even do that, so I'm grateful."

"I'm not done." He took her hand. "I called the mayor's wife, and she's on board with merging the girls' art show in with the auction at Bid for the Cause."

"Are you for real?" She dropped his hands and threw her arms around his neck in a hug that was so sweet and genuine it brought on a strange kind of chest pain. "Thank you," she whispered. "Thank you, thank you, thank you."

He let her hold on for a moment longer, because she seemed to need it and he seemed to need her up against him. Maybe it was the little scare with Rebecca, or maybe it was the way Piper looked at her as if she'd once been in the teen's shoes that twisted a knot deep in his gut.

Transparency. Don't blow your chance now.

"It's not a done deal. We still have to convince my mom," he said, and her smile vanished. "Hang on, that's the easy part. I know that I can get her to agree, I prom—"

She covered his mouth. "Please don't say that word."

He wanted to argue, but his heart hurt too much for the breathtaking woman with the sad smile. He knew she didn't ask for a lot from the people in her life, but she was asking him for patience and understanding. Those were two things he had in spades.

He took her hands away but held them in his clasp. "I won't. But only because you asked me not to."

She went up on her toes and kissed his cheek. "You're a good man, Josh Easton."

14

Piper watched Josh pull away from the curb and then walked into her house. Rebecca was at the kitchen table. Her back was straight, her backpack was in her lap, and she looked closed off and scared.

Piper didn't blame her. She wasn't sure what had transpired, but based on her scraped knee and bruised cheek, it had been a crappy night. And that wasn't taking into account what had gone down between her and Josh.

"I didn't mean to chase off your boyfriend," Rebecca said.

"He's not my boyfriend."

"He wants to be."

"What makes you say that?" Piper asked, going for casual, when inside she felt anything but. She'd been on one impromptu date-ish night with the guy and, while her heart raced every time she thought of him, she didn't want to get ahead of herself.

"You know, you really don't have to feed me. I already ate at Skye's." The girl was clearly lying.

"Well, then how about you help me cook my dinner, and if

you're a little hungry afterwards, you can have some." Piper hung her camera bag by the front door. "I also have brownie mix I was thinking of making."

"Whatever."

"Do you know how to make a salad?" Piper asked, setting her purse on the kitchen chair closest to Rebecca. She was jumpy enough without feeling as if Piper didn't trust her.

"It's a salad," she said, the *duh* implied.

"Good, everything's in the bottom drawer. If you get started on that, I'll get the pasta going."

Piper pulled out a bowl for the salad and handed it to Rebecca. She filled a large pot with water. "How did you find my house?"

Rebecca hesitated while washing her hands at the kitchen sink. "Are you mad?"

"No, just wondering."

"There's a big neon flash card with your name and info on Skye's fridge. It says 'In case of emergency, call Piper'. And it has all your info. You can even see it through the window."

Piper was touched that she was Skye's emergency contact, but also a little concerned that anyone who was in Skye's house could find Piper.

"Is that how you saw my address? Through the window?"

Rebecca shrugged. "Skye would freak if she saw me, um, all dirty."

"I used to think that too. But eventually, Skye wore me down until I realized that she wanted me the most when I was *dirty*."

"She's kind of big on the hugs."

Oh, Piper knew. Just like she knew that Skye was starting to break through Rebecca's walls. And that was a good thing. No one could love the way Skye did, and Rebecca needed a lot of love if she was going to make it.

Piper swallowed hard. She knew what it was like to grow up without even a single person to give a rat's ass where you were and if you were safe. Her earliest memories were of waiting on the front porch for her mom to come home. Sometimes she did, and sometimes Piper made herself a toaster waffle, then tucked herself into bed. No matter where her mom landed, she was always drunk.

Every so often, when her mom was between men, she'd make Piper feel as if she were the center of the universe. Then Boyfriend Next would come along, and Piper was nothing more than a footnote in her mom's life. Being made invisible by the people who were supposed to love and protect you left behind lasting scars, which shaped every moment of every day until being invisible was less painful than being discarded.

"If you want a place to crash, I have a guest room. The mattress is kind of lumpy and I only have basic cable, but it's yours if you want it."

Cutting a cucumber, she asked, "Are you going to hound me about that stupid art show?"

"It's not stupid, and yes. You're too good not to enter. Plus, it's going to be held at this fancy house in the hills. And if you sell anything, you get half the money."

"Oh, goodie," she said with forced cheerfulness. "I can imagine how my jeans and hoodie will play out."

Piper hadn't thought about that. She'd been so excited about the chance for the girls to show their art in a place fitting of budding artists, she never considered that the majority of the girls wouldn't have anything to wear, let alone feel comfortable. Hell, Piper had felt like an imposter the moment she set foot in Belle Mont House, and she'd been there in a work capacity.

"You and I are about the same size. You can borrow something of mine," she offered. Rebecca said nothing. "I'm not really a dress person. I kind of live in pants and boots, but we can raid my closet while the brownies are baking."

Rebecca gave a noncommittal shrug, but Piper knew she was getting through to her. Half of anything was more money than what Piper had ever had in her pockets when she'd been that age.

"Do you like tomato sauce or butter and cheese?" Piper asked just as a knock came from the front door.

"Twenty bucks, it's your boyfriend," Rebecca said.

"Ten bucks, and you have to put the pasta in the water when it boils."

Piper didn't wait for an answer because she knew, instinctively, it was her boyfri . . . Josh. Smoothing down her hair, she opened the door and there he stood. Wearing the hell out of a pair of black slacks, a white button-up, and shiny patent leather shoes.

"Why do you look like a penguin?" she asked.

"My mom and dad used to take dance lessons at Strictly Ballroom. After he passed away, I became the Fred Astaire to her Ginger Rogers. Once a week, I become her dance partner. I forgot that this week was moved to tonight."

Warm tingles filled her chest. "So when you said you wanted to dance with me at the engagement party, you mean you wanted to *dance*. I'm afraid my dancing skills end with the Macarena and YMCA."

"You just need a good partner," he said, and all she could think about was him partnering her right into a tangled sheets tango. "Maybe I can teach you someday soon."

"Why are you back?"

Hands in his pockets, he rocked back on his heels. "After I changed, I came back, then pulled around the block, circled it three times, and came back."

"And the tux?"

"Just imagine. I'm able to go from daytime litigator to nighttime Sinatra."

"You did all that for me?" she asked, then bit her lip.

He pushed off the railing and stalked toward her. "For you."

His eyes did a long, slow once-over, and his expression said he liked what he saw. Piper's nipples gave an excited welcome.

The afternoon had been warm, so Piper was in a yellow tank top, denim shorts, and teal Converse. Her hair was loose and finger-styled, her lashes mascara-ed, and her lips strawberry. On the way home, she'd parked around the corner and touched herself up in anticipation of seeing him again.

It appeared that he'd done the same.

She walked out onto the porch and shut the door, holding on to the handle with both hands behind her. It was a strategic move, so she didn't do the whole reach out and touch someone move since she didn't know why he'd come back.

"I didn't want to leave until I knew you were okay," he began quietly.

"I should be asking you that." Getting a better look at his bruise, her restraint fizzled, and she reached out. She couldn't help herself; she touched his cheek. He sucked in a breath. "Did Rebecca do that?"

"More like Owen." He put his hand on hers and held it to his cheek. "Are you sure this is a good idea?"

"Me touching you? Not at all. I'm beginning to question my five-date rule."

She felt the apple of his cheek rise beneath her hand. "We'll put a pin in that and circle back, but I was referring to Rebecca staying here. How well do you know her?"

"Well enough to know she's a scared kid who got her butt whupped and needs a safe place to sleep."

"I think we should call her parents."

"I don't think there's anyone to call. She's clearly been on the streets for a while."

"How do you know?"

Josh studied her as if trying to figure out how she had such intimate details of homeless teens. "I just know. If her parents cared, she wouldn't be on my doorstep holding her life's belongings in a backpack."

"There's always the teen shelter on Tenth," he suggested.

"The bigger kids wait until the smaller kids fall asleep, then steal their stuff."

"Were you one of those smaller kids?" he asked, and she tried to hold his gaze but somehow couldn't. "I want to know you. No judgment. No hidden agendas."

She'd been judged her entire life, so even though she wanted to believe him, she was a little leery. "It usually works better when people get to know me in smaller doses."

"I'll take you in any dose you're willing to give," he said, and a flutter started deep in her chest.

How did he do that? Make her feel special and desirable? It produced a dilemma of the most complicated kind. Getting wrapped up in a man who was her opposite was never a good idea.

"I don't get to say this very often, but thank you for coming through on your word."

"I always come through."

Her history warned her not to believe in that either, but the usually silenced romantic part told her she was safe with him. So, just for tonight, she decided she should go with it.

He took a piece of her windblown hair and let it slide through his fingers. "How do you normally celebrate?"

"Alone."

"How about Friday, after you get off, you come with me and celebrate at my family's bar?"

Definitely (maybe) Dating

"You mean, celebrate alone together?" she teased.

"I've come to like being alone with you."

She'd come to like a whole lot of things when it came to Josh. "I'm teaching at Urban Soul and have a late portrait session Friday, so I won't be home until seven."

"Then I'll pick you up at seven."

At the prospect of going on a real, pick-you-up-at-the-door date, rocket-powered hormones blasted through her better judgment. "You can come inside now if you want. I'm making brownies for dessert."

"I love brownies," he said, as if she were a plate of chocolate, chewy goodness and he was going to eat her up whole. "But I'd better not."

"Why? Because of Rebecca?"

"Because of this." His big, beautiful body pressed her up against the doorway, and he ran his hands through her hair, gripping her head and holding her steady. Then he kissed her.

Their lips made contact, and all logic flew out the window, making room for all kinds of feelings. All the feels all at once. Need, lust, desire, and something more tender that had her head sounding the alarm: *In case of an emergency, save yourself first.*

He opened his mouth on hers, and she decided she could save herself later. Like after this game of *get to know you* later.

His hands raked through her hair, to the back of her neck, before he started the long, slow descent south until he had a palmful of her butt—which seemed to be his favorite place on the planet. He squeezed, and she let out a low hum of arousal, which made him squeeze a little harder. And just when she thought they could take this interlude to his car, he abruptly broke the kiss.

They were both breathing raggedly, and they were both fired up and ready to go. It was just like in the park, only better. The pull was intense, like two magnets daring science to keep them apart.

"I think I see the problem," she said, and he pressed into her. "*Oh,* it's a really, *really* big problem."

His gaze dropped to her lips, then her nipples that were pressing against her top. "A problem for another night. When you don't have company."

"Maybe I should invite you over for company some night soon."

"Is tomorrow too soon?"

With the promise of tomorrow, Piper barely slept a wink. Every time she closed her eyes, she relived that kiss. Which was why she'd kept her lids tightly shut as long as possible, even sleeping through four alarms.

Wanting to shoot the chalk art downtown before the city came alive and the sidewalks were bustling with people, her morning started early. She thought about waking Rebecca and asking her if she wanted to join in for a fun field trip exploring Portland's beautiful street art. Piper knew of a few mural paintings in the warehouse district that had popped up. She was hoping it would help inspire the teenager and show her how beautiful and powerful expression could be.

After a quick shower, she slipped on a pair of jean shorts and a faded rock tee, then headed downstairs to make some breakfast. Normally, Piper would make herself cereal or yogurt, but she wanted to get as many calories into Rebecca as she could.

Chocolate chip pancakes, country potatoes, and bacon. Only when she tapped on Rebecca's door, the girl didn't make a sound, so Piper decided to leave a covered plate on the counter with a note telling her to stay as long as she wanted.

Packing some bacon to go, she gathered up her things. But when she slipped her equipment bag over her shoulder, she noticed that it was too light.

Closing her eyes and praying she was wrong, Piper opened the bag to find her camera, her 1972 Leica, was gone. And so was Rebecca.

15

"You're here!" Darcy said, sounding so excited Piper looked behind her to see who she was talking to. The only people behind Piper were a group of fraternity guys sharing a pitcher of beer, eyes glued to the screen.

It was game night, and Piper was at Stout. The place was wall-to-wall Seahawks fans, the bar standing room only, and if there was any doubt as to which team was the crowd favorite, the banner above the bar read: IF YOU DON'T LIKE THE SEAHAWKS, THEN YOU'RE IN THE WRONG PLACE . . . SO GET OUT BEFORE YOU GET PUNCHED IN THE FACE.

Piper hadn't seen or heard from Rebecca since yesterday. In passing, she'd asked Skye, who hadn't seen her either. Piper wasn't mad at Rebecca. Disappointed? Maybe. Heartbroken that her camera, which had once meant everything to Piper, was gone? Absolutely.

She didn't tell Skye what had happened, and she sure as heck didn't call the cops, but she did drive around for two hours after her last client looking for Rebecca. With no luck.

She'd even called Josh to say she'd meet him at the bar.

"How did you know I was coming?"

Darcy looked at her as if she'd sprouted a wedding veil out of the top of her head. "Girls' night?" Darcy studied her. "Wait, why are you here?"

Wasn't that the question of the hour?

"Right! Girls' night," she said with an overly bright smile, wondering what was going to happen when Josh showed up talking date night. She hadn't meant to double book, she just wasn't used to being this social, which sounded pathetic. In reality, she wasn't pathetic, she'd just never nailed down the art of being social. It fell under the peopling umbrella—both of which gave her hives.

Piper glanced from one giant flatscreen to the next, all set to the Seahawks and all showing highlights of the game. "I'm late." *Really late.* "Like bottom of the fourth quarter late."

Piper didn't know all that much about football, but she knew she'd missed enough of her date that she wouldn't blame Josh if he'd given up.

"It's *end* of the fourth, not bottom, and unless a team is celebrating on the field under a confetti cannon, you can't be late," Jillian said. She was dressed in black, strappy sandals, a cute khaki skirt, and a Seahawks-green, M. I. L. F, MAN I LOVE FOOTBALL tee. She was that sweet, girl-next-door kind of beautiful that Piper couldn't manage on her best of days.

"My job ran over, and I had something I had to do, so I did a quick change and rushed over." Yes, the family part of the family portrait didn't play nice, but the truth was she didn't feel right about going out when Rebecca might show up.

When, after an hour passed and Rebecca was a no-show, Piper left a note on the door saying she'd be home after ten and the key was under the mat.

"You look, um, wow," Jillian said.

"I don't know about wow. You're just thrown because I'm not in my usual black-on-black gear."

Knowing how much Josh liked an exposed tank strap, she had on a rock tee that fell off one shoulder, a spaghetti-strap tank, denim skirt, and her thigh-high boots. They were heather-gray suede, with a dark-gray silk ribbon that ran up the back and tied in a bow at the top. A little girlie for her usual taste, and it was date five standard issue footwear. But the boots were sexy and feminine with a touch of bad-ass—and she needed a little bad-ass in her step tonight.

The moment she walked in the bar, she knew she didn't fit in. She didn't look like the other women there, a mixed crowd that fell somewhere between *Cosmo* and *Better Homes and Gardens*, with a few boardroom babes thrown in. In fact, it was becoming clearer by the second that Piper was unlike anyone else in Josh's life. Even dressed up, she had an edge that was extremely polarizing. A single glance, and people either liked her or they didn't.

Piper was an introvert who didn't like large crowds and had yet to learn how to people. Peopling didn't come naturally. It was a skill she'd worked incredibly hard to fake. Successful peopling required being open and vulnerable, finding ways to connect on a level that stemmed from shared experiences.

Piper's experiences were unique. Growing up, she didn't watch *American Idol* with her family or go to prom. She didn't even graduate high school like everyone else, earning her GED when she'd been nineteen.

So connecting was hard. It often turned into a one-sided conversation where Piper nodded and said *Uh huh* as if she too had vacationed to Disneyland for a milestone birthday. On the bright side, she had mad listening skills.

"Oh no, you're a definite *wow*," Darcy agreed and, when Piper tried to argue, waved over Owen.

"What can I get you?" Owen faded off, his brows disappearing into his hairline. "Wow."

"See, told you." Jillian beamed.

Owen didn't exactly give her a once-over, he'd been raised too well for that, but he did lock gazes in a way that made her nervous. The awkward, palms-sweating, not-sure-where-to-put-her-hands nervous. The kind that reminded her why she didn't like bars—or large crowds—or flirting.

"I've got it now, Picture Girl," he said, his expression dialed to light-bulb moment. "A whiskey sour."

Jillian snorted. "Does anything about her say sour? My grandma drank whiskey sours."

"Does she look like a rookie?" Darcy asked.

Piper could have pointed out that she was, in fact, quite the rookie when it came to drinking. With an addict for a mom and witnessing firsthand the stupid choices people made while drunk, Piper had promised herself to do better, be better than her childhood. Even when she'd been an angry-at-the-world teenager with a rebellious side a mile wide, she'd never dabbled in anything that resulted in a vulnerability that people could exploit.

"S'more martini." Owen pointed to Jillian, then to Darcy. "Gin and tonic." He paused to scratch his head. "You're a hard one to peg, Picture Girl." Owen tapped his finger to his lips in deep thought. "Less Manhattan and more rock and roll." He snapped his fingers. "A Stiletto. Bourbon, amaretto, and lemon juice."

"Not really a Stiletto girl," she said. Owen narrowed his eyes, then leaned over the bar to look at her boots, making her wrist itch. "Actually, can I have a water?"

"Water?" Jillian gasped. "We have a sitter. You made it to your first girls' night. You can't have water."

"How about a bubbly water?" When Jillian looked unapproving, she amended, "How about a bubbly water, with a lime in a wine glass?" *To go?* So she could lie on the couch in her sweats and eat the entire plate of brownies while reminding herself that this was a colossal mistake. Hives were forming, her camera was gone, and she didn't know what her friends wanted, but she was sure she'd blow it.

She was building up the courage to bug out when two arms came into view and a set of big, masculine hands rested on the bar top on either side of her. She didn't have to look over her shoulder to know who it was.

Josh.

His fresh scent of shaving cream, the heated wave of testosterone, the familiar way her body melted at his touch. It was intoxicating. Even though he was barely touching her, it felt as if she were encased in a Josh-cocoon.

"Lemon juice, sugar, muddled strawberries on the rocks," Josh said, his voice a sexy rumble.

"What the hell kind of drink is that?" Owen asked.

"Strawberry lemonade," he said, and Piper's heart did a little flip. He'd remembered.

"Is he right?" Owen asked Piper.

She looked over her shoulder and met Josh's very steamy gaze. "I do love strawberry."

She opened her mouth to apologize for being late before he asked, "Can I borrow you for a sec? There's someone I want you to meet."

Josh didn't wait for her answer, just took her hand, lifted it to steady her while she slid off the bar stool, then led her through the crowd.

"Introducing a chick to your mom?" Owen called out. "Rookie move, bro."

"Please tell me you aren't introducing me to your mom," she said over the noise of the bar. "I already met her, and it didn't go so well for either of us."

He glanced over his shoulder and leveled her with a look so

manly, it made it clear that he was no rookie. But she already knew this. His patience, the way he held her, the way he kissed her—*Lordy*—Josh was the real deal.

At some point, the crowd became thicker, and moving through was like being engaged in a game of bumper cars. Piper shrank in the crush, her body instinctively curling in. She couldn't see over everyone's heads, and she couldn't spot an exit. Panic slowly wrapped around her neck, and her hands went a little clammy.

In a fluid move, like they were dancing, Josh maneuvered her forward, so he was behind, his arms surrounding her. "I've got you." She looked up at him, and he was looking back, very serious. He lifted her hand and kissed the inside of her wrist like he knew.

He winked at her and then, using his body like a battering ram, he moved them toward the back of the bar, out of the crowd, through the employees-only door, and down an empty corridor.

"You okay?" he asked.

She was now. "Yes."

Without another word, he shimmied her right up against the wall, making her the middle of a Josh sandwich. The air around them became sex charged.

"I thought this was a strictly date five conversation." His gaze slid all the way down to the tip of her thigh-high boots, then back up, taking his time everywhere in between.

It felt different than earlier. She wanted him to look, had worn these exact boots for him. So she bent one knee, resting the heel of her boot on the wall behind her, and said, "I changed my mind."

"Do you think maybe you could have warned me?" His hands slid to her hips. "I came here expecting date two boots, and you jumped directly into date five. How is a man supposed to prepare?"

"Some of the best things in life are unplanned, Mr. Assistant District Attorney," she said, although he didn't look like an assistant district attorney tonight. In a dark-blue Henley, button-fly jeans, and enough male pheromones to seduce a nuns' choir, he looked like sex on a stick.

"I'm beginning to see that."

"Eyes up here," she said, but he kept them on her boots.

"I'm good."

"If you're looking in the wrong place, you'll miss it."

This got his attention. "Wouldn't want that to happen."

She shook her head, then planted one on him so bold and big his hands immediately launched into action until she was plastered against his body.

He slipped a finger under her spaghetti strap and traced it from front to back, then trailed it down her arm. "Pretty."

Right then, she felt pretty.

"Who is this person you wanted to introduce me to?" she asked conspiratorially. He leaned further into her, *all the way into her,* and she may have sucked in a breath. "Oh, we've been acquainted. Just the other night, on my front porch. It was brief but memorable."

"He remembers."

"He?" She laughed. "Does he have a name?"

His hands swept down her back and lower until his finger was toying with the bow at the back of her boot. As difficult as it was for her to lace up, one tug of the ribbon and they'd undo like a corset. "Depends on if these boots are going to stay on."

"And that depends on—" She paused, unable to finish that thought. "It depends on a lot," she whispered.

His expression turned serious. "I'm good with a lot. I'm good with whatever makes you comfortable."

She cupped his face. "You make me comfortable." And this time when they kissed, it was a gentle exploration, a promise. She didn't know what kind, but for once the idea of a promise didn't scare her—all that much.

"I can do this all night," he said against her lips, then proved it by languidly driving her right out of her mind. "But I don't want to hog you. I know Darcy has been asking all night if you were going to make it."

Piper laughed. "She has it in her head that this is girls' night."

He took her hand and kissed her fingertips—every one—teasingly nipping as he went. "Then let's not disappoint her."

"You don't mind?"

"I'm with you. Why would I mind?" he said, and she almost snorted. There wasn't a guy on the planet who would be okay with his almost sister-in-law cock-blocking him. But when Josh said it, the way he said it, Piper believed him.

And that was how Piper found herself in a booth wedged between Darcy and Jillian. Both women were shooting question after question about Josh, who was standing at the bar a few feet away, talking with his brothers. Every few minutes, he'd glance over at her, gauging how she was doing, then send a secret smile where his dimples popped out. Which was incredibly thoughtful. And sexy.

Piper was engaged in one of those silent conversations from across the room fantasies, where the connection was stronger than the distance.

"I knew there was something going on between you two," Jillian said. "I saw it at the party. The way he smiled at you."

"He never smiles." Darcy sounded amazed. "Like ever. He's so buttoned-up and serious."

A month ago, Piper would have said the same thing. But she'd come to learn that there was a wonderful emotionally in tune man beneath the suit and tie. A man who liked to hold hands and go for walks in the park. A man who shared his opinion, but respected hers. A man, if she weren't careful, she could totally fall for.

"He's like that *Fifty Shades* guy," Jillian said.

He's like my guy.

Piper froze, unsure where that came from. There was this insane chemistry between them, and they'd shared some personal conversations, but as for him being her guy? When did she start thinking like that? The moment he'd kissed her, that's when.

"He's his own guy," Piper said, realizing that was the truth. Yes, he had a high-profile job, which defined his public persona. And yes, he belonged to a tight-knit family. But those were only parts to the multi-faceted man. When it came to the people in his life, he listened, and he loved. Not for the first time, Piper wondered what that must feel like.

"And tonight?" Jillian waggled a brow. "He practically dragged you through the bar."

He hadn't had to drag her anywhere. Piper had gone willingly. The moment he'd put his arms around her, her brain misfired, and all she could think about was touching him.

"The guys joke that Josh is married to his job. And from what I've seen, he keeps it strictly casual with women."

"Are you telling me I should be careful?" Piper wasn't ready to walk away, but she had the distinct feeling Darcy was delivering a warning.

Darcy reached across the table and rested her hand on Piper's arm. "He's a great guy with a huge heart, and when he falls, I know he'll fall hard. He's an all-in kind of guy. Look at his career. What kind of thirty-something runs for district attorney?"

The kind of guy who went after what he wanted. And while

he'd made it clear he wanted Piper, she wasn't sure if it was more than physical. A terrifying realization.

She'd already shared far too much with him—secrets she'd never told another living soul. Not even Faith, who had been Piper's best friend when she'd desperately needed one. He was so easy to talk to. When they were apart, all she could think about was Josh. When they were together, all she could think about was kissing him.

Warm tingles made themselves known in her belly. Stupid tingles.

"We're just having fun," she said, not feeling the fun at that moment.

The other two women exchanged another look, like there was an entire conversation happening at the table that Piper wasn't privy to.

"It's okay if it's more," Jillian said.

"It's not. Now, can we talk about something else?" Unable to look at Darcy when asking such a huge favor, Piper closed her eyes. "Like how my permit fell through."

Darcy's eyes became as big as saucers. "How?"

"I didn't meet the timeline and criteria for an emergency permit."

"I am so sorry, Piper," Jillian said. "I know how much this meant to you."

"Thanks. And it does, which is why I'm going to ask the Ladies of Portland to merge their charity event with Urban Soul's art showcase. But I need to get your support first, Darcy."

"I think it's a great idea."

"Before you say yes, there's more. I know you said I could use the grassy knoll, but I was hoping"—unable to look at her friend, Piper closed her eyes—"to use the observatory."

"If the LOP agrees, I don't see why not," Darcy said. And when she realized Darcy was dead serious, she opened one eye.

"Seriously? Because I can't pay much."

"Of course." Darcy laughed. "Not only will it help a charity that means a lot to you, but you're my friend."

Piper swallowed past the emotion building in her throat. "I don't know want to say and—can you two stop that whole convo through the ether thing you do?"

"Sorry. It's a mom thing," Jillian said. "We've had to get good at talking without actually talking when the kids are playing."

"We used to spell things out, but preschool ruined that. And mouthing to each other is a joke. The other night, Gage mouthed, 'Lace or silk?' and Kylie turned and asked me what silk was. I told him he was in trouble, and his solution was for me to ditch the panties altogether."

"In my house, the word *panty* refers to cotton." Jillian sighed dreamily. "Oh, to have someone to buy lace and silk for."

Piper felt her face heat. She'd bought some silk and lace just today—and decided to wear them tonight. After that kiss, she had a feeling she'd be showing them off soon.

"How did you get the Ladies of Portland to agree?" Darcy asked, referring to the society group Margo belonged to.

Piper grimaced. "I haven't."

"Oh boy. You do know that this event was started twenty-five years ago by Margo and, up until this year, she's had full control."

Piper let her head thunk against the table.

"I told Josh it would be a no-go, and he assured me Margo would cave."

"Josh, huh?" Jillian teased.

Piper looked up. "We moved on to a new topic, remember?"

"You moved on to a new topic. I'm still caught up on you and Josh."

"There isn't a me and Josh. Fun, remember?"

"Barely." Jillian sighed.

"You did it," Piper said to Darcy, remembering how Margo watched her p's and q's around her. Gone were her horns and bad attitude, leaving a pleasant mother of the groom. Grandmother. "What magic did you weave?"

"My adorable daughter."

She thunked her head again. "So there's no hope for me." She looked up. "Actually, failing isn't an option. I have a whole lot of people who I refuse to let down."

"Then you have to get her to think it was her idea," Darcy advised. "Tell her stories of the girls she'll help. And if you can't appeal to her softer side, don't be afraid to show your fangs. Margo is like a bulldog with a bone when it comes to her ideas. She's only playing nice because of Kylie. But for her to agree, you're going to have to make a good case."

"That shouldn't be hard. The girls' art won't be anywhere near her auction."

"My advice? Meet on neutral ground and go into the meeting with a few votes in your pocket."

Jillian took a sip of "mommy juice," then leaned in to whisper as if anything could carry over the crowd. "How is it that all the Eastons are so freaking hot? Every single one. It must be some recessive gene. There's not an average one in the group."

"Any one in particular you find hotter than the rest?" Darcy asked, and Jillian was suddenly interested in her drink. "That's what I thought."

"Who?" Piper asked, relieved to be out of the hot seat.

"Clay, that's who. Every time he's around, Jillian gets all flustered and finds a reason to go to the opposite side of the room."

Jillian rolled her eyes. "I don't get flustered. Besides, I'm like a married-divorced-now-single-mom older than him." She looked at Piper. "Plus, flirting with a guy who's in my social circle is nothing but trouble."

"Then flirt with someone else," Darcy said. "You've been divorced over two years, it's time you had some fun."

"Agreed," Piper said, and Jillian became flustered.

"I'm more interested in who Josh wanted you to meet earlier," she said.

Piper shrugged. She wasn't going there.

"My guess, it was a ruse," Darcy said.

"Based on the lack of lipstick and the way she's turning beet red, I have to agree," Jillian said.

"Do you think this is a date?"

"Absolutely," Darcy said. "First, maybe second. She still has that collided with an Easton look about her."

"Seriously, I'm right here," Piper said. "And I don't blush." But she was so blushing.

"Here's how girls' night works," Darcy explained. "Either you spill, or we keep asking questions until we figure it out."

"Plus, I haven't been on a date since Obama was in office." Elbows on the table, Jillian stacked her hands under her chin. "Let me live vicariously."

Piper looked over at Josh, who was looking back. He lifted a questioning brow and then, as if he knew exactly what was happening, sent a cocky grin in her direction.

You like me, he mouthed, and she rolled her eyes, then looked back to the table of awaiting expressions.

"We may have agreed to be here tonight at the same time," she said, hoping Fate didn't strike her dead for that lie.

"That sounds like a date," Jillian said.

"Not a date so much as being alone together."

Both women exchanged looks, then laughed. Darcy was wiping the humor from her eyes when she said, "That's an Easton explanation if I've ever heard one."

Piper swallowed the lump in her throat. "Like a line?"

Because it hadn't felt like a line. Nothing between them felt shallow like a line.

"Not at all," Darcy assured her. "Josh would never put something like that out there unless he felt something."

"I don't know if we're at the *feel* place." Another white lie. "But he's sweet, and I'm enjoying whatever this is."

"You two have totally kissed." Darcy leaned forward, her eyes going narrow as if trying to gather information from the cosmos. "And tonight wasn't the first time."

"What? Is this some parlor trick? Let me guess what base you've slid across?"

"No," Darcy said at the same time Jillian said, "Yes."

They both looked at Jillian, who shrugged. "What part of 'since Obama' did you guys miss?"

A server came by and asked for their order. The girls were ordering another round when Piper's phone pinged.

Josh: Do you need to be rescued?

PIPER: Are you offering to be my Prince Charming?

JOSH: I LIKE THE TERM 'KNIGHT' better.

PIPER: Prince Charming gets to kiss his lady. 'Knight' rides off. Alone. With only his sword for company.

JOSH: Have I mentioned that knights are overrated?

Piper considered carefully what she wanted to say next.

To his core, Josh was a savior, and she didn't subscribe to the whole concept of being rescued. Her mom spent her entire life waiting for a man to save her. To make her happy and solve all her problems. She wound up a miserable and lonely black-out drunk. Piper wouldn't make that mistake.

Piper: So are princes.

Josh: . . .

The dots disappeared, and she felt his gaze on her. She wanted to look up and show him that she meant what she said, but in the end, she wasn't able to look him in the eye. Afraid she'd blown it, she was about to call it a night when the dots reappeared.

Josh: Maybe you're not the one who needs to be rescued.

16

"Are you following me?" Piper teased as she climbed out of her car.

"I'm following the boots." *Hot damn*, those boots. "And their owner," Josh added as he walked over to hold the door open for her while she rummaged through her back seat. He couldn't help but stare at her fine ass as she bent inside to gather up her things, the skirt riding high on her thighs. The further she disappeared into the back seat, the more skin he saw.

"You were trying to get away from your brothers."

That too.

"You need a new power-steering pump," he said. "It was like you were sending smoke signals to the entire downtown."

That wasn't the only kind of signal she was sending. They'd been slowly undressing each other from across the room all night. It had been so blatant at times, his brothers gave him shit. But he didn't care. The second he spotted those mile-long legs sitting at the bar, encased in toe to mid-thigh suede, he'd been a goner.

Josh was an ass man all the way, with legs coming in a close second. However, Piper in those boots, with her never-ending legs, was causing him to reassess the exact order of his *Hell Yeah* list.

"POSH and I have an understanding."

She straightened, and he slammed the door, the car letting out a low groan. "Like a death pact? Because she's one strip of duct tape from the giant junkyard in the sky."

He took her bags out of her hands, halting when he noticed one missing. The one she never left home without. "Where's your other camera?"

"Oh." She waved a dismissive hand. "I must have misplaced it."

Josh held her gaze. She was upset, but trying to hide it. "Where's your camera, Boots?"

She let out a huge sigh. "Before you say I told you so, I think Rebecca took it."

He cradled her head. "I am so sorry."

She shrugged as if it were no biggie, but he could sense just how upsetting this was for her. "All I do know is that I hope she's okay."

A frustration grew in him. Piper had opened up her house to a virtual stranger who'd taken advantage of her and stole what was likely the most treasured item she owned.

"If you want to press charges—"

"No way! She made a mistake, plus we don't know for sure she was the one who took it. I might have left it somewhere," she lied.

"I can at least have someone come over so you can make a report. That way if it's found, they'll know who it belongs to."

Piper met his gaze. "You and I both know it won't turn up unless someone wants it to. And I'm not going to do anything to put Rebecca in danger. I promised I wouldn't call the cops."

"That was before she stole from you." What was so hard

about that? Josh understood the loyalty and why Piper was hesitant to press charges, but it was better Rebecca was given a slap on the wrist then to get into serious trouble later.

"Until I hear her story, I'm not going to assume." She looked up at him. "Isn't that what you'd hope someone would do if your family member was accused of something?"

Like a sucker punch to the chest. It was like his dad was speaking directly to him about hearing people out, asking what their story was before passing judgment. Josh liked to think he was a good prosecutor, but suddenly he felt as if he'd lost sight of what the law was intended to do. It should be the last resort, not the starting point.

Had just one person along the way asked to hear his dad's story, he wouldn't have had to spend the last year of his life fighting to save the bar and his reputation. Instead, one employee's bad judgment led to two years of legal hell.

"You're right," he said quietly. "And if someone I loved was accused of something, I'd hope they had someone like you in their corner."

"I just think that everyone deserves to be heard out. I mean, let's say Rebecca did take my camera, I want to at least know the *why*. To me, that's more important than the *what*."

"It should be to everyone." Including him. Especially him. With his professional aspirations, he should know better than to go off halfcocked without knowing the full story.

"Then promise you won't say a word," she whispered. "I want to handle this my own way."

He stilled. By her own admission, she never used the word promise, so who was he to deny her when this might be the only time she'd ever ask him for something. "I promise."

"Now, I think this is where I thank you for following me home." She wrapped her arms around his neck.

She started to kiss him, and he said, "Not here." Hand on her hips, he walked her backward, up the steps to the front porch, directly under the porch light. "Here."

She looked up and smiled. "Is this where you kiss me goodnight?"

He wanted to do a whole lot more than kiss. Getting her out of that skirt was *numero uno* on his *Hell Yeah* list. Scratch that. Getting her out of those boots obliterated the list. But she was looking up at him with reluctant desire, and he had promised her a proper date, and that ended with a kiss under the porch light. What happened after that was up to her.

"This is where I tell you that I had a good time. No, a great time, and I want to see more of you," he said.

With a smile, Piper closed the distance, her skirt brushing his thighs as she turned him so she could walk him backward until the door was pressed at his back and she was pressed at his front, causing a whole lot of pressing to build in his pants.

She rose up on her toes, leaning into him until she was plastered against him, stopping when they were close enough to share the same breath. The night surrounded them, creating a sense of intimacy, the air crackling with growing sexual heat.

"This is where I invite you in," she whispered, her mouth brushing his with every word.

"For brownies?"

"That too." She turned the key in the door behind him and the lock disengaged.

Piper looked up at him as if brownies were code for mind-blowing sex and that she wanted more than one helping, making his body practically high-five out of his pants.

The still night air hung thick, nothing between them but moonlight. She sank her teeth into her lower lip, those whiskey-brown, oh-so-trusting eyes meeting his, and his brain clicked. Beneath the sexual bravado was a hint of shy vulnerability which had him pausing.

It was no secret that Piper's life had been a revolving door of disappointment, and he refused to be another person who let her down. He remembered that first night at the party, the way she'd looked at him with equal parts interest and indecision. She'd felt cornered, out of her comfort zone, and had lumped him in with every other guy who had blown into and out of her life.

"I'm okay taking this slow," he said.

While he wanted her in a kick-in-the-door and tumble-into-bed-fast kind of way, it was more important that she knew this wasn't a sprint for him—he wanted to go the distance. Bad timing be damned, he wanted to see where this thing between them went.

"I figured my boots were the equivalent of me scribbling 'I want you' on a cocktail napkin."

Before he could add cocktail napkin notes to his *Hell Yeah* list, her lashes fluttered closed, and she pressed her mouth to his.

Her kiss slayed him. It was everything that he needed and nothing that he'd ever felt before. The crazy emotions from the evening and the shy way her lips caressed his tangled into one big, complicated lump in his throat.

Josh wrapped his arms around her and deepened the kiss until he didn't know if he'd be able to let her go. His hands slid down the back of her thigh before traveling back up and under her skirt, his fingers stopping right before things got interesting. She was all soft skin and glorious curves.

Wrapping a single arm around her waist, he lifted her until her feet were off the floor. Her arms tightened around his neck, her legs dangling, as he opened the front door and let himself in.

"Rebecca?" Piper called out. "Are you here?" When no response came back, she called out again. Silence.

He sent up a silent *thank you* to the Universe. "Coast is clear."

"Then what are you waiting for?"

Taking her mouth, he kicked the door shut behind him, walked down the hallway and into the first bedroom he came to. His guess must have been accurate, because she didn't object when he set her on her feet right next to the bed. Not that either of them let go.

He moved her back, back, back until her legs bumped the bed and she fell onto the mattress. He pulled back to look at her. And look he did. So long his brain short-circuited.

Look, then touch? Touch, then look? Indecision hit hard.

"Maybe this will help," Piper said and—*what a woman she was*—lifted her arms in invitation. Josh RSVPed to that party in no time. He took the hem of her camisole, sliding it up inch by inch, exposing more and more skin as he went until he reached a little hint of black lace. Then there was a whole lot of black lace as he pulled it over her head, leaving him with a one-of-a-kind view—of two perfect tens begging for attention.

"Two little straps, and it's go time." She didn't look away, didn't fiddle with her clasp, just flicked one strap off her shoulder, then the other. "Unless you're looking for a little showtime."

He ran a hand down his jaw. "I've been thinking about this moment for so long, I need a minute."

"Then while you gather yourself, Mr. Assistant District Attorney, how about we make this an even playing field." She did a little swirly action with her fingers, gesturing for him to lose his shirt. He wanted to, he really did, but there'd come a time when the shirt would go up and over his head, blocking his view. And there was no way that was happening.

"I showed you mine, it's only fair you show me yours." She slid her palms under his shirt and, running her hands up his abs and over his pecks, she tugged the fabric as she went. When she pulled it over his head, she had to stand and roll up on her toes, bringing their bodies so close he could feel her nipples brush against his skin.

And, *magic of all magic*, when his shirt hit the floor, she was missing a bra. Next came her skirt, lowering the zipper, tooth by tooth. She let it hang on her hips, low enough that a hint of light-yellow lace peeked out. He wasn't expecting yellow. Black, maybe red, but she had on light, feminine yellow, and suddenly he saw this soft side to the tough girl that he always knew was in there buried beneath the impenetrable armor she used to keep her heart safe.

Looking both uncertain and embarrassed, she bit her lower lip. "Not what you were expecting?"

"Nothing about this was expected, but you're one hell of an incredible surprise."

"Incredible, huh?" she said, pushing him down on the bed. "That's a lot to live up to."

Before he could reassure her that she'd already blown his expectations, she did a little shimmy action with her hips, which sent the tiny scrap of denim to the floor, leaving her in nothing but a yellow thong and lace-up boots. It was like girl-next-door collided with *Pretty Woman*, revving up his body until it was ready to break through the gates. She slowly turned around, making a complete three-sixty, showing him every single, solitary inch of skin.

"Come here," he said, pulling her into his arms and kissing her in a way that told her exactly how the rest of the night was going to play out. With her losing her mind over and over and over again.

He laid her back on the bed, crawling up her body until he was settled between her legs—the only thing between them was her thong and his jeans.

His hand glided up her rib cage, sneaking around the back side, inches from her breasts. Her breath caught and she smiled, following the same path, skimming but avoiding direct contact.

"You're playing dirty," she whispered.

"I was testing a theory."

Piper did some testing of her own, rubbing over his jeans, then under his jeans until—*bingo*—he groaned, his eyes rolling all the way back. He was certain he'd pass out from the sensation of her soft hands on his hardness.

Not letting up, she stroked him again, this time cupping him and giving a little squeeze. Then not so little. And just when he thought she couldn't get any sexier, she wrapped her legs around him, locking her ankles behind his back.

Being a ladies first kind of man, Josh held her still as he kissed his way down her collarbone to her breasts, worshiping one, then the other, tugging her into his mouth until her back was arching off the mattress.

Not wanting to rush, he worked her into a frenzy as his hand moved lower, tracing her hip bone until finally coming up against the waistband of her sexy lace. He teased his way inside, all the way inside, adding a second finger to the mix.

"Josh." His name was a breathy moan.

"What happened to Mr. Assistant District Attorney?" he asked against her breast.

"Too." Her hips move with him. "Many." Pumping against his hand. "Words." Her legs tightened around him.

Josh upped the pressure and the tempo, loving how her breath caught, the way her lips parted. She was so close, all it would take was a little swirl of the fingers and—

"More!" she cried out, and he gave her more until her body was clenching tighter and tighter. She started to tremble, panting for him to keep going, and then she went off like a firework, exploding around him.

A few moments later, her lashes fluttered open, and she

smiled a sated smile. Her hand was still down his pants, and as she came to, it slowly started stroking him. He stilled her.

"How about this next theory we try together?"

"Together," she whispered. "I like together."

Hell, he loved together.

He started removing her thong at the same time she began tugging at his jeans. They were a big tangle of arms and legs, somehow managing to get him wrapped and sliding home in record time. Both of them sighed in pleasure.

Her heavy-lidded eyes deepened to a dark brown and locked on to his. "I like this theory."

With a grin, he began to move. Slow and steady, neither looked away until his heart opened up in a way he hadn't expected, bringing fathomless possibilities to the forefront of his mind.

Her hips moved with his, matching his rhythm, staying in perfect sync as the strokes became deeper and the pace became faster. Lacing their hands, he pressed them into the mattress, taking her mouth as he continued down this pathway, further and further, until looking back was no longer an option.

Right, he decided. Everything about this moment felt right. Right time, right woman.

He was determined to stay with her, right up until the moment she tumbled off the edge. By the way she was clenching, her legs so tight the heels of her boots pressed into his ass, he knew she was as close as he was. So close he could see that finish line, and they were both racing toward it with a raw need that made breathing impossible. He moved faster, and she held tighter, winding up until one more move and they'd both shatter.

"Josh," she said, a hint of vulnerable hesitation coming through. She was scared, needing reassurance, and that broke his heart.

"I've got you," he promised her. "It's okay. Let go."

She did, and it was so sexy he exploded with her. They both continued to move through the orgasm, not letting up until they crossed right through that line and even further. Further than he'd ever gone, until he stopped thinking and all that he did was feel.

And she felt damn near perfect.

17

"I don't see this working out," Margo Easton said from the opposite side of the table, placing a dramatic hand to her chest.

"I assure you, we're perfectly matched," Piper argued.

September had arrived, and Mother Nature was showing off. The mums were in full bloom, the sky was a brilliant blue, but Piper was a complete wreck. Even before she was called to make her case, she'd begun sweating in uncomfortable places.

The day after tomorrow was the final meeting for the Ladies of Portland before Bid for the Cause, and Piper had been invited to present her idea to the board. Only two slides into her fifteen-page presentation, which she'd compiled in an effort to sway the board, and Margo was already poo-pooing the idea of partnering with Urban Soul. And she was taking board members with her.

This was one of the reasons Piper hadn't wanted to face down Satan's Keeper at the last location the two had sparred. While Darcy owned the venue, Margo acted as if it were her private garden, even directing the staff while they passed out samples for the tasting. Darcy had pointed out that Belle Mont was better than Margo's house, where the old bat would've had the home court advantage.

But Piper had a secret weapon. Her handsome, hard-packed muscle plus-one, who'd unexpectedly shown. He was seated to her left, so close she could smell his fierce protectiveness and so stoic that everyone knew whose side he was on.

The gesture was moving and romantic. He'd promised her he'd come through, but never in a million years did she imagine that, with a seat available right next to his mom, he'd pull up a chair next to Piper.

"It's moving way too fast," Margo said. She was dressed in white linen slacks, a classic mauve button-up, and a clunky gold necklace. She was starched, refined, and shooting Piper the eye. "We already have the event planned, right down to the last detail."

Piper thought back to the advice Josh had given her earlier about how to state her case in a way that made it difficult for the opposition to rebut. "I can only imagine how much work y'all have put into the event, which is why I'm not asking you to change a thing."

"You're not?" Kitty asked.

"No, ma'am," Piper said, hearing her accent slip again. She glanced at Josh, who sent her the merest ghost of a smile, igniting those silly tingles. More than that, it calmed her nerves, made her feel like she wasn't alone. "All I'm asking is that you allow me to use the conservatory as a gallery to display art from local artists."

"I was promised that the conservatory would be open for guests to wander through during the appetizer part of the evening," Margo said.

"It will be," Darcy said, sitting on Piper's right. Next to her was Jillian, who said she had a voice in the matter since she'd volunteered to make mini bundt cakes for the event. Their support was a bit overwhelming and intimidating. It had been so long since Piper had had a good and loyal friend, she'd forgotten what that kind of sisterly bond felt like. And it felt great. "In fact, I think Urban Soul will add a fresh, youthful feel that will appeal to the next generation of bidders."

"Teens wandering about?" Margo blanched. "When my family started this charity twenty-five years ago, there was no wandering. There was a specific goal, which we met every time. Do you know how?"

"No, ma'am." But Piper suspected she was about to learn.

"By maintaining focus on the important things. It's easy to get distracted, be pulled in other—flashier—directions." Her gaze landed on Josh. "If we get pulled in too many directions, we lose our effectiveness." She put her hand to her chest. "At least, that's what my Benji would have said."

"Maybe a fresh take is exactly what this organization needs," Kitty said, and Piper knew they were no longer talking about the fundraiser. "We've been operating under the same stale ideals and agenda for years, rendering us nearly irrelevant."

All eyes landed on Margo, of the stale and irrelevant ideals. The woman's face went red, and her eyes were a little too misty for Piper's liking. And while Piper would rather chew on manure than side with Margo, she was a sucker for the underdog. And right then, Kitty was coming after Margo, partly because of Piper.

"Nothing that has raised as much money for the community as this organization has could ever be seen as irrelevant," Piper said gently, meeting Margo's gaze. "And merging the two events will be a way to honor tradition while embracing the problems that young people face."

"The number of younger attendees has gone up over the past few years," Ms. Dalton, the oldest and most respected Ladies of Portland member, said. She was also the senior adviser to the board, so her opinion was golden. Winning her vote would ensure that other members would side in Urban Soul's favor.

"They rarely bid because it's the same old stuffy items," Kitty went on. "Plus, as a local artist myself, I feel inclined to support other artists."

"And isn't that what this is about? Supporting others. I mean, look at this." Piper clicked to the next slide, which was shown on a monitor that Gage had brought into the conservatory.

She looked at the photo facing the room, which showed a stunning piece of the underside of the bridge crossing the Columbia River, the cement piles speckled with glimpses of tagging art and the waters beyond. The whole piece was drawn as if captured through a fisheye camera lens, compressing the top and elongating the sides, like looking through a peephole.

"This is the work of a fifteen-year-old girl, Samantha, who only started drawing last year. She's a junior in high school and comes to our after-school program three days a week. And the photograph was taken by Clive Kessler."

At the mention of the famous photographer, impressed murmurs came from the table. Clive wasn't only known in artist circles, he was one of the most revered landscape photographers on the west coast—he was also Piper's mentor.

Confidence bubbling that maybe she could pull this off, she flipped to the next slide. "This is a spray paint art piece titled *Cinderella's a Lie*. The artist is sixteen and, with no formal training, she's likely the most talented person in the program."

Every time she looked at that photo, that euphoric feeling in her chest, which always appeared when looking at beautiful art, began to warm. She had to make this happen. Those girls were counting on her. Rebecca was too good to be passed over, and Piper refused to be another person who let her down. "Rebecca got lost in the foster system until Skye's the Limit stepped in."

She felt Josh's eyes on her but refused to look his way. It had been four days since anyone had heard from Rebecca, and Piper was starting to get worried. Just talking about the teen's art made Piper want to cry. Josh must have sensed her sadness, because he rested his hand on her knee beneath the table and gave it a little squeeze.

Piper placed her hand on top of Josh's and squeezed back.

"Is that vandalism?" one of Margo's minions asked. "It looks like vandalism."

There was a chorus of "Uh huh"s and "It does"es, and Piper was certain her boat was sinking.

"I'm sure Piper can set our minds at ease," Margo said, and Piper felt her forehead start to glisten. Margo would spray-paint a Mercedes if it meant getting her way. The only reason she would let someone defend their case, especially Piper, was if she thought she'd already won the argument. The woman had an ace up her linen-cuffed sleeve, and that made Piper nervous.

"The piece you are referring to was painted on a garage door, which was approved by the owner," Piper explained. "I understand that to you this just looks like graffiti. But it's so much more. Urban art tells the stories that we often, as a society, overlook. It's a visual history of the people who walk those streets. Their story is as important, if not more so, than ours. If not for art, it might never be told."

Margo looked out at the group—and they were all looking back, rapt by the drama that was about to unfold. She cleared her throat. "We have already chosen a well deserving charity that benefits stray animals and local shelters."

Piper wasn't sure if the woman was comparing her girls to strays, but a seed of anger the size of a stone began to burn in her stomach, and that same determination, which had served her well when she lived on the streets, solidified. She was going to win over this crowd, even if it meant taking on the mother of the man she was definitely, maybe dating.

"I'm sure People Against Purebreds is a deserving charity, which is why I'm not asking for any of the money this event earns."

"But you are," one of the ladies, who was seated at Margo's right and wearing a button that read PUREBREDS with a big red line through it to state her allegiance, said. "If we agree to put those photographs into the auction, it might take money away from the other items."

"They won't be in the auction. Each work will have a set price and if there is interest, a person can pay the asking price or they can offer any amount over, whatever they feel the piece is worth."

"You're expecting us to hand over all the money from the sales," Margo said. "Who knows where it will end up?"

"Ten percent would go to your chosen charity."

"They were promised all of the proceeds of the auction," Margo shot off. "This charity was selected a year ago when I was the president. And I won't have the decision undone because someone wants to benefit from my hard work."

And there it was, the reason Margo was sinking her teeth in. She'd lost her crown to Kitty, and by splitting the attention of the auction she felt as if she were losing her legacy.

Piper put as much sincerity as she could in her expression as she said, "I understand your hesitation, Margo. You have worked hard to create an event that has helped so many people over the years. Let me address your concern. In no way will Urban Soul distract from the amazing evening you have planned. And it won't affect the auction. I've spoken at great length with Darcy about how to lay out the showcase."

At the mention of Darcy being on board, Margo's lips puckered as if she'd bitten into a lime.

"And we're not asking for a dime from the auction or the per-plate cost for each guest," she explained. "We're only talking about the money raised by Urban Soul."

"What *will* you do with it, dear?" Ms. Dalton asked.

"Fifty percent will go into an account for each girl, so when they age out of the system, they'll have funds for college or starting their independent lives. Because when they age out, they are on their own." Piper hoped no one else heard her voice crack on that last part. Only Josh had, because she felt him shift closer. "The other forty percent will go to help Skye's the Limit."

"That was another concern. I took the liberty of researching this Skye's the Limit and the woman running it," Margo said, her necklace swinging with contempt. "Some things popped up, and I was hoping you could put my mind at ease. How would it look for the Ladies of Portland to support an organization run by a woman who was hosting an illegal half-way house out of her home and was arrested for unlawful gathering?"

A fierce protectiveness overtook her, and Piper was about to say something she'd regret when she felt Josh's hand turn over to lace with hers. She met his gaze, touched to realize he was asking if he could take this one. She gently nodded.

"Mom, the house is a home for girls who need a safe place to land. She rescues girls who would otherwise have no one in their corner," he said, and Piper was relieved that she'd never mentioned to Josh that Skye took in younger girls as well. Not often, but 'no' wasn't in Skye's vocabulary. "I can't even imagine what that would feel like, not having a loving and supportive family, but we have the chance to help change some lives."

"I used to be one of Skye's girls," Piper admitted, leaving out that she'd been barely seventeen at the time. Lost, hungry, and young enough for Skye to lose her homeless shelter status. "Skye might be a little eccentric, but she's dedicated her life to rescuing girls from a life you couldn't possibly imagine," Piper said, but Margo crossed her arms defiantly. "Girls like me who needed a safe place or even just one person to be kind and care about whether they lived or died."

Piper watched as Kitty and three of the other board members teared up. She didn't need Margo's vote to win, but she wanted her vote. Not only because the woman needed to be informed of what was happening in her beloved city, but also because she was Josh's mom. And while Piper hadn't given a rat's ass at the engagement party, things had changed.

She'd changed.

"You have raised a wonderful family, but not everyone has that. Can you imagine what it would be like to have nothing? Not a toothbrush or book or even a second pair of shoes?"

"Well, from what I understand, you had a pair of shoes that landed you in some trouble."

Piper sat back in her chair as if she'd been shoved. While her past would always be an important part of her, she was no longer the girl from that juvie record, which was supposed to be sealed. Was this what happened when you became friends with someone in power? They investigated you?

No, she decided. They'd just investigate someone like her.

"They were boots because it was winter and I was cold, and they landed me in Skye's house, which saved my life. She's saved many girls over her lifetime. Maybe not girls you would even acknowledge, but they exist, and they need help." Piper addressed the board. "I need your help to help them."

"I think this is an interesting opportunity for our organization," Ms. Dalton said. "Would you mind if we discussed it among ourselves?"

"Of course." Piper stood.

"We'll take a vote at Thursday's meeting and notify you of the outcome."

"Thank you." Piper stood, then paused. "There are thousands of Rebeccas in Portland, and we have a unique opportunity to help a few of them feel significant and special." She handed Kitty her remote. "I have some more samples of what would be showcased in my presentation. Feel free to scroll through them. There are some really amazing pieces."

"You promised you'd be nice," Josh said, putting his arm around his mom.

When it looked as if the board was leaning in Piper's favor, Margo had excused herself to the conservatory. Josh knew how much this event meant to her, just as he knew how hard change was for her.

"It's difficult to be nice when she shows up uninvited and derails something that is twenty-five years in the making."

"She was invited. By Kitty, Darcy, and myself."

"But no one asked me." Margo leaned into him. "This event used to be your dad's favorite night of the year."

"Actually, I think the first day of Oktoberfest was his favorite day of the year." Josh laughed, but his mom stayed silent. "Mom, what is this really about?"

"You blindsiding me today."

Josh blew out a breath. "I didn't blindside you. I offered to help Piper secure a permit. Things went south. I owed it to her to fix things."

"So you decided to support her scheme to take over my event?"

"She isn't scheming to ruin your event, Mom. She's looking for a way to help a few girls go to college. And before you say anything else about Piper, this whole thing was my idea."

Margo clutched her heart dramatically. "*Your* idea? How could you not come to me first?"

"It all happened so fast. When Kitty was in favor of merging the two, I moved forward."

"I knew Kitty was behind this," she whispered through her teeth. "This whole thing used to be my committee. I started this committee. Your dad and I started this charity event. The only reason Kitty was elected board chair is because her husband's the biggest donor for the auction and she said he'd pull his support otherwise."

Josh steered her toward a small seating area at the far end of the conservatory. They both took a seat and looked out the glass walls at the skyline. The afternoon was so clear they could see snow-topped peaks of Mount Hood in the distance.

"I know it's hard losing things that remind you of Dad."

"We've just had so much loss," his mom whispered. "When we started this event, it was a simple auction in our backyard to raise money for the Ackerman family."

Andy Ackerman had been Josh's childhood friend. They used to ride bikes at the park and get into trouble down by the pond. When Andy was eleven, he was diagnosed with leukemia. The medical bills alone forced his parents to take out a second mortgage on the house. Had it not been for Josh's parents, they would have lost their home.

"Dad would be proud of what you've turned this event into." He paused to give himself time to really consider how to broach the topic of the hour. He understood his mom's need to control her world for fear of losing the things she cherished and love. But he'd also made Piper a promise. "You started this to help one family in need. What better way to honor Dad's memory than to once again focus on a few people with whom we can make a huge difference?"

His mom turned to look at him, her eyes glassy with emotion. "Are you saying that because you believe it or because you want to impress your lady friend?"

"Can't it be both?" he asked honestly, and Margo lifted a frail shoulder that was so weighed down by the grief she clung to.

"Your dad would have been by my side no matter my decision. Right or wrong."

"Dad's not here, Mom." He took her hand in his. "And he wouldn't want you to hurt like this. He'd want you to move on and have a happy life. Play with your granddaughter, look forward to Gage's wedding, embrace your daughter-in-law. Let go of things that no longer bring you joy." Hell, he sounded like Rhett.

"You kids spark joy. This event sparks joy. Anything I used to do sparks joy. I feel like everything's changing," Margo admitted. "Rhett's either gone or with Stephanie. Gage is busy with his new family. Owen's at the bar as much as your dad was. Now you're missing family dinners."

"I noticed you didn't mention Clay," he teased.

"You boys all know Clay is my favorite." She didn't sound guilty in the least. "The baby is always the favorite. It's the law of birth order."

"I thought the firstborn was your favorite."

With a watery smile, she reached over and patted his cheek. "You're a close second."

"Your family is growing and changing. That's what families do. That doesn't mean they love each other any less. And the bigger we become, the more love there is to go around."

"Your dad would have known what to do. He was the flexible one, always loving everyone so freely." Margo hung her head, and Josh heard a sniffle. "I'm barely holding on to Benji's memory as it is. And it seems you boys moved on in a flash."

Talk about crushing his heart. He knew his mom was stuck somewhere between denial and anger on the steps of grief. Her sons had moved on to acceptance, but Margo felt as if she'd been left behind.

"You know that's not true," he said, and Margo looked up. "I'm fighting to get Dad's good name back, Owen's running the bar, Rhett is doing what Dad wanted for him. And Clay? Dad would have lost his mind to see Clay play for the Seahawks. Don't you see? Everything we do is somehow connected to Dad and doing right by his memory."

"Maybe I do need to let go a little. I just don't know how."

"How about with this event? I met the girl who painted the garage door. She's pretty special. Strong-minded and tough, and just needs someone to give a damn."

Very much like another feisty female he knew, who had left the veranda and disappeared into the house. He knew she was nervous and irritated at his mom, and rightfully so. Margo had been a pill, but Piper had managed her with class.

He lowered his voice but stressed the immediacy of the moment. "I need you to vote in favor of this."

Margo let out a suffocated breath. "As long as it's tasteful art and not stolen road signs with graffiti."

18

Twenty minutes later, Josh found Piper in the kitchen, elbow deep in a sink of dishes. She was wearing black ankle boots, matching black pants that hugged her body to perfection, and a pretty, yellow top, which reminded him of a certain pretty, yellow thong.

Her hair was twisted up in an intentionally messy knot, leaving her neck—and that tattoo—exposed. He wasn't sure what was more of a turn on, the tattoo or the mystery behind it.

He walked up behind her, his arms circling her waist. At the touch, Piper tensed as if startled. It was a brief, instinctual reaction to being caught off guard, but it told him another part of her story. A part that made his chest ache.

"Are you a Christmas fan?"

"Christmas?"

"The F. *Fa la la*?" he teased.

She laughed, but it was half-hearted. And he hated that. "Forget about it."

"Can't." He nuzzled the back of her neck. "What are you doing?"

She didn't take her attention off the dishes. "Patricia from the catering company was telling me how one of her servers called in sick, so I'm helping out."

"Helping out or hiding out?"

"Maybe a little of both," she said quietly. Her body was tense, nerves rolling off her in waves.

At the unexplainable need to soothe her, Josh curled his body around her like a shield. "My family is a lot to take in."

"I figured that out."

He feathered a kiss at the base of her neck, then rolled up his sleeves, grabbed a dish towel and started drying the clean dishes. She gawked at him as if he'd morphed into some kind of alien. "What are you doing?"

"Didn't you hear? Patricia's short-staffed."

She reached for the rag, and he held it above his head. "Seriously, you don't have to help."

When she lowered her arm, he went back to drying. "You're not the only person who likes to help people."

Except, she didn't only help people—she changed lives and she didn't boast about it, like people in his office would. She actually made an impact on the same communities Josh had become a lawyer to protect. But since meeting Piper and Rebecca, he had begun to wonder if maybe he was missing the bigger picture.

He hadn't busted his ass to be an errand boy to a mayor who believed Josh's time was expendable. And throwing back a few with a guy who believed he was entitled to a different set of rules was as bad as being one of those entitled guys. Even more irritating, for all his diplomas and contacts, Josh had been acting like an idiot.

She stopped and looked him in the eye. "Please tell me the apple fell far, far from the Easton tree."

Without wavering, he said, "I won't make excuses for the way my mom behaves. She changed after my dad passed, and then when Kyle died it got worse." He shook his head. "She gave in to the anger and loss."

"I know what it's like to be angry at the world. Your mom isn't the only one who can be judgy and harsh. I don't dislike her, Josh." She met his gaze, hers soft with understanding. "In fact, I respect her. The way she is with you and your brothers kind of makes me like her."

He chuckled. "Kind of?"

She studied the dishwater. "My mom never protected me the way your mom protects you."

Piper was such a caring person it hurt his gut that she hadn't been cared for the way she deserved. It also made her all the more impressive. Josh was the man he was because of his dad. Piper had achieved everything she had, and who she was, all by herself.

"What would your mother have done?"

She looked up at him through her lashes. "Depends on the guy she was with."

His heart broke for the girl she'd been, and his protective instincts wanted to hold and soothe the woman she was.

"Thanks for being here with me today," she said.

"I don't know if it helped." It better have helped. If he found out his mom voted against the idea because of his relationship with Piper, there'd be words. Lots and lots of frustrated words.

"It helped me," she admitted, and before he could answer, she moved away to finish the dishes. "You showed up, and that means a lot to me."

"I'll always show up," he said, and she went silent.

He could have said more, but he gave her the out. Like he had the other night when, after a long and steamy night under tangled sheets, she'd all but kicked him out. Then gone radio silent, not even calling him about today. Best guess? She got scared. Hell, he'd left a little shaken. A relationship was the last thing he needed right now. With all the moving pieces clogging his life, his overall plan didn't leave room for much else. Coming today hadn't been a mistake, but it cost him a meeting with a potential donor. And if he wasn't careful, it could cost him the election.

If he wanted to help people at the same level as Piper, then he needed to keep his eye on the target. But the minute he had walked in, watched every emotion cross her face, all thought of his schedule faded.

Her expression had started with surprise and quickly morphed into relief with a touch of gratitude thrown in. He'd been hoping for something a little closer to affection, but when she'd gripped his hand under the table, holding on to him as if there were no one else she'd rather have by her side, it made him both smile and ache.

"They're going to say yes."

"Then why can't they tell me today? I keep telling myself that if they understood what I was saying, they'd come to a decision, vote to take a chance on me."

Take a chance, as if believing in her was a risk. "You were amazing today."

"But was I amazing enough?" She handed him a plate. "I mean, it's a simple yes or no."

"When it comes to my mom, nothing is simple." Again he moved behind her, setting down the rag to hold her in his arms. "Believe in your work. I do."

She looked at him over her shoulder, and he got that same punch to the gut he always did when touching her. He'd like to think she felt it too, but she kept her feelings locked up tight. "How did you know it was my work?"

He kissed her nose. "*Cinderella's a Lie*. You took the photo."

"But there were a handful of photographers represented in there."

"Didn't matter. I saw you the second you flicked to Rebecca's slide," he said. "The photo was strong, bold, edgy, and feminine. It was you."

She turned in his arms, staring at him as if what he'd said didn't compute. "That's how you see me?"

"That's just one layer," he admitted. "I want to see all the layers, Boots. But you've got to let me in first."

"I don't know how," she admitted softly.

"Maybe start with knowing I'll show up for you when you need me."

"I don't do need so well. And trust?" She shook her head, loose strands of chocolate-brown hair escaping its confines and falling around her shoulders. "That's something I don't think I'm capable of."

From what he'd learned about her past, he didn't blame her. "Then know that I am. I always come through for the people in my life."

He could see the cautious disbelief in her eyes. "I'm in your life?"

"I want you to be."

She looked him in the eye. He wasn't sure what she was looking for, but she must have found it because she ran her fingers through his hair and delivered a tender kiss. No deflection. No pretense. Just Piper, kicking the door open a small crack and letting him in.

19

The next day, Piper spent her morning at the farmer's market, distracting herself from worrying about Rebecca and the afternoon of driving around looking for Rebecca. When she was about to start checking shelters, Skye called to let her know that Rebecca had slept there last night.

It was as if a dump truck worth of fear and worry had been lifted, and Piper could finally take a deep breath. Her biggest worry had been solved—she knew where Rebecca was, at least for tonight.

Which brought her to worry number two. The Ladies of Portland. Their monthly board meeting should be coming to a close and, good or bad, Piper would have her answer. If it were good, she'd celebrate with an entire batch of brownies. If the outcome was not in her favor, she'd allow five minutes of feeling sorry for herself, then strategize a new solution. She might even call Jillian and Darcy—or maybe even Josh—for a brainstorming session.

The skill of relying on others wasn't in her genes, but these past few weeks had shown her that asking for help wasn't a sign of weakness—it was a signal to others that she was open to forging connections, and connections led to some pretty amazing things.

Piper spent the past few days going back over every second of that meeting. The things she'd said, every look and comment the ladies made, and the way Josh had been there for her.

She was a big *show don't tell* kind of person—mainly because promises were rarely, if ever, kept and her policy protected her from further disappointment. Regardless of the outcome, Josh had come through. He'd gone the extra mile, and he'd shown up when she'd needed him most.

For Piper, a family wasn't in the cards. But friends, romance, and maybe even the chance to make an impact on other people's lives no longer seemed impossible.

She pulled into her driveway to find someone sitting on her front porch. The sun had turned in for the night, and the air had turned crisp, but Rebecca sat there, in nothing more than battered Converse, ratty jeans, and her thin, dark-blue hoodie.

Thin clothing was a good way to get around without lugging a suitcase. Piper had survived two winters without a proper coat. It was also a good way to freeze.

She grabbed her emergency raincoat and mittens from the floorboard of the back seat, then hopped out of the car and tossed it to Rebecca.

She caught it. "What's this?"

"Peace of mind. It's supposed to get down in the forties tonight." Piper unlocked the door and stepped inside. She didn't make a big deal about extending an official invite—girls like Rebecca didn't do official. Instead, she left the door open behind her. "I've got chili going in the slow cooker."

Relief hit hard when the teen followed her inside. "You pissed at me?"

"For what?" Piper left her purse and camera bag by the door and walked into the kitchen.

"For borrowing your camera." Rebecca hung the jacket on the rack, and a minute later, she walked to the threshold of the kitchen.

Piper turned and lifted a brow. "Borrowing implies you asked permission."

"It's not like I hocked it or anything." Rebecca rustled through her battered backpack and pulled out the camera. "Here."

Piper hadn't known until that second just how much the camera meant to her. The shutter button was form-fitted to her finger, the sides of the camera smooth from years of use. This camera was the start of her new life, a physical history of her journey. Starting with the day she left Georgia to the moment she sold her first photo and, finally, the moment it had been returned by a girl who could have sold it for a month's worth of food.

"Thank you."

"Whatever. It's yours," Rebecca said, her expression challenging her, like *Go ahead and yell at me for lifting the camera.* Piper didn't take the bait. When she'd invited the teen into her home, she knew there was a high chance the girl would walk off with something. It was a risk she was willing to take to ensure Rebecca had a safe, warm place to sleep.

"You could have stayed the other day."

"I figured you wanted me out of your hair." She was still standing at the threshold of the kitchen.

"How about we make a deal? We'll both be straight up with each other. If I want you gone, I'll tell you."

"What do I have to do?"

Piper aimed the camera at Rebecca and snapped a photo. She was caught off guard with how young the teen looked.

Beneath the attitude and anger was a scared sixteen-year-old who was all alone in a big, terrifying world. A girl who should be stressing about homework, not where her next meal would come from.

"Clean up after yourself and maybe help with the laundry. I hate laundry. It's one of those chores that even when you're done, it's never really done." While that was the truth, she wanted Rebecca to feel comfortable to wash her clothes. Laundromats cost money, and why waste it on cleaning clothes when showers were hard to come by? "You like chili?"

"Sure." A fib.

Piper lifted a brow, and Rebecca sighed. "Not really."

"You like pizza?" Rebecca's eyes lit. "I'll take that as a yes. Why don't you call and place an order for anything you want while I go and change? Number's on the fridge."

"I don't need a handout," Rebecca said, so much defensiveness in her tone that heartache fisted in Piper's chest.

"No handouts here. Everyone pulls their own weight. Tonight, you can pay me back by putting the chili in Tupperware." Piper opened the cupboard and set two glass mason jars on the counter.

Cautious surprise lit Rebecca's face. "And tomorrow night?"

"We're having chili." Piper dropped two twenties on the table. "And the dishes are on you."

Rebecca eyed the money, then Piper. Wanting to give the impression that Piper trusted her, Piper also dropped her camera on the table and turned to leave. "Be sure the pizza's a large. Oh, and those cheesy breadsticks!" she called over her shoulder. "And dessert. Anything chocolate." Whatever was left, she could package up and send with Rebecca if she decided to ditch before breakfast.

By the time Piper showered and put on sweats, pizza was on the table, her kitchen was immaculate, and Rebecca was sitting on the couch watching television. Piper opened the box and there was still a fully formed pizza.

A nagging feeling washed over her. The coat on the hanger, waiting for everyone before digging in. Until recently, someone had cared for Rebecca. Piper wondered where they'd gone and how she'd ended up on the streets.

"How many slices?"

Rebecca said one, but Piper gave her two, which the girl inhaled, along with three cheesy breadsticks and another slice of pizza. When Piper was finished, Rebecca surprised her further by taking both their plates to the kitchen and doing the dishes.

Instead of slicing the chocolate lava cake, Piper grabbed two forks and set them on the coffee table, then ate a bite straight from the container.

"So good," she groaned, and when Rebecca didn't move for the utensil, Piper forked off a big bite and handed it to her. "Are you from Portland?"

"Is this the part where, because you fed me, I have to spill my guts?" Rebecca's expression was a complete challenge. She was waiting for Piper to use her authoritative adult tone and demand answers.

"Just curious. I'm from Georgia," she said. Maybe if she opened up, Rebecca might do the same. This was another show-not-tell moment. "I moved to Portland when I was about your age."

Rebecca picked at the cake. "With your parents?"

"No, my mom and her boyfriend, who had octopus hands, are still in Georgia. I think." Honestly, Piper hadn't a clue. She'd lost contact with her mom the day after she'd arrived in Portland. "When I got here, I called to say I wanted to come home, and she said it wasn't a good time for her."

"Parents suck."

"Some of them do."

Rebecca appeared to disagree, and Piper didn't blame her. Parents seemed to fall into two categories: amazing or awful. She knew where her mom landed on the spectrum, and she wondered what Rebecca would say about her own parents.

"My mom's in jail. She killed my dad."

Piper's heart stalled, her lungs pinching painfully. "I am so sorry."

"Me too." The way she said it, so matter of fact, as if it was buried so deep that she couldn't access it. "My dad was a drunk, a mean drunk. One night he came home and was swinging his gun at me. My mom grabbed the gun, and somehow it went off and—"

"Isn't that self-defense?"

"She had a shitty lawyer. One of those appointed ones. But it was okay, I got to live with my grandma."

Piper understood mean drunks firsthand, as they seemed to be her mother's man of choice. There was something about bullies that her mom gravitated toward. Piper wasn't sure if her mom had passed along her addiction gene, but she wasn't taking any chances. Which was why she rarely, if ever, drank.

"My grandma was pretty cool," Rebecca said into the silence. "She died in May."

Rebecca's entire lifeline had likely died with her. It explained the manners and seed of hope in the teen's eyes. The longer kids were on the street, the more hardened they became, the worse their decisions were—until eventually they were caught. Few of them by people like Skye.

"I'm sorry about your grandma. I didn't really know mine. Were you close?"

"I mostly lived with her. Until, you know . . ." Rebecca lifted a slim shoulder.

"That must have been hard when she passed."

"Sometimes I wonder if she'd be disappointed in me," she said, and Piper was humbled by how brave Rebecca was being, opening up about something so personal. If a teenager could do it, then why was it so hard for Piper?

Josh had said as much. He'd done so much for her, been open and vulnerable, even came through on his promises—no one had done that for her. All he asked in return was to get to know her. But she'd been so closed off, hiding the things she was embarrassed about and skipping over things she was scared to admit aloud. If a teenager could be open about such painful and personal things, then Piper didn't have an excuse.

"From what you've told me, I think she'd be proud of you for taking care of yourself."

"You think?" Rebecca was doing her best to keep the tears at bay, and it reminded Piper of how it felt to have no one. How a combination of bad decisions by the people in Rebecca's life would shape the rest of her world. Every day, every decision, and every interaction would forever be impacted by these next few years.

It took a lot to rob someone of their ability to trust, but once broken, coming back was nearly impossible. All because Rebecca had been dealt a shitty hand.

"Are you in the market for a room to rent? I've been thinking of renting out the spare bedroom."

Rebecca snorted. "Yeah, I'll apply right after I win the lottery."

"I'm looking for an assistant. It's nothing glamorous. More like grunt work. You'd help with lighting, scouting locations, directing tipsy clients into the right position, babysitting any rug rats from photo-bombing the shot, and sometimes reminding me to eat. Like I said, grunt work. But it pays well, and you'd learn a lot about composition and lighting."

"I don't really know a lot about cameras."

"Neither did I when I started. But someone took me under his wing and taught me everything I know." Piper aimed for real. "Look, I was going to look for a roommate anyway, it might as well be you. You already understand perspective, color palettes, and you think out of the box, which will help me. I was taught by a very traditional mentor; it would be nice to get a youthful perspective. Most importantly, I already know you and have seen what you can do. Even this photo you took of your new piece I imagine is amazing."

"*In Numbers We Hide.*"

"*In Numbers We Hide.* It sounds amazing. In fact, I was thinking tomorrow morning we can go downtown and shoot some chalk art. You can use my digital camera. The place I want to take you to faces west, so the best time to shoot would be when the sun comes up."

"You're probably busy," Rebecca said, but she held Piper's gaze, wanting to watch Piper's expression when she answered.

"I am." She was insanely busy, booked up for the next two weeks. "I'm willing to wake up at four if you are."

That hope in Rebecca's eyes flickered. "Sure."

"Is that a sure to the four A.M., or the roommate, or both?"

Piper watched the onslaught of emotions cross the teen's face. Hope, disbelief, all leading to the final expression: fear. Fear that the offer had strings, that if she said yes, she'd open herself up to even more hurt. Fear that the offer was real.

"What's in it for you?"

"A roommate. Someone to help with the chores." Piper stopped with the BS. "Honestly? Because I wish someone would have done that for me. I mean, in a way Skye did, but I'd been on the street almost two years before she scooped me up. I was nineteen when I finally passed my GED, twenty when I got my own place, and twenty-two when I started college. I never went to a school dance or kissed a boy."

Piper had gone from sophomore year straight into adulthood. And that wasn't any way to grow up.

Rebecca seemed to take it all in, carefully considering what other angles there might be. Piper kept her face carefully neutral.

"I'll clean up after myself and help with the chores, and working as an assistant wouldn't suck. Do I have to go to school?"

"That's a nonstarter." Piper wasn't sure how she'd get Rebecca enrolled without her mom's consent, but that was a problem for another day. Right now, it was about getting Rebecca off the street and giving her a safe place to land. To pay forward the kindness Skye had extended to Piper. "Do we have a deal?"

"Don't you want to know why I took your camera first?"

No, she was more interested in why the girl brought it back. "If you want to tell me."

Rebecca studied her fork, pushing her bite around the plate. "I wanted to take the picture for the showcase. That is, if I can still enter."

20

Piper had just put the leftovers in the fridge when her phone rang. She didn't recognize the number. Praying it was the Ladies of Portland, she answered right away.

"Hello?"

"Is this Piper?" a voice asked—that voice belonging to one Margo Easton, who was likely calling to gloat.

Piper closed her eyes and told herself she would not let Satan's Keeper make her cry. She'd faced bigger and tougher bullies, and this one wouldn't take her down. Period.

"Hello, Margo."

There was a long pause, and Piper could practically hear the bangle bracelets jangle. "The board has voted on your art show."

"And?" Piper held her breath.

"It was a five to four vote." Piper hadn't been expecting a landslide, but five to four didn't imply a strong sense of confidence. "In your favor."

Piper nearly dropped to her knees. "Oh my god." She turned around. "Oh my god. Thank you. Thank you so much. You have no idea how many girls' dreams you just made come true."

Piper being one of those girls. And Rebecca. God, Rebecca

was going to sell at least one of her pictures; she knew it. Piper was going to have Clive retake the photo of *Cinderella's a Lie,* increasing Rebecca's chance of selling for a high price, which would give her a good solid start for her college fund. And that's when the first tear formed. Rebecca could actually finish school and go to college if she wanted.

"I can't thank you enough. Can you please pass along my thanks to the board?"

"I can," the older woman said. "And I want you to know that I voted in favor of combining the events."

Piper froze, mouth hanging open. "You did?"

"I did."

"But why?"

"My son. He told me that your art program means a lot to a lot of people." Margo sighed, and Piper knew this was hard for her. Piper coming in and screwing up her plan was difficult, so the vote of support meant even more.

"It does. It means so much to these girls."

"I know. Josh told me that it meant a lot to you and that I need to be nicer."

"Well, we don't want to go *too* far," Piper teased. "I don't know if I'd recognize you if you weren't sparring with me."

For the first time in the conversation, Margo laughed. Piper wouldn't call it a guttural, from the heart laugh, but it sounded less strained than when the call had begun.

"There are rules."

"I wouldn't expect less."

"No street signs and no vandalism allowed. Any funny business, and the showcase is out."

"I promise you that there will be nothing shady included." Piper stilled. She'd said the word promise and didn't break out in hives.

"I hope so because I went out on a limb for you," she said.

"I don't know what to say."

"Thank you is the appropriate response," Margo said primly. "And the next time you see my son, could you pass along that I did as told?"

"Depends," Piper said, and heard the woman sigh. "What's his address?"

Still in her pajamas, Piper arrived at Josh's place. She had to circle his neighborhood twice to find parking and ended up finding a spot two blocks over.

She double-checked the address and triple-checked, and when she was about to call Margo a liar, someone in an expensive suit exited the building.

"Excuse me, is this a hotel or residential living?"

Expensive Suit looked up at the golden sign over the awning. "Both. Depends what floor you're asking about."

"Twenty-ninth floor?"

"Residential."

Nerves ignited because *Just Josh* lived in an elegant high-rise in the Pearl District on one of the Brewery Blocks. With upscale restaurants and a bustling night life, it was one of the most desirable areas in the city for young professionals. His building was modern and intimidating—a world that was light years from her daily reality. She'd passed this building a thousand times, never once imagining she'd be invited inside.

Well, she hadn't been invited exactly—more like crashing, she thought as she slipped into the elevator and hit the button for the top floor.

After making sure Rebecca was settled, Piper had come over to give Josh a heartfelt thank you that could only be delivered in person.

"You've got this," she whispered to herself. "I promise you, this is real."

It was the second time in as many hours that Piper had used that word. In fact, she could count on one hand the number of times 'promise' had come out of her mouth. To her, it wasn't something said in passing or to pacify a situation. When she made a promise, it was an unbreakable bond between Piper and the person in question.

Some unkept promises led to devastating results. Like the promise she'd made to Faith that everything would work out when it didn't. She was older now, wiser, and would never make that kind of mistake again.

On the other side of the coin, Piper's life had been filled with people who came in making big, lofty promises, which, in the end, rarely panned out. Reason number one why Piper was promise-averse.

Reason two was the sense of intimacy that came from sharing a promise. The same kind of unexpected intimacy she felt whenever she was around Josh.

"It's now or never." Piper took a deep breath and knocked, then immediately regretted her decision.

She was in her pj's with damp hair, no bra, no makeup, and no idea what she'd do when that door opened.

Footsteps sounded behind the door, and her palms went damp. When faced with the decision to stay and see how this played out or make a stealthy escape, Piper did what any cornered chicken would do—she turned to run like hell. Only the elevator door had closed, the stairs were at the end of the hallway and—

The door opened, and her breath hitched. Bathed in a soft glow from the lights overhead, Josh stood in the entryway. He wore a faded T-shirt, jeans, bare feet, and a look of surprise.

Piper started to rethink her stealth attack when he smiled,

those sea-blue eyes twinkling her way.

"Hey." His rough voice brought on an onslaught of tingles.

"Hey," Piper said, and before she knew what was happening, her feet were moving forward until she was toe to toe with the most incredible man she'd ever met. She slid a hand around to the back of his head and pulled him down, fusing her mouth to his in a greeting that came right out of a movie.

If he was caught off guard, he didn't show it, pulling her close and groaning low in his throat. It went from hot to scalding, and she was still on his doorstep. Walking him backward, she took his lower lip between hers, delivering one hell of a bite, which he seemed to like. So she did it again.

"Now we know why you've been skipping out on poker night," someone said from inside the condo. Piper froze.

Gage.

"Oh my god," Piper whispered, looking up at Josh, horrified. She tried to move him away, but he didn't budge.

"Poker night's over," Josh announced.

"That doesn't work for us," Rhett said. "Things are just getting good. You got any popcorn?"

"You've got thirty seconds before I throw you out."

"Okay," she said and started to move backward. His arms tightened around her, holding her in place—some serious muscle action happening up top and down below. Reminding her of just how big he was.

With a sexy, sly grin he said, "Not you. Them."

"You don't have to cancel poker night."

His gaze dropped to her lips, dark and intense. "Yeah, I do." To the guys, he said, "Fifteen seconds."

There was some grumbling and a whole lot of chuckles, but finally cards were tossed on the table, and everyone stood.

"Lemonade, huh?" Owen asked as he walked through the door. "I'm going to have to add it to my repertoire."

As the guys passed, Josh turned his body, shielding her from what had to be the most embarrassing moment of her life.

Josh closed the door and walked her backward until she was pressed against the wall. He stroked a lock of hair behind her ear, his thumb tracing down her cheek. He watched the motion as he brushed her lower lip. "Now, where were we?"

"I was about to thank you."

"That was one hell of a thank you."

Her belly fluttered. "Your mom called. The showcase is a go."

"That's great." His smile was genuine and warm.

"You're great," she whispered, a little embarrassed when her voice caught. Because he was amazing and honest and a man of his word. He was all those things and so much more. And right now, he was hers.

Wrapping one arm around his neck and placing a palm on his chest, she kissed him again. This time it was a gentle exchange of gratitude that lasted from one kiss to the next, blending into so many she lost track. And when her heart finally rolled over and exposed its soft underbelly, Josh kicked up the heat and took over. Which worked for her.

She'd gotten herself this far, always being the one in control, the one making everything happen. It was nice to let someone else be in the driver's seat.

He cradled her lower lip between his, nibbling and teasing before sliding his tongue across the seam. She opened immediately on a throaty groan.

He rested his hand low on her back, cradling her to him. Of course, she willingly fell into his arms and into an unspoken promise.

His fingers embraced her head, holding her to him as his mouth moved down her throat to the vulnerable spot at the base of her neck. He kissed his way to her shoulder, working the strap of her tank down with his teeth.

"I'm starting to love straps," he said, his lips brushing her other shoulder, and when that strap slipped, he smiled against her skin. "No bra?"

"I didn't bother to change. I hope you don't mind," she said. "Oh, and I like a matching set."

He was teasing his tongue down to her cleavage when he stopped and looked up at her. "Matching set, huh?" His hands were on the move, down her back to inspect for himself that she was, indeed, commando beneath those pajama bottoms. "This changes things."

"What things?"

"We're not going to make it to the bedroom."

With his arms around her waist, he bent down, and when he straightened, he was holding her. She laughed as she wrapped her legs around him, loosely locking her ankles at his lower back. "Your couch looks comfy."

"Too far." She had a few other suggestions on possible locations—against the door, pressed into the wall, perhaps the big, overstuffed chair facing the fireplace—but before she could tell him, he moved.

It happened so fast she barely saw it coming. One moment she was in his arms, the next she was sitting on the entry table, Josh standing between her legs.

"That urgent?" she asked, and he pressed all the way into her. "I see."

"Oh, in about five seconds you're going to see. And in about five minutes you're going to be screaming my name."

"Tick tock, Mr. Assistant District Attorney. Tick toc—"

His mouth crashed down on hers, urgent and hungry—and with a whole lot of challenge. She'd thrown down the gauntlet, and he was going to deliver. The mere thought made her quiver.

He scooted her so that she was arched off the table, and then without warning, he dropped to his knees. He kissed her belly, her ribs, lifting her shirt as he went before reaching the undersides of her breasts. He peeled her shirt up and over her head, and this time he pressed opened-mouth kisses down her body until, *bingo,* he reached her second favorite kissing spot ever.

Pulling her deep into his mouth, scraping the tip of her nipple with his teeth, he gently blew on her heated skin. She shivered, so he did it again and again and again until she was halfway toward that orgasm he'd promised.

"My word," she moaned.

"Josh," he corrected, and all she could do was nod.

Josh indeed. Working his magic until she was panting and desperate for release. Her stomach trembled with anticipation, and she couldn't look away as his hands traveled south, easing their way into her pajama bottoms on a direct course with pleasure central.

He took her mouth again as one finger disappeared inside her, and it did something to her. The hunger, the intensity morphed into something—a desperation for his touch, a deep need that only he could fill.

She ground against his hand, then placed hers over his to tilt it upward and angle it so that when she came down it created a sweet, sweet friction. The pressure built, her need soared, and she held on to his hand, creating an erotic bond. She gasped, finding it impossible to breathe as his talented fingers did a swirling action.

"Oh my!"

He looked up at her and smiled. "Closer, but not quite right. Maybe if I did something a little more like—"

Her body shook, her head falling back as he added a second finger into the mix. Not caring about the stupid challenge, she pushed her hips forward until his fingers disappeared all the way, pressing on the little bundle of nerves. "Right there."

"Right there, who?" he mused, but got down to business. He

had her so wound up, her vision started to blur, but he didn't pull back. Not when she squirmed on the table or pressed up to get the right amount of pressure.

The man was all practiced grace and deliberate finesse as he led her closer and closer toward the most sensual experience of her life. Unable to wait, she slid her hand lower, linking fingers and moving them in and out in a rhythm that had her so tight she was going to snap.

"Damn!" he said in awe, watching their hands.

"Piper," she corrected.

That's when he picked up the pace, and she knew his name was right there, just out of reach. All he had to do was move a little to the left and up—she shifted her hips—and yeah, right there, right there where—

"You got it, Boots. Let go," he whispered.

"What if I fall and nobody's there to catch me?" she asked, tears stinging the corners of her eyes.

He threaded his free hand into her hair and looked her dead in the eye. "Do you trust me?"

She trusted him unlike anyone in her life. She nodded.

"Then trust me when I say I'll be there. Every time."

Full-blown tears choked her throat at his sweet words. More importantly, he meant them. She could see it in his expression, the intense way he held her gaze, the secret smile that was always just between them. And that was all she needed to let go.

She was on the verge of embarrassing herself when the emotions spilled over lashes and down her cheeks. What was wrong with her? She never cried, but now that the floodgates opened, she couldn't stop them.

"I promise, I've got you, Piper."

She didn't correct him, didn't tell him to take it back as she fell fully and completely, like an avalanche, over and over, fast and out of control.

"Josh," she whispered. Then she groaned, his name becoming a mantra, as if she'd be safe if she kept saying it. From the emotions and the blind hope and the inevitable disappointment.

The tears didn't stop, just kept coming as their bodies moved as one, bonding like some essential molecule.

"Josh," she said over and over with every tremor that rocked her world. And he didn't stop. Diligent and deliberate, Josh moved. Slow withdrawal and even slower thrusts, deeper and deeper, until she was riding yet another high before the delicious crash.

Then something miraculous happened. She fell so hard and blindly, all she could do was cling to him, her limbs wrapped around him completely, her heart beating with his in perfect sync.

"Josh!" she screamed as she saw the past and present rushing up at her, the future right there. All she had to do was reach but, like before, it was right out of grasp, this elusive thing she'd never managed to touch.

Neither broke eye contact, and the moment rose to meet them, and it began. First, it felt like a little stumble, but instead of struggling for footing, she gave herself over.

To Josh, to this insane connection, and to the security and safety that could only come from love.

Love. The word didn't scare or make her want to run. It made her want to hold on even tighter, stay right there in his arms and memorize what it was like to feel cherished.

She'd loved many times over the past thirty years, but she'd never been on the receiving end. For her, love had always been followed by a 'but,' never given freely or forever.

But this felt different. Her heart swelled against her ribcage. Piper closed her eyes and leaned into Josh, her breathing coming in fast puffs, exhaling the residual fear and breathing in his scent and strength.

A while later, when she came to, she found herself leaning against his chest, his arms around her, his mouth languidly kissing her neck. Slowly, her lids opened to find a pair of honest and tender eyes locked on hers.

"A two-fer," she breathed.

"A two-fer, who?"

"A two-fer, Josh. But I was supposed to be thanking you."

He chuckled. "That was the best thank you in the history of thank yous." He looked at the clock above the fireplace. "Ninety seconds left, and you still have your pants on."

The sun was rising, casting a soft glow into the loft and over Piper's beautiful naked body. They never made it to the bed, working their way around the living room until they ended on his couch.

Piper lay in his arms, her body sated, her breathing slow and steady—but he couldn't stop touching her. Her stomach, her back, the tattoo at the base of her neck, and her breast—holding it as if he owned it. When what he wanted to own was her heart. He was pretty sure she already owned his.

A shocking realization. Especially after that last time, when they'd moved to the couch. It hadn't been rushed or frantic but had been a slow merging of two bodies making love under the rising sun.

Making love? Where had that come from? Before the question had fully formed, he knew the answer. Knew he was falling for her. Hell, he'd already fallen. And fallen hard. She was funny and smart and caring—so damn caring. Instead of letting the world chew her up and spit her out, she reached out to others in need.

And he needed her. More than he'd ever needed anyone. His mom, his brothers, his career—all things he loved, but his love came at a cost. When his father passed, Josh had stepped into the role of head of the family and a lot of people counted on him —relied on him to keep their family together and their worlds turning.

With Piper, the noise, the constant barrage of requests, the overwhelming responsibility—it all dimmed. Around her, all he had to do was just be. A state that was as foreign to him as the feeling in his chest. Like he wanted to run away and come home at the same time. He liked how she kept him guessing, how she made him laugh. More than that, he liked who he was around her. And that was something he hadn't felt in a long time.

He nuzzled the back of her neck, right on the tattoo that was as mysterious as the woman herself.

"Faith," she said, her voice rough with sleep. She turned in his arms, her eyes so serious behind those lashes. "The F, it stands for Faith. She was my friend. My best friend."

The way her voice quivered told him this story had a horrific ending. He tightened his hold and rolled, pulling her on top of him. Running his hands through her hair, he cupped the back of her head. "Tell me about Faith."

"We knew each other in high school. We both were living in unsafe houses, so I convinced her to run away with me. We made it from Georgia all the way to Portland, watching each other's backs. Only when we arrived, it was so much harder than I thought. We were only fifteen and thrust into a sea of uncertainty."

"How old were you when you moved in with Skye?"

"Seventeen." Jesus, she'd been on her own for two years. A kid, no older than Rebecca, lost in a world that had abandoned her. "Skye found me, and Faith found meth. She overdosed three weeks before her seventeenth birthday."

"Piper," he whispered, brushing away a tear with the pad of his thumb. "I am so sorry."

"I was the one who convinced her to come with me. I made it sound so cool, not understanding what we were really getting ourselves into. Do you know why the park benches are filled with sleeping people during the day?"

"No." And he didn't think he was going to like the answer. He'd already learned why he saw so many kids hanging out in the park after dark, and it had changed the way he looked at his city and all the people who live in it.

"Because it's too cold to fall asleep at night." She swallowed. "Faith's situation was bad, but not so bad that she needed to run away." Which made him wonder, not for the first time, exactly how bad Piper's past was that she'd have to put two thousand miles between them to feel safe.

His fingers skated down her spine and back up only to repeat the motion. He loved the feel of her soft skin. "Did she live with Skye too?"

She folded her arms on his chest and rested her chin there. "No. Even though we weren't technically adults, Skye had been trying to get me and Faith to move in, but Faith thought we were safer on our own. Really, it was Skye's zero tolerance rule. The day after Faith died, I moved in with Skye."

"I'd like to meet her. When you're ready," he added. Piper was jumpy when it came to feelings, so he'd be patient and let her come to terms with what was between them at her own pace.

"She'd like you," Piper said with a watery smile. "Skye's the closest thing I've ever had to a family."

"I'm glad she found you," he said, and Piper rested her cheek on his chest, her gaze avoiding his. "Hey, where did you go?"

She looked up at him, and the raw heartache he saw there gutted him.

"I wasn't honest with you," she began. "I didn't lie, but I left out a few details about the showcase."

Instead of his chest filling with the kind of dread that usually followed someone who'd admitted to withholding information, he felt hopeful. She was opening up to him, and that was all he'd asked of her.

"An omission isn't a lie," he assured her.

"It is to me," she said with so much conviction he finally understood how she'd survived her childhood. With a rigid set of rules and guidelines. "I like to think I'm better than that, but I got scared that you wouldn't help."

"Life isn't a ledger, Boots," he said gently. "When I offered to help, it was with zero expectations. Whatever you want to share, and whatever pace you want to share it, is your call."

"Skye's world isn't black-and-white. She lives in the gray zone, which is the only way she's able to help so many girls. It's why they trust her. Following the rules, waiting for the red tape." She shook her head. "That all takes too long and only hurts the people who are already hurting. Like me. If she'd waited for me to age out of the system, I wouldn't have made it. But she took a chance. And now I'm asking you to take a chance on her."

She took a big, weighted breath and let it out. "She's going to lose her house, and if she does, all those girls will lose their safe haven. That's why the showcase is so important. The money raised from Urban Soul will go to pay off the second on her house."

"And you've been doing all of this by yourself?" he asked, amazed at the lengths Piper would go through for the people she loved. Kind of like the unwavering support he and his brothers share.

"Don't you see?" she said. "You helped me, so I wasn't alone."

21

Spending three delicious, sexy, mind-blowing nights with Piper in his arms in the past five days had fried his brain. Josh had all but forgotten that tonight was dance lessons with his mom—and he couldn't bail and leave her the only single in its Foxie Silvers' Salsa class.

Needing a quick shower and change, Josh closed the case he'd been working on and powered down his computer. While the view of the Willamette River and downtown was killer, he wasn't necessarily sold on high-rise living. But Gage had been on him to diversify for years, and the owner had been highly motivated to sell, so Josh had purchased the penthouse for a song.

Even saying the word *penthouse* sounded pretentious. And Josh was learning that pretentious no longer looked good on him. It probably never did. Once upon a time, when he'd been starting out as just another lawyer in a sea of crabs who were willing to crawl right over him to gain the advantage, it had been all about the impact and positive change.

Somewhere along the way, between law school and being appointed to the Office of the District Attorney, he'd deluded himself into thinking that if he toed the line, he'd come out on top—and he had.

Now it was about something else. Something incomprehensible and transparent.

Being the front-runner for district attorney should have left him feeling excited and fulfilled. And sure, when he'd first been asked to run, the rush of adrenaline went straight to his head, leading him to believe that if he had the right house, the right car, and the right woman on his arm when he rubbed important shoulders, he'd be satisfied.

He wasn't wild about his loft, his car was uncomfortable, and the only woman he wanted on his arm was Piper—who would rather chew glass than mingle with country-club types. People who Josh had spent his life around and people who had a huge influence on his career. The old "it's who you know" adage was alive and well in the Easton family.

There were those who'd known and respected his dad, there were those who wanted a free pass because of Josh's connections, and then there were others who wanted an introduction to his more famous, wealthier brothers. Which was why Josh was so careful about asking them for favors. Brother to brother was one thing, but once that circle began to spread, things got more dicey—and more dirty. Two things he planned to avoid if he were elected.

Running a hand through his hair, he padded down the hallway. Workwise, it had already been one hell of a week, and it was only Wednesday. Thanks in part to Russell Heinz, his days had turned into catastrophic calamities of error. Starting with misrepresenting evidence and twisting Josh's witness into a pretzel of misspeaks and ending with Josh stuck in a U-Haul for a grand total of nine hours—since the five-foot sculpture destined for the auction, made of chewing gum and rubber bands, was too large to be picked up in a car. Something his brothers found hilarious.

He didn't know how it happened, but it seemed as though every time he walked into his office, he was thrust into a shitstorm of other people's problems he was expected to resolve. None of which had anything to do with his actual job. Which was why he'd decided to work from home today, for some uninterrupted time to make headway on his ever-growing caseload.

He'd spent the past twelve hours at his desk and was looking forward to a cold beer, a hot shower, and ten hours in bed.

Strike that.

A cold beer, a hot shower, and ten hours in his bed—with Piper. But she was at Belle Mont House shooting her first wedding at the venue, and he was expected at ballroom dancing in an hour—their schedules weren't playing nice.

Walking into his front room, he came to an abrupt stop. Gathered around his coffee table, with a cornucopia of take-out on top, like this was Thanksgiving dinner, were a handful of Eastons.

"Nice socks," Owen said, taking in Josh's faux wingtip socks his mom bought him for Christmas. "Do you have a matching top hat and monocle?"

"I was going to ask to borrow yours." He shoved Rhett, who was in Josh's favorite chair. "Glad to see the small fortune I pay for building security is being put to good use."

"You should complain," Clay said, resting his feet casually on the edge of the table.

"Somehow I doubt it would help. I hear the property manager's a real ass," Josh said.

"Or his brother is charming." All Rhett had to do was smile one of his million-dollar smiles or offer to take a selfie, and he'd be granted access to the Oval Office. Then again, the lax security had brought Piper to Josh last week, so he really couldn't complain.

Josh purposefully remained standing, hoping that they'd all take the hint and get out. Not that there was any place to sit. Even if he wanted to pull up a cushion—which he most certainly did not, Clay and all six-foot-four of Owen pretty much consumed the entire couch, and Gage and Rhett were cozy in the overstuffed chairs.

"Mom showed up today asking for Darcy," Gage said. "She had a new set of bedsheets wrapped up with a bow. Told Darcy it was a family tradition for the mother of the groom to provide wedding sheets for the honeymoon."

Josh did his best not to laugh. "Mom's cock-blocking you on your own wedding night?"

Rhett shivered. "Can we please not use those words in the same sentence?"

"Laugh it up. There's more." Gage leaned forward and rested his elbows on his knees. "And since you started this tidal wave, it's your job to fix it." Josh wasn't sure exactly how to solve cock-blocking sheets, but since Gage's tone gave him the feeling that this would be a big-brother-saves-the-day kind of talk, Josh decided to take that seat.

"Remember that advice you gave me? *You come on the road with me, and I'll fly out to see you,*" Rhett said in his best Josh voice, then leaned in real close. So close Josh could see the crazy flash in his brother's eyes. "I've spent the past thirty-six hours in the air to spend two hours with Steph while she was getting her makeup done for some shoot. Instead of *Honey, this surprise is so thoughtful; let's go have sex,* I got a look that clearly said, *I wish you would have called first, since I have a mixer with other influencers tonight and I don't want to be overshadowed by you. So rain check? Now, go jack off in the shower like you do every night because you're married to a jet-setter and your balls are about to permanently retire."*

"You think that's bad," Owen said. "Mom told me that she wanted to work at the bar three nights a week. Do you know what will happen to my sex life if she starts working there? It will fall on hard times. My sex deficit with collapse."

"The funny thing is? Everything she's doing she said is to spark joy. Any idea where she got that idea?" Gage asked.

Oh boy. "So I may have mentioned that, between Darcy and Steph, the family is growing, and that's a good thing. She just needed to go with the flow instead of fighting it head on."

"Which explains why we're all here," Owen said. "In addition to changing the cocktail menu, she dropped that she's decided to move in with me."

They all laughed. Well, except Owen who looked ready to punch someone. "I woke up this morning and found her folding my underwear."

Gage bellowed, "Been there! My advice? Shut it down, bro."

"Oh, I shut it down." He looked at Clay. "I told her that Clay missed home so maybe she should go to Seattle for a few weeks."

"Not happening," Clay said. "I'm planning on meeting up with a cute flight attendant I met on the way here."

"Good luck finding the time because she's already packed. And she has plans to spend quality time with each one of you," Owen announced to the room, and they all groaned.

It wasn't that they didn't love their mom, but when she set her mind of a task, she went all in. And right then, the last thing Josh needed was his mom going all in with his private life. Piper startled easily and was already wary of Margo and anything family related. And how could he blame her? Her life hadn't been conducive to overbearing relatives who meant well. Or the kind of family dynamics where love always prevailed, even if it did include a little smothering.

"Hang on," Clay, always the prevailing voice of reason, said. "Did she say why the sudden need to be all up in everyone's lives?"

"No. Just that it would spark joy." Everyone looked at Josh. "You want to tell me how she spends one afternoon with you, then goes off on some Marie Kondo journey that is screwing with our lives?"

Josh felt his stomach bottom out. Followed by his chest. Out of all the talks they'd had over the years, why had she decided to listen this time? "I only encouraged her to embrace new things."

"Things like helping you get laid?" Gage asked. "Because you getting laid is putting a serious cramp on the rest of us."

Josh was delirious. He had to be. Because it took everything he had not to laugh. Or point out that screaming about wedding sheets and sex deficits while strategizing how to handle their five-foot mother like she was the leader of a terrorist cell was ridiculous. Then again, Josh was wearing black-and-white wingtip socks that looked like dancing shoes.

"I'll talk to her."

"Can you do that before she gives Darcy a copy of *It Starts with the Egg*?" Gage asked.

"Or buys Littleshit a sibling. Last night I was at her house, and I caught her googling Cockapoo breeders in Portland. I also found a collar in the present closet."

"You know not to go in the present closet. Ever," Owen said, like they were five and scared that Santa would skip their house. "And how do you know it's for you?"

"Prancy was engraved in the tag."

"Fancy and Prancy?" Owen snorted.

"There was also a pack of guitar boxers. Glow in the dark." Rhett's fingers made like explosions.

All four brothers looked at Clay, who shrugged. "What can I say? I'm the favorite. By the time Mom gets through the four of you guys, I'm smooth sailing."

"Asshole."

"Lucky asshole," Clay corrected.

Josh, who'd been listening to nothing except his brain churning on how to correct his screwup, said, "I'll fix this."

The door burst open and there stood Margo. "Yes, you will."

All five men stood. Josh glared at Owen. "Is there a vending machine in the lobby with everyone's house keys in it?"

"Nope, just yours," Owen said. "I might have made a few copies when you were on that business trip and asked me to watch your plants."

"You made copies for everyone?" he whispered.

"You asked me to watch plants, bro." Owen shrugged. "Seemed the right thing to do."

Margo slammed the door and narrowed her eyes. Right. In. On. Josh. "I just got off the phone with Kitty. Is it true you're helping her with the auction?"

And the night just kept getting better. "The mayor asked for my help."

"So, it's true," Margo chided, hand over her heaving chest. "My own flesh and blood, helping the enemy."

"I'm not helping the enemy. I'm helping the event."

"Bullshit!" Owen coughed into his hand.

"That I had to hear from Kitty Caldwell . . ." Margo shook her head.

Josh walked over and kissed his mom on the cheek. Then, shoving Owen aside, he set her on the couch. "I was kind of unwillingly drafted into the position. The mayor was there, and it all just kind of happened—" He stopped himself. "I should have told you."

"Yes. You should have."

He could go on about how stretched thin he was, how the mayor's endorsement seemed to come with more strings than a traveling marionette company, and that Josh was drowning in responsibility. But the truth was, family should always come first. He owed it to his mom to come clean.

"I'm sorry. When Kitty asked me, I should have come to you first. While a part of the reason I offered to help with your committee was guilt, the other part is because I love you and wanted this to be a success."

"Didn't you wonder why Kitty was on board with merging events?" Margo asked. "Because she knew that if it went off without a hitch, she'd get the credit. If it fails, she'll redirect the blame onto me."

"Then it's a good thing it's working out," Josh said, and Clay waved his hand across his mouth in the universal sign of *zip it.*

"Is it? My son approached the board, my son pushed for this idea, my son made a promise that it would be amazing. Now suddenly, my son's idea is coming into question." Margo breathed deep through her nose and out through her teeth. "I'm head of the oversight committee. Which brings me to this."

Margo smacked the day's issue of the *Portland Tribune* against his chest. "First you help Kitty behind my back. Now's she's out to set me up and secure her position for next year."

"Kitty might be a lot of things, but she's not going to sabotage her own event to prove a point." The same event the mayor was supposed to publicly make his allegiance clear.

"Always looking for the best in people." Margo patted his hand, then smacked the paper against his chest again. "Read."

Josh took the paper, unfolded it, and looked down at the headline and the six photos that followed. "Biggest turnout in Bid for the Cause history. With sold-out seats and the largest collection of rare pieces, Kitty Caldwell and the Ladies of Portland are estimated to raise groundbreaking numbers to help with this year's cause, People Against Purebreds, a non-profit that supports local animal—"

Margo flapped her regal hand impatiently. "Kitty's getting all the credit, and thanks to my sons, she's auctioning off items from A-list celebrities, fifty-yard-line seats, and a host of other things donated by the . . . how did they put it? Oh yes, the Men of Easton."

"Mom." Rhett squirmed in his seat. "I was just trying to help. I know how much this cause means to you and—"

"Keep reading."

Josh continued. "A self portrait of the mayor's—"

"Cheap self-promotion. For God's sake, get to the important part. Here." Margo jabbed her finger at the bottom of the page with so much force she nearly punched a hole right through it. "Margo Easton, the founder of Bid for the Cause, has extended her generosity to Urban Soul, an after-school art program for local teens, that will be holding an exclusive charity showcase."

The article went on to explain how the showcase would work and how prospective buyers could help send at-risk teens to college. It even had a few photos of the entries featured at the bottom of the article.

"This is great press," Josh said, trying to see the problem.

Margo silenced him with one arched brow. "It's a disaster! I received a call from the paper earlier, asking if I wanted to go on record about this photo."

Josh looked at the stunning picture of a three-story silo on the river's edge. On the tallest cylinder was a picture of a starling. The bird's crown was a brilliant blue, its chest iridescent teal. From a distance, it looked like one giant image, but upon closer inspection, each feather was an individual image, making the bird a mosaic of smaller starlings.

Woven into its chest were the words *In numbers we hide*, and down the bird's beak was the artist's signature: *Bex*.

It was impressive and stunning and, according to the article, it was another way vandalism was scarring Portland's urban terrain.

"Defacing the city? Are they serious? This is amazing. The article posed the question of how to distinguish art from graffiti, and if the Ladies of Portland were making a stand in favor of trespassing and vandalism."

"I find it odd that Kitty had lunch with the journalist, and next thing, my name is mentioned in a controversial article." Margo turned the page. "And candidate Russell Heinz makes a pledge to clean up Portland."

Of course he did. Heinz would make a pledge to imprison his own mother if it would win him a few votes. Even worse, Josh had a pretty good idea who Bex was and that he'd seen more of her work spray-painted around the city.

Rhett took the paper and studied the photo. "I think these are the silos on the riverfront. I know the owner. If you want, I can give him a call since he owes me a favor. I booked his kid for a show at Stout."

"You will do no such thing. I had one rule. One." Margo flicked a single finger in the air. "That everything must be approved and vetted. Your lady friend personally agreed she would oversee each and every new entry from Urban Soul."

"We still have no idea if the property owner gave Rebecca permission," Josh pointed out, praying to hell that Rebecca hadn't done what he thought she'd done.

"The owner notified the police, who came to see me about this *Rebecca,* whom I assume is one of these Skye's the Limit girls."

"She is."

"Of course, she is," Margo said, as if the information excited her. "Kitty played innocent about the entire matter and sent them my way. I have been told that the only way to access the property is by either scaling an eight-foot barbed-wire fence or cutting their way through. They located a hole on the back entrance and wire cutters. As far as I'm concerned, this young lady is lucky she isn't getting arrested."

"Arrested?"

"Then there's Piper. Since I doubt Clive Kessler would break and enter, Piper must have been the one to take the photo. What was her plan? She had to know we would find out."

"First, we don't know if she took it." Josh thought back to Rebecca and the missing camera. "And we don't know if there were any nefarious plans. It's some teenager painting a rusting glorified tin can. And I don't think Piper shot it. Rebecca took— uh, borrowed her camera a couple of weeks back."

Josh knew he should have tried harder to convince Piper to file a report. Not that he wanted to see Rebecca get in trouble, but at least Piper's name wouldn't be attached to the incident, and it wouldn't blow back on her.

"Well, then you might want to tell someone because if anyone will be held responsible, it will be Piper."

Josh ran a hand down his face. Piper was going to be livid, then she was going to be devastated because Josh knew where this conversation was going. "Before we make any rash decisions, let Rhett reach out to the owner. Mom, you and I can talk to the Ladies of Portland."

"Oh, the board made their stance clear. They want to get as far away from this mess as possible, and I suggest, for the sake of your campaign, you do too."

"Can't they at least give me a couple days to make this right?" he asked. Margo's expression wasn't all that encouraging.

"I doubt it. My mind is already made up, as I'm sure the other members' are as well."

Josh understood why his mom was taking such a drastic stance; it came down to his dad's memory. But why were the other members digging in? It was a puff piece on page eleven of the society pages. Margo avoided his gaze, and a sinking feeling hollowed in his chest. "Mom, what did you do?"

"I did what was best for the charity and what is best for you." Margo smiled sadly. "You might not care about the optics, but I know how these things play out."

Josh scooted forward and took his mom's hands. "This isn't about Dad."

Margo yanked her hands back as if burned. "Of course this isn't about your father. But we all saw how one misappropriated comment can take down an entire family."

She was talking about how Heinz nearly toppled Stout because of one employee's mistake. The employee had sold alcohol to a minor who had a fake ID. Heinz got the Oregon Liquor Commission involved and temporarily froze Stout's license, which almost bankrupted the bar. The employee was immediately fired, but his dad spent the last years of his life fighting a lawsuit that was eventually thrown out of court. But the damage had been done, and his dad passed not knowing if he'd had a legacy to pass down to his sons. So he understood his mom's over-the-top concern, but like Piper had reminded him, the *why* was more important than the *what*, and until he heard the entire story, he wasn't about to pass judgment.

"No one is taking down anyone, Mom. This is about teenagers showing their art, and until we know what happened, let's take a breath."

"And if the story is true?"

"Then we'll deal with it then. But even so, maybe it was just a teen who made a mistake. Screwing up is a part of life."

"And you don't find this particular oversight a little convenient?" Margo asked, and Josh's gut reaction was to say no, but then she added, "Kitty, the board seat, the graffiti—that's a lot of mishaps in an election year. You've been spending so much time resolving that woman's problems, you've barely had time to do your job."

"She has a point," Owen said, and Josh wanted to punch him.

"Owen, you're whining because Piper didn't fall for your BS."

Owen considered that. "True."

Margo stood. "Well, I'm not going to allow someone else's lapse in judgment to ruin this event or my standing in the community. Portland might be a big city, but my world is a tight-knit community." Margo took his shoulders. "You are this close to making your dream a reality. To making sure people like Heinz never have the power to hurt families like ours." Her breath caught. "You say you want to clean up the city? Then clean it up. And that starts with the stance you take right now."

"You mean my stance about Piper?"

"If you connect her to any of this, then yes."

Josh stood. "Mom, you can't be serious. I doubt Piper even knew about it, and I'm sure she's as surprised as we are."

"Doesn't matter. I put my neck on the line, and she guaranteed that all art would be on the up and up." She pointed at the lower picture. "This is not on the up and up, so I can't see how she's surprised. Who knows how many more broke the rules?" Margo patted his cheek. "I'm sorry, but my hands are tied."

"All it would take is you getting behind this," Josh argued.

She gathered her purse. "And all I need is for you to get behind me."

"I'm always in your corner." Even when her allegiance was misplaced, Josh had promised that he'd always put his family first. And it was a promise he intended to keep. He just had to find a way to make sure he had Piper's back as well.

"You're a good son, and I'm sorry about how everything worked out. I really am," she said, and he could hear the sincerity in her tone. Just like he could hear the absoluteness.

"But I need to do what's right for the charity, and the last thing we all need is bad press. And the last thing you need is to be extending favors for actions such as this." Margo kissed him on the cheek. "You're so close to your dream. Don't get distracted now, not when the finish line is in sight."

"Maybe the distraction is I'm running toward the wrong finish line."

Margo gasped. "That isn't a distraction. That's you being rewarded for your hard work."

Josh sat back and ran a hand down his jaw. Damn, he was tired. His family meant well, but sometimes they drove him nuts.

"I think I'm too tired for dance tonight. Maybe next week." With a hug, his mom walked out the door.

"Jesus." Josh collapsed onto the couch and wondered what had just transpired. And since when did his dating life include political platforms and family alliances? "Rhett, can you really call the owner and try to smooth things over?"

"I'll see what I can do," Rhett said. "If that's what you want to do."

"What do you mean? 'If that's what I do'? Of course, I want to help."

No one moved. They all sat there staring at him, for what he didn't know, but he got the distinct feeling that he'd missed something important.

"What?" he asked.

"Rhett has a point." Owen held out his palms. "When you first decided to run, you said no deals, no favors, and no extending markers. You wanted to be transparent and fair. Do you really want to start your race helping your lady friend get out of a bind?"

He hadn't thought about how it would appear, and optics, as

he was learning, were more important than his actual platform. Which, when he thought of it, was total BS.

"Could you at least ask the guy if he's going to press charges?" It would give him solid footing when he tried to resolve the matter while pleasing both women in his life.

"Done," Rhett said.

He gripped the back of his neck. "Thanks. I'm going to call Kitty and find out what's really going on. Depending on how that goes, I may need to schedule a meeting with the mayor about the article, which he will likely pin on me. Then somehow, I'm going to fix this. So what if one entry violates the rules? That doesn't mean the event should be canceled."

Gage let out a low whistle.

"You telling me you wouldn't do the same for Darcy?" he asked.

Gage looked at the guys, then back to Josh, who felt like everyone was in on some big, cosmic joke. "Didn't know you were that far. Everything makes sense now."

"What makes sense?"

Gage laughed hysterically. "Bro, if you don't know, you're worse off than I thought. But a word of advice? You can't fix everything for everyone. Sometimes you need to pick a side."

22

Piper was on the hunt for romance.

The lighting, the setting, the way the sun crested the horizon, shining down on Mount Hood, casting a perfect golden glow for romance and ballgowns. All her planning, the bartering, the hustling. She'd cashed in every favor she had and paid it all forward. Clive was bringing the art scene. The Bid for the Cause would bring Portland's upper crust, and even a boutique in town donated dresses for each girl to feel like the belle of the ball.

A little over a month ago, she would have told Darcy she was the exact wrong person for the resident photographer job at a wedding venue, but lately she'd begun to wonder if Cupid was more than just a fat baby with a crossbow.

The auction was in a week, so she was making her trip count, doing double duty by testing lighting through The Cave for the auction and setting up the Urban Soul showcase. Darcy had track lighting installed and strung industrial cable against two of the exposed brick walls. All that was left was to arrange the photos in a way that told a unique part of a much larger story.

This was Piper's strong suit. Telling a story with a single

image. Today, she had three dozen images to work with, and the overall aesthetic was going to be breathtaking. The raw and timely take on Portland set against the backdrop of historic wealth. This was an experience most artists dream of but rarely achieve. She couldn't have asked for a more perfect setting.

The only thing that would have made this more perfect was if Piper hadn't volunteered to shoot the Bid for the Cause. It would be great exposure for her, but she wanted to be there for her girls, act as gallery manager. But Skye had offered to handle any and all sales from the event, even walk prospective buyers through the story behind each photo.

If they sold even half of the photos for the asking price, those girls would have enough for a year at the community college and Skye would have enough money to make a huge dent in her back property tax. Still, Piper wanted everything to be perfect, which was why it was critical that everything be situated ahead of time. With Belle Mont's insane schedule, today was the only time Piper would have to test the layout.

She'd picked up the glass-mounted photos on Saturday from a local framing company who had donated the cost of the frames. Then Clive Kessler and each of the well-known photographers had signed the bottom of each respective photo. Piper had a few last-minute entries that she had to shoot which still needed her signature, then she could finalize the order.

"What are you doing here?" Jillian asked, confusion in both her voice and expression.

"Trying to get the overall aesthetic right and failing miserably." She laughed. Jillian did not. "Why are you looking at me like I forgot to put pants on?"

Darcy and Jillian walked over to look at the photo Piper had strung, and their jaws went slack.

"It's . . . wow," Jillian said.

Darcy shook her head. "I had no idea they would be this stunning."

Piper took a step back to absorb a photo taken by Clive Kessler of a three-dimensional chalk-art piece, of a waterfall streaming over a two-tower skyscraper connected by a fifty-foot glass corridor and situated in the heart of downtown.

"The artist is fourteen and has been doing sidewalk art with her dad since she was seven."

"That's amazing," Darcy said, then turned to Piper, her eyes full of pity. "Please tell me that Josh explained what happened."

"What happened?" she asked, her windpipe struggling to open enough to pull in oxygen. This was it. The other shoe that had been dangling. After the call with Margo, she'd allowed herself to believe that she was on steady footing.

"The Ladies of Portland called this morning." Darcy looked skyward. "I so did not want to be the one to tell you this. There was an article in the *Portland Tribune*."

"What article? And who still reads the local paper?"

"The *Tribune* ran a piece about the auction and showcase, with a couple of the photos," Jillian explained.

"Really? That's great exposure for those girls." She'd hand-selected them to showcase the different types of art that would be displayed.

"There was a picture painted on the side of a silo."

"Isn't it beautiful?" Piper leaned in conspiratorially. "I'm not supposed to have favorites, but I think that one will be the belle of the ball."

Her friends exchanged a look that rubbed Piper the wrong way. Pity. An emotion that Piper had long ago divorced herself from. "Just be straight with me."

Straight gave her a chance to pull on her tough-girl armor. Allowed her to protect herself from the impending hit she was about to take to the chest.

"The owner of the silo didn't give the artist permission," Jillian explained.

Piper shook her head. "No way. Reb—I mean, the artist—wouldn't enter something that she knew broke the rules."

Right? A strange sensation wove its way around her throat. Piper never said outright that Rebecca needed permission; she'd just assumed, after the run-in at Skye's, that the girl would know. Plus, she knew from the beginning Rebecca had her eyes set on the prize. Not that Piper blamed her; it was enough money to secure a sixteen-year-old a leg up and off the streets.

Piper remembered the photo in question. It was the one she'd come across going through the negatives from her camera.

It was bold and risky and so beautiful it had moved Piper to tears. It captured the strength and fear of what girls like Rebecca lived—what Piper had lived. She wished she'd had it earlier to use in her presentation and prove to those stuffy ladies how beautiful urban art can be and how art can provide girls a voice.

Then she'd gotten greedy, entering it in the contest without consulting Rebecca first. It was supposed to be a surprise, but had she asked Rebecca, this whole thing could have been avoided. God, this was all her fault.

"Rhett knows the property owner," Darcy said. "And he said that he most definitely did not approve a three-story bird on his silo."

"Rhett knew?"

"Margo told them the other night at Josh's house."

"The *other* night?" A bitter taste filled Piper's mouth. "Josh knew about this?"

And he hadn't told her. They hadn't seen each other in a few days, but they'd spoken by phone. And he hadn't said a word about the article or the silo—or any of the possible outcomes.

Piper sat down on one of the leather barrel chairs. *Think. Think.*

"I'm not going to jump to conclusions. Until I hear the story from the artist, and she tells me she broke the rules, I'm not even going to contact the board."

And she wasn't going to say Rebecca's name and land her in trouble in case the paper had gotten it right. Rebecca was starting to open up, and there was no way Piper would assume anything or point any fingers.

"What am I going to do?" she asked Darcy.

Darcy took a seat. "I can try to squeeze you in some afternoon in October. Maybe an early afternoon showing."

"We're right back to the permit issue, and it's too late." Skye wouldn't have the money for the payment and those girls wouldn't have a proper showing. Piper pressed her palm to her stomach, which was knotted with panic. "The girls are going to be so disappointed."

And Rebecca. She could potentially be in trouble. Wanting to get the teen's side of the story and give her benefit of the doubt, she dialed Rebecca, who answered on the first ring but said nothing.

"Rebecca?" There was a long silence. "Are you okay?"

"I screwed up," the quiet voice came, and she could tell Rebecca was crying.

Ah, shit. "We all screw up. The good news is we can fix it."

"I don't know if we can fix this," she said, and in the background, Piper heard banging. Loud banging. "Where are you?"

"Skye's." While Piper was relieved the girl was somewhere safe, the banging and shouting in the background had her concerned.

"Where is Skye?"

"Barricading the door."

"Gotta go," Piper said to her friends, leaving her camera bags, her purse—everything— behind and heading straight for POSH.

"What's wrong?" Darcy called out.

"I think Skye's getting herself arrested." Piper jumped in her car and started the engine. Before she could back out, Darcy and Jillian were both inside and fastening their safety belts. "What are you doing?"

"Coming with you," Darcy said. "In case you need someone to post bail."

"No. This is my problem."

"This is what friends do for each other," Jillian explained. "Good times and bad."

"Aren't those wedding vows?"

"Friends are just as sacred, and you're our friend, Piper," Darcy said.

For the second time that week, Piper found her eyes misting over. She looked at Darcy through the rearview mirror. "Don't you have a wedding tonight?"

"Yup. So you better get a move on," Darcy said. "I've never been arrested before."

Jillian looked at her friend. "Who said anything about getting arrested?"

"The look on Piper's face. It's the same mama bear look you got when Coach Dickwad benched Sammy for being too small."

"Gage is going to have to make my bail since Dirk is two months behind on child support," Jillian said, referring to her douche of an ex.

Piper tore out of the parking lot. She made the fifteen-minute trip in ten, screeching up to Skye's house right as a second patrol car arrived.

Skye had her arms and legs spread in the doorway like a big X of a barricade. Behind her was Rebecca, tears streaming down her face, with so much fear in her eyes that Piper's heart ached.

She raced up the porch, and a police officer put out her arm. "Ladies, you'll have to stand back."

"I live here," she lied. "And that's my mother and sister," Piper said, and that didn't feel like a lie. "I need to know what's going on."

"Censorship!" Skye hollered, her palazzo pants blowing in the breeze. "This is about censorship, plain and simple. Call the paper, the press, and that sweet brunette on Channel 5 who always does the pieces on amazing animals!"

"Ms. Ezra." The police officer sounded at her wits' end. "No one is under arrest." Piper heard a big *yet* headed their way if Skye didn't come down from her Big Government soapbox. "We just want to ask Rebecca Fontanilla a few questions."

"It's Miss. The Universe calls me Skye Luna, and whatever you want to ask Rebecca, you can ask me. Because within the Universe we are all one, sisters and brothers."

Because Piper didn't want the whole *make love not war* speech, she looked at the officer and explained, "She won't answer to anything else."

With a sigh, the policewoman said, "Miss Luna."

"Skye, please," Skye said, patting her chest sweetly, as if this were suddenly a pajama party and Officer Miller was the guest of honor.

"We're here because we believe that Rebecca has information on a street tagger named Bex, who recently defaced two buildings downtown and an industrial mill."

This was worse than Piper thought. It wasn't a single location. Rebecca had been keeping herself busy around town.

"I didn't think anyone would see it," Rebecca said softly enough that no one else heard, and that's when Piper knew *she'd* been the one to screw up. She'd been so sure that the photo would catch a chunk of change, she'd handed it over to the journalist.

"Defaced?" Skye said, horrified, and Piper knew she was

winding up for the big finish. "It's a work of art, and while the Universe calls me Skye Luna, my street name is Bex."

Oh boy.

"Bex the, uh, Hex." Skye lifted a can of spray paint, which happened to be less paint and more anti-rust primer.

Piper rolled her eyes. "Okay, Bex the Hex, put that down and get out here so we can straighten things out."

Skye's face crumbled in disappointment that Piper was ruining this oh-so-fun game, and Rebecca went ghost white. Both women walked down the porch steps.

"I'm sorry," Rebecca whispered. "I didn't mean for anyone to see the picture. I wanted to show you, but then I got scared you'd kick me out of the art show, and I forgot the second rule of vandalism. Don't take incriminating photos."

They both knew that Rebecca wasn't worried about the art show. She was terrified that Piper's offer had been too good to be true and now she'd blown it.

"You always have a place at my house. Remember? Roommates?"

Rebecca nodded, a few sniffles escaping. "I knew what I did was wrong, so I can't let Skye take the blame." The teen walked straight toward the officer and met her gaze. "I'm Bex."

Piper's heart pinched for the girl who was trying to do better, only to do something ridiculously stupid, but for all the right reasons. And intention was nine-tenths of the law. Or at least, that's what they always said on *Law & Order*. Or was it possession was nine-tenths of the law?

Either way, intention had to count for something, and Piper wasn't going to let Rebecca get brought up on charges that a little bit of white paint could fix.

Piper faced the officer. "I am so, so sorry about this. The mess, the confusion, and wasting your afternoon, ma'am."

"I'm sorry too," Rebecca said.

"She can't be more sorry than I am because I'm Bex," Skye repeated.

"No, ma'am. I really am," Rebecca said honestly. "I'm really Bex."

"She can't be." Darcy and Jillian stepped forward, arm in arm. "We're Bex."

Everyone looked at Darcy in her chinos, ballet flats, and preppy ponytail and Jillian in her Cake Goddess apron. Piper sighed. "Guys, you're only making this more complicated. I don't want to have to explain to Gage how you are now a wanted vandal."

"Wanted?" Rebecca croaked.

"I've got you," Piper said, repeating the words Josh had told her.

"Link hands, ladies. We'll make a body chain in protest," Skye said, reaching her arms out to the sides.

Piper smacked Skye's hand down. "Whatever 'Hands Across America' picture you have in your head, let me remind you there are only five of us."

"Picture you're larger than life, the strength of our foresisters sharing their wisdom and power."

Piper looked at Darcy and Jillian. "I am so sorry I dragged you into this."

"Dragged me? Are you kidding? I feel like I dragged you into this," Darcy said. "If it hadn't been for my engagement party, you would have never been in Margo's sights."

"Well, it looks like we got ourselves a problem, Officer Miller," Skye said with a big grin. "If you can't prove beyond a reasonable doubt who Bex is, then you have no case. Court adjourned."

The officer reached for her cuffs. "I'm not the DA, so I don't have to prove anything. As far as I'm concerned, I might as well take you all downtown."

The officer led them toward the car and Piper's throat tightened with concern and a little panic. "Before my friends get dragged further into this, you need to explain to me. Everything. Understood?" she said to the teen.

"Officer," Rebecca said, and when Skye tried to step forward, Piper stopped her with a stern shake of the head. "They're just trying to help. It really was me. I was the one who painted the silo, and I'm really sorry."

"We'll still need to figure this out downtown," Officer Miller said.

"How did they know it was me?" Rebecca asked as they were walking to the patrol car.

"Margo," Darcy said, sliding an arm around Rebecca in a maternal and gentle way Piper hadn't even considered. She was so busy being tough, she hadn't realized that what the girl needed was something gentler.

"I don't even know how Margo would know. I just found out," Piper said.

"Josh must have said something."

"Josh said I can trust him, and even though this goes against who I am, I'm giving him the benefit of the doubt." Even as Piper said it, a bad feeling jumped up and grabbed her by the throat.

"Saying it doesn't make it true, Miss Piper," Rebecca whispered.

"Maybe not, but I know I can trust him. He's different."

Rebecca looked up at Piper, her eyes filled with tears. "It's never different for girls like us."

"Maybe this time it can be."

23

Piper hadn't been in the back of a cop car since she was sixteen and had a momentary affliction of sticky fingers and shoplifted those galoshes. It had never landed her behind bars or with the possibility she'd have to spend the night in jail, so she wasn't sure of the exact protocol, but she did know she was granted a phone call.

Only, she wasn't sure who to call. Skye was one cell over. Rebecca had, thankfully, been allowed to sit in the bullpen with a nice and understanding female officer who just wanted this all to disappear.

Piper could get behind that but wasn't holding her breath.

"Can I have my phone call?" she asked, not sure who she'd call. Her one-call person was behind bars, hollering about civil liberties, trying to incite a protest in the bullpen, refusing to be silenced until the city of Portland recognized the time and passion that artists put behind their work.

Then there was Josh. Not the ADA who could easily pull a favor to make this all go away, but the man who'd told her he always showed up for the people in his world and had promised her that when she fell, he'd catch her.

Well, she'd fallen and had no idea if the safety net would appear.

"Hello?" she called out, feeling as if she'd just helped negotiations between two warring countries.

Darcy's call had been to Gage, who'd let it slip that all of this was, indeed, Margo's doing. He hadn't wanted to tell her the entire story, but Darcy had ferreted out enough to make Piper's chest tighten painfully.

First, the owner of the silo hadn't been the one to notify the police. In fact, he hadn't even known that his silo had been painted. Nope, the caller in question was Neighborhood Watch Commander, Margo Easton. When she couldn't get a rise out of the property owner, she'd called the police station personally, even trying to connect Rebecca to a tag on the stop sign at the end of Margo's street.

The second thing, and most devastating, was that Rebecca's name came from Josh's mouth. She hadn't heard that from him and wanted to give him a chance to explain himself when she saw him next, but today it seemed explanations only complicated everything.

"I don't get it," Piper said quietly. "Why did she single me out? Even using a teen to get to me. Who does that?"

"Margo," Darcy said quietly from inside her cell. "My guess is that she saw the fireworks between you and Josh and got nervous about losing another son."

"I'm not taking him away. We're not even really dating." Even as she said the words, she knew they weren't true. Josh felt like more than a real boyfriend than her last real boyfriend—and they'd lived together.

"You are most definitely dating," Jillian said. "If he's seen your O-face more than three times in a single week, you're dating."

"It's true," Darcy said.

"Three times equates dating," Gage said, walking over to Darcy's cell. "Then what does that make us?"

"Engaged," Darcy said, light and flirty, and like someone who knew exactly who their one call would be to.

"I can't wait for marriage then," Gage said. "And I never thought I'd be into the bad girl vibe, but I'm looking forward to tonight."

Piper worked hard to school her features, because she was the bad girl Gage was referring to. More disheartening—it was the truth, wasn't it? No matter how hard Piper tried, trouble found her, or she found it. She'd never done well with authority, was too scared of not measuring up. She was terrified that all the weight she carried would drag the people around her under.

Just look at Darcy and, in a way, Rebecca. Yes, the teen had painted the silo and yes, she knew trespassing was against the law. But Piper had gone behind Rebecca's back and used a photo she had no right to make public.

She'd gotten so far ahead of herself she didn't consider the girl's right to privacy. Even worse, she'd assumed Rebecca stole the camera and told Josh about it, swearing him to secrecy, but he'd told his mom, who practically used a blowhorn to tell everyone she came across. It was like graffiti telephone.

This whole situation could have been avoided had she and Josh kept their word. Wasn't that the theme of her life lately? Getting too far ahead of herself.

The deputy unlocked Jillian and Darcy's cell, and Gage took Darcy into his embrace. Piper had to look away. Watching a real unbreakable bond, a love that would go the distance, was too much right then.

"After adding hardened criminal to your street cred," Gage said to Darcy, "how about we go home and take a nice, hot shower. Cuffs optional."

Darcy looked from Jillian to Piper to Skye and shook her head. "I can't leave them here."

"Honey, this isn't my first rodeo." Skye waved her off. "Plus, Officer Miller said dinner's Salisbury steak and smashed potatoes from Phil's Diner. That means the potatoes have roasted garlic and a pound of butter and cream."

Gage turned to Piper. "All of your bails have been posted."

"Thank you," she whispered.

"Don't thank me. Thank Josh, who made a lot of promises to get this handled quietly."

And there it was. The reminder that she was a complete idiot for ever thinking this could work. They were two freight trains headed for each other with no emergency brake.

Just look at today. She'd landed herself in hot water and now, according to Gage, Josh had to use favors to get her out. The exact kind of thing he'd avoided doing, especially for his campaign. And if that wasn't enough to have her feelings solidified, then seeing him, dressed in his courtroom best, standing at the entrance to the holding cells had her heart lodging itself painfully in her throat.

She'd rather stay in there all night than have this conversation in a cell with witnesses to overhear.

He walked toward her, his shoes clicking on the concrete floor, gripping the bars when he was in front of her. They stared at each other for a long while, and she couldn't decipher what he was thinking, holding everything close to his chest. She had a feeling none of it was good.

"How are you?" he finally asked.

Piper's heart pounded against her chest so hard and fast she was afraid she might pass out. Panic welled up, and she was mentally struggling to keep it together when his intense blue eyes locked with hers. She wasn't sure if it was a low blood sugar thing, since she hadn't eaten since last night, or if the huge lump in her stomach had slowly expanded its way to her throat, cutting off her air supply. But Piper knew that if this was Karma, she packed one hell of a punch.

"Confused," she said, her voice full of so much emotion she had to look at her boots to hold back the tears.

"Me too. We need to talk."

Piper looked up. Josh did not look happy. He didn't look mad either. He appeared uncertain and a bit concerned, which was a new look on the confident and sure-of-himself lawyer.

"About?" *Please say us*, she thought. As in I-didn't-break-my-word us.

"About the silo."

She went very still. "You want to talk about the silo?"

"Not really, but I need to know if it was Rebecca," he said, and Piper's pulse skidded to a stop. *That's what he wants to talk about?*

She watched his expression. "So it's true," she said quietly. "You told your mom about Rebecca."

His expression told her everything he needed to know, and the truth of the moment churned in her stomach until she swore she'd be sick.

"Why?" she asked. "Knowing how your mom would react, why did you tell her?"

"She was upset and scared about how it would blow back on her."

"*She* was scared?" And just like that, the ray of hope that he was there for her went dark. "Your mom. A wealthy, sixty-year-old woman was only worried about how this whole thing would blow back and cost her her little club, so she went after a sixteen-year-old girl. Destroying everything Rebecca might have been able to do with her life."

"I didn't know she'd call the cops."

"I've known your mom for less than a hot minute, and I knew exactly how she'd react. Just like she knew what I'd do. And here we are." She motioned to the cell. "And where's Margo, by the way?"

They both knew that his mom was sitting happily in her garden sipping tea.

Josh scrubbed a hand down his face. "You and I know you didn't break in to take that picture."

"We don't know anything because that's how the system is supposed to work, remember? It starts with questions before accusations."

"You're right," he said quietly. "But this has gone past that. You're an adult, Piper. Rebecca's a teen, they'd just let her go with a warning and maybe some community service."

"Would that be before she got a permanent ding in her file or after they threatened her with juvie that they'll never follow through on, because *Why not scare some sense into her*? What better way to spend a Friday than to scare the shit out of a kid who made a mistake that can be painted over?"

His expression said she'd nailed it. "I'm working something out."

"Working something out to save Skye's? Or working on something to soothe your mom's delicate feelings?"

"I'm trying to do both, but it's hard when everyone is making things complicated."

She took a step back. "I'm sorry if real life is complicating things for you. And your mom," she said. "Because that's what this is about, right? Your mom and her event and reputation? God forbid she doesn't get her way."

"This isn't about my mom or the event."

"Then tell me what it's about," she said, trying so damn hard to keep the tears at bay. She didn't know what was worse, that a single conversation with his mom could have averted the situation or that he wasn't even aware of what he was doing. To Rebecca. To Skye.

And to her.

"About holding people accountable. I'm all for hearing Rebecca out. But letting her skate?" He shook his head. "We only learn from our mistakes."

"And how did you learn? I mean, as an upper-class kid with a powerful family at his back? Tell me, Mr. Easton, what would your punishment have been? A slap on the wrist, a warning, maybe mowing lawns for a month?" Piper's chin went up. "I've dealt with scarier than a misdemeanor charge, and I've faced down people scarier that you."

He looked as if she'd just punched him. "You're scared of me?"

"I don't know." She shrugged, and that's when the first tear slid. "Gage took Darcy and Jillian, and you come in here asking about how I wronged your mom, the whole while with me in here and bars between us."

"Some advice?" Skye said. "You're blowing the landing there, sonny."

He looked at the bars, as if only realizing the barrier between them, whereas the entire time she couldn't think of anything else. He in his Italian fitted suit and fancy degree, and she in overalls behind bars.

"Look, let's make things easy. We don't match, Josh. I don't match."

He tilted his head. "Why would I want you to match?"

Even though he'd signaled to the guard to open the door, they still stood there on opposite sides of the law. She toed the invisible line still between them. "This situation right here should be your answer."

"But I haven't asked you the question I came here to."

A stupid thrill zinged and zagged at the idea of a question, but in the end she squashed it. "First, *I* have a question. When you made those promises about Rebecca, about the event, about us, did you ever intend on following through?"

"Yes. God, yes. And I will." He reached out for her, and she instinctually stepped back. Holding it together was difficult, holding it together with his gentle hands on her would be impossible.

"Boots?" His voice was filled with question and uncertainty.

"I don't know what hurts worse, that you can't fix things or that you don't even see why you can't. Either way, I'm not interested in your solutions." Her throat caught. "Why don't we skip to the end where we both realize we don't work before anyone gets really hurt."

"I'm already hurt," he said quietly, and Piper's heart cried out for things it shouldn't wish for.

"You and me. Our lives. Your family. Your job. Don't you see?"

The officer appeared with the keys to unlock the cell and when it slid open, each clink of the metal further chipped away at her heart. The moment an exit was clear, her instinct was to run, but the part of her that was so tired of running begged her to hear him out. Listen to his why. Then he stepped inside —with her.

"I see everything that's important," he said.

"You're supposed to see that nowhere in the equation is there room for me. I see how hard it is for Darcy, and she already fits. Me? My world doesn't work like that."

"Fitting in is boring," Skye said. "Tell her."

"I think I've got this," he said to Skye, who gave a disbelieving *tsk-tsk*. Josh took Piper's hand. "You fit. With me, you fit."

"How?" She laughed, but it came out more a sob. "Your mom

was upset over some stupid picture, and instead of giving me the benefit of the doubt that I was handling it, you decided to make her feel better and use Rebecca as an out. You shared something I told you in private. To your mom."

"Rebecca spray-painted the silo. We both know this."

"That's not what this is about. Had you kept your word, Rebecca would have come clean on her own terms and walked into the station to give a statement. Which she already did, by the way. But instead of giving people the chance to right their wrongs, your mom had her hauled off in cuffs. The kid is so scared she's ready to run, and I don't know how to make it better. And that's on you."

Without another word—there weren't any that would be able to get past the emotions strangling her—she walked out of the cell. She'd heard him out, listened to his why, and it hurt more than if she hadn't known.

Josh watched her go, and the confusion in his eyes, as if he hadn't a clue as to what had transpired, created an ache so vast it swallowed her whole.

Her heart shattered like glass, Piper kept her gaze on the floor as she passed the other cells and made it to the women's bathroom. She didn't look back, didn't even say goodbye, just held in the pain until she closed the door. And as she clicked the lock into place, the first sob escaped. It was quickly followed by a second and a third as the raw and all-encompassing emptiness hollowed out her chest.

Josh hadn't only broken a promise, he'd broken his word, and in turn, he had broken her heart.

Piper had finally allowed herself to love someone, a soul-deep love that wouldn't ever fully disappear. She knew her heart would never fully heal, because this kind of love was the kind that broke people. And while Piper had survived a lot of things in her lifetime, nothing would ever compare to this.

He may not have broken her—she was too strong for that—but Josh had asked her to open up and let him in. And she had.

Now she was paying the price.

24

The showcase had finally arrived, and Piper couldn't be prouder of her students. There were over thirty entries, most of them stunning and photographed by the fabulous Clive Kessler, and the girls looked beautiful in their dresses.

The showing wasn't at Belle Mont like she'd hoped but at a downtown brewery that donated the use of their terrace for the evening. The owner was an old friend of Clive's who graciously offered his rooftop terrace free of charge as long as he could sell wine and beer at the event.

"Where is everyone?" Jillian asked, scanning the room.

"Once Clive arrives, more people will show."

That was the hope anyway. While there were a lot of people milling about, most of them were family or friends of the students—not potential buyers. Margo had dug in, and the board had refused to allow Urban Soul to be a part of their evening. Which was okay, Piper told herself. The girls were more comfortable this way, and Piper didn't have to worry about dealing with Satan's Keeper all night.

Nor did she have to see Josh. It had been four days since

she'd walked out of that cell. And even though he'd left messages and texted, it had been four days since they'd last spoken, and her heart still ached as if she were reliving the whole ordeal over and over again.

She'd never been stupid enough to believe he would choose her over his family, but she was stupid enough to believe him when he made a promise. When he had agreed that intention was more important than actions. Now she had not only let down Skye and Rebecca, but she'd let down herself.

"I swear, I invited everyone on Sammy's football and school roster," Jillian said. "And trust me, those moms can't pass up a kid-free night with the promise of alcohol. Once bedtime is done, they'll show, and then these photos will sell like flapjacks at the Tiny Tyke Annual Pancake Breakfast."

Piper hadn't been that ambitious, but she'd hoped that there would be more sales than passes. "This is how shows go. People look, they drink, they look again, then they go to a bar and drink while they talk about the art they should've bought."

"Then we need more alcohol," Jillian said.

"And maybe some of the diners from downstairs," Piper joked.

"On it."

Piper watched her friend, who had withdrawn her donation for the Ladies of Portland auction in solidarity, disappear down the stairwell. Making sure everything was being handled, Piper silently escaped to the back of the terrace, where she could have a private moment to collect herself. Yes, when Clive showed, he'd bring with him a few of his most devoted fans. But she didn't want Clive to walk into a gallery showing where not a single piece had moved, especially after having to deliver the embarrassing blow that the event was no longer at Belle Mont but above a brewery. Which was catty-corner to Josh's apartment building.

From the terrace, she could see the darkened windows of his loft—remember the way he'd held her after they'd made love. And it had been love. At least on her part. Her heart still felt as if it were shattered, shredding what was left of her ability to trust. She'd never be open to someone like that again. In the end, the price of that kind of vulnerability was way too much.

And it didn't just cost Piper her heart. The ripples of her mistake went far and wide. Skye's home was in danger, the girls who lived there were vulnerable, and her students were facing a huge disappointment if this evening didn't turn the corner.

Then there was Rebecca, who had gotten off with a hundred hours of community service repainting over graffiti at inner-city schools but had also been dealt a terrifying hand. Scared straight didn't even cover it, and while Josh was right and she needed to learn from her mistakes, the learning curve had been steeper than necessary.

This event and the possibility of raising the funds had all sounded so easy around a cup of dandelion tea. She had made her own promises to people she loved, and she wouldn't be able to keep a one.

Something in her stomach clenched, making her wonder, not for the first time, if that was how Josh had felt. Stuck between his mom, his career, and his promises to her . . . promises he'd made about them. Not that there was a 'them' anymore. She'd seen to that, pushing past him and walking away without so much as a goodbye.

Her without-even-a-second-glance exit had been from her tough-girl arsenal, a leftover from her childhood, and she knew exactly how cutting it could feel. So why did she do it?

She'd expected him to take her as is, but at the first sign of Josh being Josh, an ADA with a fiercely loyal family who lived within the walls of the system, she'd called it quits. She could claim it was because she was protecting Rebecca, but in reality,

Piper had been afraid of the possibilities and the possible disappointment.

Questioning Rebecca's intentions, even though the teen was guilty as charged, reminded Piper of what it was like to be that terrified, a rebel of a teen who pushed everyone away. It made her wonder what Josh would have thought of her then. What his family thought of her now. She'd let her fear and stubborn pride get the best of her. But he'd played his part in the whole fiasco.

Piper dropped her head to stare at her knee-high leather boots and felt the first sniffle threaten. "Why do you always have to ruin everything?" she whispered and, *great, just great*, she was about to cry at her own party.

"From where I stand, everything looks pretty damn perfect," a sexy, low voice said.

Piper closed her eyes and felt a single tear slip out.

A rough finger wiped her tear away and when she looked up, there he was. Josh. Standing in front of her dressed in a tux, complete with a handkerchief and bow tie—the whole works.

"What are you doing here?" she asked.

"I came to see my girl."

"Your girl?" she whispered.

"Yeah. She's about yay high." He held his hand to his chest. "Dark hair, tiny nose ring, this sexy tattoo right here." He reached out and ran his fingers behind her neck, tracing the tattoo. "Did I mention her eyes? Brown when she's happy, green when she's testy, and golden whiskey when she's turned on."

"What color are they now?"

"Sad." He stepped closer. "And for that, I will forever be sorry."

And just when she thought it couldn't get any worse, his hands rested on her hips and he pulled her closer. She opened her mouth to tell him that she was fine, but instead her entire body began to tremble with emotions so encompassing they were screaming to escape.

"I shouldn't have walked away before we'd finished talking, and I should have given you a chance to explain your intentions. I did to you exactly what I accused you of. I was too afraid to hear what you'd say."

He tucked his hand beneath her chin and lifted her gaze to meet his. "I should have come after you to explain myself." He took a big breath. "When you left, I realized how hard I was struggling to become the person I want to be. That man who I am around you. The man you make me. But instead, I got sidetracked by my mom, the mayor, the race."

"You have a lot of people counting on you." And that would never change, especially if he won the election. "I know your family means the world to you, and that's really amazing," she said honestly. "I'm just not sure there's room in your life for me."

A terrifying thought because it reminded her of the scared girl who would rather live on the streets than be discounted again and again by the people she loved. People who didn't love her back enough to come looking for her.

"You are my life. That's what I should have told you. You remind me what it's all about, why I'm doing this." He stepped closer. "You remind me of the why, Piper."

"But you still picked your mom?" Something she was having a hard time getting past. Not his loyalty to his family, but how easily he allowed his mom to control the entire situation. "When Margo dug in and cost a group of girls an amazing opportunity, you didn't stop her or at least set her straight."

"I know, and I am so damn sorry. What Rebecca did was wrong, but what I did was even worse. You gave me your trust, and I didn't keep my word. I messed up big time, but I promise we—"

"Stop, just stop." She plugged her ears. "Promises are made

to be broken. You won't mean to, but you will." She turned around, facing the skyline. "This is why I hate promises, they always hurt too much."

"I didn't come the other day for my mom or the silo." He slid his arms around her from behind and whispered in her ear. "I came for you. You, Piper."

Her breath caught. "Why?"

"My family, my job, all the crushing responsibility. I let all those things lead me down the wrong path when all I had to do was look up and see you."

A tiny beacon of hope lit in her belly. "When you look at me, what do you feel?" Please say that with her he felt found because that's how he made her feel. Seen and heard, and not so alone in a world that was designed to make space for the past.

"With you, I feel like I'm coming home." Large hands settled on her hips and slowly turned her until she was nestled in the most glorious chest she'd ever felt. Wanting to grab on, but terrified of looking as desperate as she felt, Piper let her hands hang by her sides, but she rested her cheek over his heart and tried to calm her breathing to match his steady beat.

And somewhere between his arms coming around her and feeling his lips press against the top of her head, Piper wondered if maybe she'd found the kind of man, a man like Josh, who saw forever in her.

And Piper might be a promise-phobe and terrified of disappointment—from herself and others—but she wasn't a coward, and she didn't do regrets.

"I don't know how home feels, but you make me want to find out what it could be like."

"This." He tilted her head up and brushed his lips across hers, igniting a million tingles—and for once Piper welcomed them. "This is what it's like."

His lips touched hers, and a warm flood of understanding

and acceptance filled her chest, and a foreign lump of something she believed to be love wrapped around her. And when he pulled back, her mind said, *He's mine.*

Piper started to tell him just that when she heard a commotion behind them. She turned to find a large crowd walking around and admiring the photos. "What's going on?"

"Me coming through on my promise," he said roughly. "I realized that I should be here with you. Not with my mom or the mayor, but here. I said I always come through for the people in my life. For me, you're it. You are my life. So I called everyone I know, including my brothers, to see if they could help, and it turns out we know a lot of people who like art."

"Is that Rhett?" she asked, spotting his brother standing next to Rebecca, asking her about her photo. And then the most miraculous thing happened. He placed a red sticker at the bottom of the frame, indicating he'd bought Rebecca's *Cinderella's a Lie*.

Tears in her eyes, Piper turned back to Josh. "You did this for me?"

He cupped her cheek. "I'd do anything for you."

"Why?" She had to know.

"I love you, Piper Campagna, so much I can't think straight. And that's not an excuse, but I was so busy trying to fix everything, be perfect for you, that I lost sight of what was important. And that's us. It will always be us."

"I like us," she whispered. "But wait. Isn't tonight your big night with the mayor?" Yet, he was there with her.

"This is a big night for me. It's the night I tell the woman I love that I want to be in love. That I am in love."

"You love me?" she whispered, her heart inflating like it was filled with helium.

"I love us," he said. "So let me ask that question I wanted to ask the other day. Do you love me back?"

"Yes!" she cried and went up on her toes and kissed him. "I love you so much it terrifies me."

"Join the club." He cupped her face. "I've spent the past month trying to talk myself into believing that this was just chemistry."

Piper froze. Healthy love wasn't exactly in her wheelhouse. But the man in front of her, the man who said he loved her, was surrounded by it. "How do we know it's not just chemistry?"

"Because I'd rather be alone with you than anywhere else in the world."

Josh kissed Piper, and when their lips touched, Piper finally understood that love, in all its pureness and intensity, wasn't something said in the middle of the night. It was something shown, something given without an expectation.

EPILOGUE

Six months later...

"Put your hand right there," Josh said, and Piper's pulse picked up.

"Here?" she asked.

"Lower," he whispered, and she moved it lower. "Lower still," he instructed.

And her palm slid even lower. His was on the move as well, skating down her back to rest on the lower curve. Then he pulled her flush against him—against all of him—sending little zings through her entire body.

"Here?" she whispered.

"Oh yeah, right there. Now, how about that dance, Boots?"

Before she could answer, Josh stepped right into her, and they began gliding across the floor. Around them, other couples moved to the music as the instructors passed, commenting on posture and body lines. Not that Josh needed any instruction; his lines were impeccable and his body mouthwatering.

"If I step on your feet, remember that I warned you," she said.

"Then close your eyes and follow my lead."

Over the past few months, Josh had done everything he could to prove to Piper that she was his number one, that she was loved. He showed her an emotion she'd never experienced before.

Adoration. Josh made her feel adored and treasured, and as if she were the most important person in his world. So she closed her eyes and let him lead her around the dance floor, twirling her and even adding a dip that made her laugh.

"What kind of dance is this?" she asked. "A waltz?"

He stopped, his hands going to her hips and holding her closer than when they'd been dancing.

"Actually, I was hoping it could be our wedding dance," he said, and Piper's heart leapt.

"A wedding dance?"

"*Our* wedding dance." He pulled something out of his pocket, and it sparkled under the lights. It was a beautiful antique ring with a deep-blue sapphire in the middle surrounded by a band of diamonds. "Piper Campagna, will you marry me?"

Piper wrapped her arms around his neck and brushed her lips against his. "Mister District Attorney Josh Easton, there is no one else in the world I'd rather be alone with."

THE END

Thank you for reading!

MAKE an author's day and consider leaving a nice review! Reviews help authors like me find new readers and gain advertising. If you enjoyed the read, tell a friend!

Review it now!

WANT MORE EASTONS?

Turn the page to check out Gage and Darcy's story, *Chasing I Do,* a humorous, feel-good enemies to lovers romantic comedy!

CHASING I DO. - CHAPTER 1

Darcy Kincaid had dreamed about this day since she was six and uncovered her mother's stash of Southern Wedding magazines in the basement. After a lifetime of planning, handpicking two thousand of the palest of pink peonies, and her entire life savings, she was about to pull off, what she believed to be, the most romantic I Do in history. The sun was high, the sky was crystal blue, and a gentle June breeze carried the scent of the nearby primrose blooms and ever after.

Today was the perfect day to be married, and the rose garden at Belle Mont House was the ideal backdrop. And Darcy wasn't about to let a tail-chasing wedding crasher ruin her moment. No matter how charming.

Not this time.

"Nuzzling the bride's pillows before the wedding will only get you escorted out," Darcy said to the four-legged powderpuff in matching pink booties and hair bow.

The dog, who was more runway than runaway, dropped down low in the grass, eyes big black circles of excitement, tail wagging with delight—her jewel-encrusted collar winking in the sunlight.

Darcy squinted, but could only make out the first word. "Fancy." The little dog's ears perked up and her tail went wild.

"Such a pretty name," Darcy cooed, taking a cautious step forward. "I'm Darcy; it's nice to meet you. I'm going to come a little closer so I can get a better look at your collar and find your mamma's number. Is that okay?"

With a playful snort, the animal's entire body was wiggling as if so excited by the idea of making a friend she couldn't hold in the glee. Darcy reached out to ruffle her ears, and Fancy, confusing Darcy's movement for time to play, snatched up the pillow and gave it a good shake.

"No!" Darcy cried, halting in her tracks while little bits of stuffing leached into the air, causing perspiration to bead on her forehead.

Fancy, on the other hand, wasn't worried in the slightest. Nope, she gave another rambunctious whip of the head before jumping up and down with the pillow as if this were all fun and games.

Sadly, this situation was about as close to fun and games as natural child birthing. Not only was the vintage silk pillow, a family heirloom passed down from the bride's great-grand-mother, in danger of becoming a chew-toy, but the bride's ring was swinging dangerously from the aged ribbon.

And this wasn't just any bride. Candice Covington was the former Miss Oregon, a Portland mover and shaker, and the first bride to be wed at the newly renovated Belle Mont House. Candice was already in the bridal suite, her beloved in the tower room, and two hundred of their closest friends and family were set to start arriving in just over an hour—and the dog looked content to nuzzle the pillow all afternoon.

With its teeth.

"Stop!" she said in her most authoritative tone, putting her hand out.

To Darcy's surprise, the dog stopped. Her snout going into hypersniffer mode, she dropped the pillow to the grass and rose up to smell the air. Seemed Fancy had caught the scent of the prosciutto-wrapped figs sitting on a chair that Darcy had been tasting, and she stood up on her hind legs, then walked around in three perfect circles.

"Someone's got moves," she said. "Not bad, but mine are better."

A decade of planning events for Portland's pickiest clients and four years in the trenches as a single mother had taught Darcy the art of positive redirection. She'd lasted through potty training, teething, and chickenpox. This stubborn ball of fluff didn't stand a chance.

Eying the flower arrangement on the closest table, Darcy grabbed a decorative stick and gave it a little shake. "Want to play with the stick for a while?" The dog sat, eyes wide, head cocked to the side in an explosion of cuteness. "We can switch toys before you destroy the pillow, okay?"

"Yip!"

Tail up like a heat-seeking radar, the dog hit the fetch-and-retrieve position, pointing her nose toward one of the open fields.

"Ready?" Darcy wiggled the stick again for show. "Go get 'em!"

The stick flew through the air, going as far in the opposite direction as it could. Darcy released a sigh of relief when it cleared the fountain and landed in the middle of the field.

A low growl sounded, followed by a blur of white fur that bolted past.

Those little legs working for the prize. A position Darcy could relate to.

Located in the prestigious West Hills, Belle Mont House was three stories of Portland history with extensive manicured gardens, six bedrooms, a grand salon, and captivating views of the city and Mount Hood—all of which needed to be meticulously cared for. And Darcy was the sole caretaker.

She had driven by the old property a thousand times over the years. But she hadn't really recognized its potential until after her world had fallen apart and a heartbreaking betrayal had left her life in tatters—much like the foundation of this forgotten house. Unable to watch something so beautiful and full of history crumble, she'd saved it from demolition, then spent every penny and waking moment renovating it back to its original grandeur. In return, Belle Mont had given her something even more precious—a future for her and her daughter.

Today marked Belle Mont's first day in operation as the year's "Most Romantic" wedding destination in the Pacific Northwest and Darcy as its planner extraordinaire—according to the editor at Wedding Magazine, who'd left a message earlier about sending a high-profile couple to check out the location.

A couple so hush-hush, the editor refused to give the name for fear that the press would show. But if they decided that Belle Mont was their dream wedding venue, and Darcy could accommodate them with the last Sunday in July, the only date that worked around the couple's hectic schedule, then Belle Mont would land a huge spread in the August issue.

The endorsement alone was enough to make her say yes on the spot. Not to mention the profit for hosting such a lavish event would go a long way toward helping pay back all the money she'd invested into the renovation—and secure her future in Portland.

A future that now resided in the jaws of a dog that could fit in her pocket.

Fancy snatched the stick and darted across the lawn toward

the twinkle-lit and peony-covered gazebo in record time—all with the pillow still in its jowls.

"Hey," she called out, "we had a deal!"

The dog's tail went up as if flipping the bird at their deal before she ran beneath a row of chairs and struck a different kind of pose altogether. A move that showed enough doggie bits to prove that under that pink bling, Fancy was all male. And about to shit all over Candice's perfect day.

A situation Darcy knew all too well.

"Had I known you had a stupid stick down there, I wouldn't have bothered trying to reason with you."

In Darcy's experience, men loved the forbidden almost as much as they loved their stick. So she fumbled with her skirt, pulling it above her thighs, and gave chase.

Fancy took off, and man, those toothpick legs could fly. Ears flapping behind him, butt moving like lightning bugs in a jar, the pooch headed straight for the rose garden, which lay directly across from the aisle runner that had Candice and Carter spelled out in the palest of pink peony petals.

"Not the runner!" she cried, only to watch in horror as Fancy raced up the center of the white pillowed Egyptian cotton, his legs pumping with the speed and grace of a cheetah in the wild, leaving a few dozen miniature muddy paw prints and a tornado of petals in his wake.

"No, no, no!" she called out. "Not the rose garden."

Terrified of the damage he could do to the roses and the pillow, she picked up the pace and rounded the white iron fencing, gravel sliding under her heels as she burst through the gate and snatched the pillow right before the Fancy dove his fancy-ass—and Candice's ring—into the fountain.

"Got it!" she yelled, but the celebration quickly faded as her momentum carried her forward—and right into the stone cherub boy's watering hole.

"Oh God, no!" Darcy yelped as water exploded around her.

Having landed ass first, she felt the cold wetness seep through her silk skirt and slosh into her shoes. Her brand-new designer shoes she'd found at a consignment store and purchased especially for today. "Please, no."

She clawed the edge of the fountain and pulled, mentally willing herself out of the fountain—but she couldn't gain any positive momentum.

No matter how hard she tried, she just couldn't pull herself out.

Refusing to give up, she looked around for Fancy, hoping to either send him to find help or pull him in with her. But he'd vanished, right before the wedding, leaving her waist-deep in his mess.

The situation was so painfully familiar, Darcy wanted to cry. Then devour the entire wedding cake in one sitting.

"Are you okay?" a husky voice asked from above.

"Thank God you're here," she said, pushing her hair out of her face and looking up, expecting to find one of her kitchen staff.

But instead of a clip-on tie with a comb-over, Darcy's unexpected hero looked like an underwear model in a dark blue button-up and a pair of slacks that fit him to perfection. And his arms—oh my, those arms—were impressive, perfect for helping a lady in need.

Although Darcy had worked hard to not be reliant on others —a lifetime of letdowns could do that to a girl—she knew that sometimes it was okay to take an offered hand. And those hands were big and solid and— whoa—reaching forward to wrap around her hips and easily lift her out.

Her feet hit the ground, and she did her best to wring out her shirt. "I'm sorry if I'm getting you all wet."

"You never have to apologize to a man for getting him wet."

He chuckled, and Darcy, realizing how that had come out, went to move, but his arms tightened, stilling her. "Make sure you're okay first. You were moving pretty fast when you dove in."

Not as fast as her heart was racing.

Closing her eyes, Darcy took stock. Her chest tingled, her head was light, and a wave of delicious thrill jumpstarted parts she'd long believed dead. In fact, she was as far from fine as a woman who had sworn off men could get.

"I'm good. Thank you," she lied, trying to gain some distance without falling back into the fountain, which was not an easy task. He was so big, he filled the space, leaving nowhere for her to go. She brushed off her elbows, which were scraped up, but she'd live, then started to straighten when a big hand appeared, Candice's ring resting in its palm.

"I believe you lost this."

"Thank you," she whispered, a wave of relief washing over her. "You have no idea how—"

Darcy looked up, and the words died on her lips and dropped to the pit of her stomach, where they expanded and churned until—Oh God, she couldn't breathe.

Her unexpected hero wore slacks and tie fit for Wall Street, a leather jacket that added a touch of bad boy to the businessman, and a pair of electric blue eyes that she'd recognize anywhere. They'd always reminded her of a calm, crystal clear lake. Today they were tempestuous, like an angry autumn storm.

The change wasn't a surprise, given the last time they'd seen each other. But the deep ache of longing it brought on was.

"Gage," she said, her heart pounding so loudly she was certain he could hear it thumping in her chest.

It was the first time she'd seen him since the funeral, a thought that brought back a dozen memories—some sad, some of the best moments of her life, but all of them a painful reminder of what had been lost.

"Hey, Pink," he said in a tone that implied that had he known it was her he would have let her drowned.

She swallowed back the disappointment, hoping he didn't notice that she was shaking. "What are you doing here?"

"It looks like I'm helping you find your wedding ring." He took her hand in his and slid the ring on her finger. The sensation was so overwhelming she jerked back.

Gage Easton was over six feet of solid muscle and swagger. He was also sweet and kind and, at one time, one of the few people she thought she'd always be able to count on. If things had gone how Darcy had dreamed, he would have made for one heck of a brother-in-law.

An even better uncle.

A swift shot of guilt mixed with the swelling panic in her throat, her reckless secret pressing down until she was choking. But Darcy swallowed it back and refused to shoulder all of the blame.

Life was filled with hard choices. While Gage's twin had chosen to be unfaithful, Darcy had chosen their daughter's happiness.

She would always choose Kylie.

Gage looked at her bare feet, then aimed that intense gaze her way. "I would have thought that after jilting Kyle like you did, you'd have started wearing running shoes to these kinds of events."

Although Gage had a big heart, he was still an Easton. And when someone messed with one brother, they messed with the whole clan. The only way to survive was to hide your fear and never stand down.

Shoulders back, chest slightly puffed, Darcy made her body appear bigger, the way she had when she'd been a young girl and encountered a stranger at her breakfast table. She'd walk into the kitchen and pretend she was big and strong—someone not to be messed with.

Her mother had a thing for rot-gut whiskey and bottom-shelf men—and made a habit of bringing both home. Sometimes they stayed the night, sometimes they stayed the year, but Darcy never knew who—or what—she'd encounter in the one place that should have felt safe.

But this was her home now, and she'd do whatever was necessary to protect it.

"After five years, I would have hoped you'd realize your family wasn't the only ones who were hurting," she said. "I may have walked out on your brother, but I wasn't the one who let him drive that night."

Gage Easton felt the truth of that statement hit hard, the power of it nearly taking him out at the knees. Darcy wasn't a confrontational person by nature, but she knew how to stand her ground. No doubt a trait she'd picked up from dealing with his family.

He hadn't seen her since the funeral. Nobody had. Not that he'd blamed her. His family had still been reeling from the aftermath of the wedding that never happened, when tragedy struck again, tearing a chasm between Darcy and the Eastons that could never be fixed. His brother, Kyle, was gone, and with the overwhelming and sudden grief that had been thrust upon his family, most especially his mom, a lot of the blame had been unfairly placed upon Darcy.

There were so many times he wanted to reach out, make sure she was okay, but he'd spent the majority of their relationship keeping his distance, certain that no good could come from letting himself get too close. And he wasn't looking to test his theory.

Not today.

"Are you okay?" he asked, waving a hand to her elbows, which were scrapped and he was certain smarting.

"Nothing that won't heal," she said, and he knew she wasn't talking about the gravel burn. "I just have to change my skirt and shoes."

"You might want to change the top while you're at it." He grinned. "Not that I mind the view, but it might cause some heart problems with the older guests."

Darcy's gaze dropped to her shirt and the two beautiful buds peeking through the translucent fabric, and she gasped. Hell, Gage was in his prime and her top was causing some serious gasping and heart palpitations on his end.

"Don't worry, I didn't peek. Much." He leaned in and whispered, "Although, if you know you're going to take a swim, you might just consider skinny dipping. You'd get the same effect, only you wouldn't have to hang-dry your lace bra and panties."

"You can't see my panties."

No, he couldn't, but she didn't need to know that. The narrowed eyes and pursed lips were enough to tell him that she was ticked just thinking about him seeing her panties. And that was a far better state than the tears that had been threatening a moment ago.

"Look," she said pointedly, crossing her arms over her chest, which did nothing except pull the fabric tighter. "I'm grateful that you found the ring and helped me out of the fountain, and I have no clue as to why you're here"—her tone said she didn't care to find out either—"but I need you to leave."

"Don't worry," he said. "I didn't come to ruin your big day. I'll get out of your way as soon as my meeting is over." And he found the abomination in bows he was stuck dog sitting.

"Oh, it's not my big day," she clarified. "I'm the planner for the wedding that is supposed to start in less than an hour."

He looked at her outfit and, while cream in color, it wasn't bridal attire. The skirt, the buttoned silk top, even her hair said professionally elegant. Not bride-to-be.

A heaviness that he didn't even notice he'd taken on lifted at her admission, and he wanted to kick himself. She wasn't getting married? So what? It didn't matter. Kyle was gone, Gage was still struggling to make peace with things, and Darcy would always be off-limits.

No matter how great she still looked. Even scratched up and sweaty, she was as gorgeous as ever.

"Well, if you'll just direct me to the manager's office," he asked. "I'm late, and don't want to keep him waiting."

She looked at her watch and froze, an expression of resignation washing over her.

"Actually, you're early," she said, so full of dread she felt sweat bead on her forehead. She stuck out her hand. "Darcy Kincaid, owner and exclusive planner for Belle Mont House. I believe the editor from Wedding Magazine said you'd be dropping by tomorrow."

Continue *Chasing I Do*

Read on for a sneak peek of Summer Affair a laugh-out-loud friends to lovers romantic comedy.

SUMMER AFFAIR - CHAPTER 1

Piper Campagna knew better than to tempt fate.

Acting as the Ansel Adams of love for even a single wedding was as risky as blow-drying her hair in the shower. It wasn't that she didn't love the idea of love or even dream about seeing something so beautiful aimed her direction. Once upon a time, Piper had given up everything in her quest for unconditional love only to wind up broke, homeless, and completely alone.

Nope, as far as she was concerned, happily ever after was about as realistic as Prince Charming riding in on a Pegasus.

She'd been to exactly five weddings in her lifetime. All her mother's. And all but one ending before the photos were developed. Making Piper the last person on the planet to take a resident photographer position at one of Portland's up-and-coming wedding venues.

Yet there she was, about to shoot a highly publicized engagement party for a local celebrity family—acting as if she were the right person for the job. As if she truly believed in something as laughable as forever. She wasn't sure what that said about her, other than she was willing to do anything to land this job, even if it meant faking it.

Piper pressed the palm of her hand to her forehead and groaned loudly. She hated fakes.

Apparently, Fate agreed because just as the fairytale of a wedding venue started to come into view through her cracked windshield, a guttural groan rattled the car. POSH—her Piece of Shit Honda—was telling anyone who'd listen that she needed more than duct tape and prayer to handle the steep hill and hairpin turns.

"Come on, girl, don't fail me now." Piper lovingly rubbed the dashboard.

The engine gave a low hum as it downshifted, pulling through the worst of the bend, handling the tight curve like a pro. POSH might have a junkyard past, but she was scrappy as hell and had an aftermarket gear-shift knob that was shaped like brass knuckles. When shit got real, POSH rallied. Break-ups, break-downs, let-downs, broken promises, and even a handful of impulsive decisions that nearly broke the bank, that car was the most reliable thing in Piper's life. Over 150,000 miles of shared history.

150,000 miles of survival.

When Piper spotted the minefield of potholes ahead, her first reaction was to slam on the brakes. As a former rebel, she might do a little roaring and rumbling when cornered, but she knew when to push forward and when to concede. Yet as the steering tightened beneath her hands, jerking the wheel hard to the left with a force equal to Goliath playing the Hulk in a game of tug-of-war, with POSH acting as the rope, Piper's stubborn side kicked in.

"Not today, Fate. Not today!" Pulse accelerating, hands slick with perspiration, Piper slammed on the brakes and tried to strong-arm the steering into submission. She'd had plenty of experience with strong-arming, which was likely why she was still single.

"Shit!" Her hot-headed impulse backfired, and instead of breaking on a dime, POSH, with her thread-bare spare and duct-taped chassis, broke traction. The back tires lost grip, spinning and kicking up gravel and dust, the car fishtailing into the oncoming lane.

Thankfully, there were no other cars on the road. Just narrow and windy with nothing but dirt and gravel to slow her down. And trees. Lots and lots of trees. Big ones, little ones, enormous ones with trunks the size of water towers.

She skidded off the road onto the shoulder and on a direct course with a pothole the size of the Death Star. There was a large white oak, its gnarled branches swaying in the wind like a bat rhythmically swinging before a grand slam.

Ignoring her rising panic, Piper reached beside her for the e-brake and, channeling the tough-girl attitude that had helped her survive her teen years, she lifted the lever, smooth and steady. POSH released a loud pop, followed by some rhythmic thumping that beat hard in tempo with her heart. The car slowly decelerated, rolling off the road, finally coming to a stop inches from the oak tree, so close the leaves scratched back and forth across the hood.

She closed her eyes and dropped her forehead against the steering wheel, no longer judging Snow White for her hysterical reaction to trees. Allowing exactly one minute to collect herself, she took in a deep breath.

It took an additional three for her hands to stop shaking, but that was from frustration. At least, that was the story she was sticking to.

Ignoring the stench of singed rubber and desperation filling the cab, she popped the hood then opened the door. Even before she got out of the car, she knew the power steering was shot.

Confirming her suspicions, she let out an impatient sigh and made her way to the trunk, grabbing the tire iron, because the belt was the least of her problems. POSH was sporting a blown back tire and, while she could technically drive the last mile uphill without power steering, no amount of tenacity could make up for a flat tire.

As if her day wasn't challenging enough, Fate sent in her official RSVP to the party, by way of a streak of lightning which cut through the inky dusk sky.

One Mississippi. Two Mississip—

The ground rumbled under the boom of thunder. The wind picked up, plastering her dress against her legs and whipping her hair around.

"Is that all you got?" Piper hollered, waving the tire iron at the sky, which was turning all different shades of furry and brimstone.

Suddenly, it stopped and an eerie stillness moved in, surrounding her as static crackled in the evening air. Thunder and lightning she could handle. It was the quiet before the storm that was the most unsettling. Knowing it was only a matter of time before the drops began to fall, she grabbed the tire iron and went to work on the lug nuts.

Ten minutes, three grease stains, and a few choice words later, she succeeded in loosening half. The other half were stubborn little assholes that wouldn't budge.

"I'm small, but I'm scrappy," she said, shucking her impractical shoes to stand on the tire iron. She gave a few bounces, willing it to budge, when another streak of lightning reached across the darkening sky, exploding so close to her car that every hair on her body became electrified.

"Lightning doesn't scare me!" she shouted over the rustling trees.

Neither did Fate. Piper had taken on tougher and survived to tell the story. Plus, fear clashed with the ball-buster vibe she'd worked so hard to perfect. Not to mention, too much was riding on tonight for anything to go array.

The beautiful bride-to-be wasn't only Piper's new boss, but her fiancé was an agent to the stars. So the guest list read like a Who's Who in Portland—the exact kind of people Piper usually went out of her way to avoid.

However, circumstances had changed, and Piper needed to adapt, so she went back to work on the flat. Within minutes, stray strands of hair clung to her skin, and smudges of break-fluid covered the hem of her dress.

She was an utter mess. And no closer to changing her tire.

Refusing to give up, she removed her blazer and placed it gently inside the car, then propped her knee against the fender and shoved. Up and down and back and forth. She worked the tire iron as if more than just her pride depended on it. And she was making headway, creating a good rhythm for herself when she heard a loud sound rip through the air.

"Shit!" She shot up, her hands going to cover her backside, her mouth gaping open.

She didn't need to look to know that she had blown the back out of her fitted "wedding photographer approved" work dress. Praying the draft made it seem worse than it actually was, she glanced behind her.

"Shit, shit, shit!"

It was bad. Pink silk with black hearts bad. And the zipper looked like it had jumped the track and split from her lower back to right below the lace waistband of her panties.

She reached behind her to unzip the dress, hoping she could somehow fix the rip, but the zipper was stuck. She tugged. And when that didn't work, she tugged while hopping around.

"I get it!" she yelled at the sky. "Message received. Now go away so I can make my own destiny."

Destiny. She snorted. Yet another thing she didn't believe in. Every decision she'd made up to that point had been hers and hers alone. Something she normally prided herself on. But today, it left her feeling vulnerable and alone. And as she took in the grease stains on her hands and bare feet, Piper knew she needed help.

Admission was the hardest part.

But with three months' rent on the line, Piper was willing to do just about anything. Even if it meant phoning in a favor.

She dialed Jillian Conner, wedding cake designer extraordinaire, the person who helped Piper land this job, and the only soul she knew at the party besides the bride-to-be.

Jillian answered on the first ring.

"Piper, oh my God, where are you?" Jillian's voice came through the phone in a hushed whisper. "The mother of the groom has been asking for you."

"I'm almost there." Piper peered over the hood of her car to the historic mansion perched on the hill in front of her.

Located in the prestigious West Hills, Belle Mont House was three stories of Portland royalty, with extensive grounds, five large entertaining rooms, including a grand salon and conservatory which captured some of the most captivating views of the city and Mount Hood. It was a premier destination for weddings, cooperate parties, and highbrow events.

No family was quite as highbrow as the Eastons, who Groom Gage, along with Bride to Be Darcy, were the couple of the night.

"Like at the door almost?"

Piper hadn't known Jillian all that long, but she could tell the woman was beyond stressed. "Like my tire blew out at the bottom of Belle Mont Drive."

"This is bad. So, so incredibly bad. Most of the family has already arrived, and Margo is demanding to know when pictures are going to begin."

"The party doesn't start for another hour," Piper stated, but a bad feeling began to grow in the pit of her belly. She had met the matriarchal dictator of the Easton family once, at her initial interview. Getting struck by lightning would be less painful that going head-to-head with Margo Easton.

"The guests arrive in another hour, but most of the family is already here."

"You've got to be kidding me!" Piper looked up at the sky and squinted at the tiny molecules of rain flittering down. A drop landed on the tip of her nose.

She gave Fate a little wave of the finger—her middle one.

"Not even one bit." Jillian lowered her voice to a bare whisper. "Margo went over Darcy's head and told the family to get here an hour early. Darcy wasn't even dressed when Margo busted in with her closest friends in tow looking for tea. Now the woman is ranting about taking a picture of the entire family in the rose garden to use for this year's Christmas card."

Rain dotted the windshield and ground, and that bad feeling grew until Piper could feel it pressing against her ribs. "She does know that a storm is coming, right?"

Jillian laughed. "I don't think Zeus himself could take on Margo when she's like this. So please tell me you're going to arrive before she begins aiming her death glare my direction," Jillian begged. "With everything Darcy and Gage went through to get here, today has to be perfect. And that means keeping Margo appeased and away from Darcy. And since Darcy's my bestie, that task apparently falls to me. When I volunteered to be Margo's keeper, I had forgotten what nightmares are truly made of."

Piper had firsthand experience with nightmares who walked in the daylight. She wasn't scared of a five-foot-nothing sourpuss in pearls. "She isn't that bad."

"She is. Which reminds me, are you wearing the dress?" she

asked as if Piper had a choice in the matter. Which she most definitely did not.

She looked down at the designer dress Jillian had made her try on—then buy. It was a little dustier—and a whole lot draftier—than it had been earlier, but with a few safety pins, a wet wipe, and lint roller it would do. "I'm wearing the dress."

"Thank God. Margo told me everyone needs to be in appropriate attire, even the staff."

"My closet was filled with appropriate photographer attire. Some of it is even press-core approved. Yet, I'm dressed as if I'm going to high tea." She tugged at the neckline and signed. "Or the Queen's funeral."

"Yeah, well, if it goes with pearls, it's Margo approved," Jillian said. "She's driving me crazy. So when I say I need you here now, I need you here *now*."

Piper took in the tire iron extending from a lug nut, then the tempest on the horizon. She calculated that she had less than fifteen minutes before the late summer drizzle turned into a Portland downpour. "I can fix the tire, but it will take time. Can you come get me? I'm just at the bottom of the hill."

There was a long pause, long enough that perspiration beaded down her spine.

"God, I wish I could. But today, of all days, my son decided he's scared of dogs and one of the brothers brought his wife's dog, who peed in my purse. Not on it—in it. And I still have one hundred twenty-six mini cakes to frost before Margo decides my dessert isn't quite right and does it herself."

Piper eyed the distance from her car to the top of the hill. It was like being stuck in the middle of the ocean in a life raft with only a whisk to paddle to shore.

Suck it up, buttercup.

"I'll figure it out. I promise."

"Before the storm hits. God, Piper, please tell me you'll get here before the storm hits."

It would be close, but she could make the hike.

"Fate herself couldn't stop me." Especially if it meant disappointing Jillian.

The two had met at the community park over the summer, during team pictures for the local Tiny Tikes football league. Piper had been conned into taking the team photo, and Jillian had volunteered enough cakepops to feed a small army. They'd bonded over the coach being a ginormous prick, which lead them to the conclusion that all men were ginormous pricks, and—several cakepops and a juice box later—they'd cemented a budding friendship.

A friendship Piper had come to treasure. She didn't have many friends growing up. Especially ones like Jillian, who not only had her life together but also cared enough about Piper to stand in her corner if the need arose.

That's because you're difficult, a little voice said from deep inside. A voice that sounded a whole lot like her mother.

Driven, Piper corrected. *Okay, stubborn.* Two qualities that had saved her life more than once.

With an unpredictable alcoholic for a mother and a chaotic childhood, Piper was wary of people's intentions. Moving from town to town, her mom burning through husbands like most people went through chips—you can't just have one—it made it hard to cement connections. Even harder to trust that the relationship could go the distance. So, she built walls. Big, impenetrable walls that were nearly impossible to scale.

But while she might be afraid to let people in, a little thunder and lightning didn't even rank on her list of things to run screaming from. If she had to trudge up that hill to get to the party on time, then trudging she'd do.

Piper opened the back door and pulled a pair of black

combat boots off the floorboard and slipped them on. She grabbed her blazer, back up clothes—just in case the dress didn't make it—and was reaching for her camera bag when Jillian squealed. "Oh wait! I forgot. One of the brothers took an Uber from the airport and the driver just left. I can have him double back to pick you up."

Piper dropped her coat back in the car and climbed inside to avoid the rain. "You are a goddess. Tell him if he gets to me before the ground turns to mud, I'll double his tip. And Jillian, thank you. I so owe you."

"Friday night is girls' night. No excuses this time, and the first round is on you."

"Done and done." Piper disconnected.

Minutes ticked by with no sign of the hired car.

"Depending on a friend is not the same as being dependent," Piper said aloud then pulled out a tub of emergency peanut butter from her purse. Because if there was ever an emergency, pink silk with black hearts was it.

And—*ah* man—just the crinkling of the cellophane wrapper was enough to send all kinds of good feels to the brain. And then, because a jar of emergency peanut butter deserved some chocolate, she dusted off her hands and grabbed a fist of candy kisses from her camera bag.

The savory smell of peanuts and salt filled the car as she dipped the first kiss in and popped it in her mouth.

"Oh my gawd!" She sighed, closing her eyes to savor the momentary bliss. She hadn't eaten since breakfast, and it was fast approaching dinner time. With the setback of the flat and the lack of an assistant, her next meal would likely be well after midnight.

When she ran out of kisses, she dipped her finger in the jar and scooped out a mouthful, then licked it off.

She was on her third pass when the sound of gravel

crunching under tires came up behind her. Piper turned to find a sleek black car headed her way.

"Thank you, Jillian," she whispered because help had finally arrived—and in Piper's world, that wasn't always the case.

With one last dip of the finger, she hopped out of the car and into the rain. Raising the jar in greeting, she gave an embarrassed little wave. The car got closer, and she sucked the remaining gooey goodness off her finger and stepped toward the road when—

"Holy shit!"

The sedan roared right past her with all four hundred of its horses powering at full tilt and nearly taking her out in the process. The car was so close it created a wind tunnel intense enough to rip the jar right from her hands. And cover her from head to toe in a fine speckling of mud.

"What the hell?" Piper yelled as the break-lights blared a steady red and the car skid to a stop a few yards ahead in the middle of the road.

Piper grabbed her blazer and tied it around her waist, then ran to the car. She'd barely reached the driver's side when the window slowly rolled down, exposing the driver within.

He was big and muscled, his body filling all the space in the car. Under the dome light she could see that his suit was freshly pressed, his dark wavy hair carefully manicured. He had the look of a man who controlled his world.

And he was gorgeous. The kind of gorgeous that made people want to stop and stare. Not that Piper was staring. Nope. She didn't do gorgeous. And she most certainly did not do suits who nearly ran her over.

"Are you okay?" he asked, his voice low and gravely.

"Do I look okay?" she asked because he looked as if he was about to climb out of the car and see for himself.

"You look like someone who was standing in the middle of

the road during a storm, at dusk, wearing black," he said. "What? Were you playing chicken or staging a car heist?"

"No, I was waiting for you."

This seemed to amuse him. He looked at her over the rim of his wraparound sunglasses and grinned—a big, smug grin that pissed her off. "You were waiting for me?"

"Don't flatter yourself," she said, wondering how he'd managed, in sixty seconds, to get under her skin. "Just looking for a ride."

"Well, hop in."

"Gee, thanks."

"I did nearly run you over," he said, a humor to his voice saying he'd purposefully chosen to ignore the purposeful lack of gratitude in her words.

"You might not want to admit that," she advised. "Some people are jerks and would use it against you."

"Are you one of those people?"

"A jerk? Usually." She made a big show of dusting off her dress, which only made a bigger mess. "But life is too short to deal with lawyers."

His lips twitched. Not quite a smile, but enough to let Piper know it was at her expense. "Noted." His voice went soft. "But seriously, are you okay?"

His genuine concern deflated any hostility she'd been clinging to. She held her arms out to the side and when she looked down she nearly laughed. "Well, my dress is ruined."

He took off his sunglasses and—sweet Mary mother of God—his eyes were the exact color of the sky, a deep stormy blue with bright specks, like the lightning moments ago. Then there was the carefully crafted five-o'clock shadow.

"And yet, you're smiling," he said.

"My usual MO would be to swing the tire iron in your direction."

That twitch was back, and this time it exposed two double-barreled dimples that sparked all kinds of tingles south of the Mason-Dixon line. Their eyes held for a long moment as if he was trying to figure out what to do with her. It was a look she was used to.

"I guess today's my lucky day."

"Mine is looking up," she said. "If you hadn't stopped, I never would have made it to the party on time."

"You also wouldn't show up looking like your dress fell victim to a finger painting drive-by."

"Who doesn't love a good finger painting?" She lifted a single, sexy brow.

"I guess it depends on who's the canvas."

Not sure how she felt about that or the growing tingles, she said, "I'm Piper. And I'm late."

"I'm Josh, and I guess I'm your driver." He reached out his hand. "You headed to the party?"

"I'm shooting it." She lifted the camera bag, then looked at his still outstretched hand. "I would shake, but my hands are covered with—"

"Peanut butter," he said, and something playful lit his voice. "I saw."

Well, wasn't that embarrassing. She wondered what else he'd seen. The way his eyes held steadfast, almost as if he was fighting the urge to veer south told her he'd most likely seen some pink and black silk.

Oh, lucky day!

"I'd offer you some but..." She pointed over her shoulder to the peanut butter-sized roadkill on the ground.

"You're mourning the peanut butter but not the dress?"

"I have other clothes in my bag. But that was my emergency peanut butter," she said.

"That would make me the jerk." He rested an arm on the

window and smiled. At her. As if their meeting was serendipitous. "How can I make it up to you?"

"How good are you with zippers?"

Continue *Definitely (Maybe) Dating*

Read on for a sneak peek of Jillian and Clay's story, Summer Affair, a hilarious and tender breach read.
Resolutions from Jillian's Journal
*Rename Resolutions to Recommendations
so that one could, at any time,
ignore them without a trace of guilt.*

JILLIAN CONNER WAS NAKED.

Not entirely naked, but her teeny-weeny teal bikini didn't leave much to the imagination. With a few scraps of material held together by a series of tug-and-they're-gone straps, she was living on the edge, about to do something thrilling—and so out of character—even if it could constitute a public indecency charge.

She tightened the silky belt of her robe and looked out the kitchen window to the pool. A giddy excitement rushed through her. The last time she was this naked outside of her bedroom or en suite was when Obama was in office. It was only a matter of time before the Homeowners Association added a new regulation prohibiting skinny dipping in one's own yard. She could practically hear the wildfire of gossip from the local mill and see the write-up in the Forest Park Newsletter: LOCAL

CAKE GODDESS TURNED MOON GODDESS IN NUDE PEGAN RITUAL.

While her backyard was open on all three sides, and its back butted up to twenty acres of state-protected forest land, her side yard had no gate, no fence, and no privacy, leaving her exposed to any passersby. But those concerns were for another time because tonight, Jillian was about to embark on something so rare and extraordinary she could scarcely believe her luck.

Me time.

An uninterrupted, unsupervised, unadulterated kid-free night. She'd heard of this white magic whispered around playgrounds and in local mommy-and-me circles. Tales of sleep-through-the-night, wake-after-noon with no-sugar-induced-tantrums kind of affair. Once upon a time, she'd been one of those carefree non-moms who frequented happy hour, spent weekends with the girls, and enjoyed a good romp with a handsome man.

Ah, sex. It seemed as foreign a concept as window browsing. And while there wouldn't be browsing or sex on tonight's menu, there would be chocolate cake, a bottle of wine, and a nice dip in the pool.

To most, a little skinny dipping wouldn't be considered bold or even pushing the envelope, but when one's envelope had been SEALED UNTIL FURTHER NOTICE, tonight's agenda was the equivalent of streaking at the Super Bowl. Especially when Jillian was a by-the-book advocate and follower. She brushed and flossed after every meal. Always used her signal, never hit snooze on her alarm, and found lists relaxing. Her hall monitor status was strong, forged from a place of necessity.

It took a fair-weathered fiancé, a Ponzi schemer, and a forensic accountant of a husband—who forensiced her right out of her alimony—for her to admit the cold, hard truth.

Jillian's picker was a lemon. An honest to God, Cupidphobic, unwilling doormat, lemon of a picker who always picked the wrong pecker. Sadly, according to her divorce attorney, and a circuit judge, bad pecker picker lemon laws were not recognized in the state of Oregon. Which left her with one solution.

Absolutely, positively, no men. No charmers, sweet talkers, bad boys, pretty boys, GQs, lumberjacks, or jack-offs. And she especially didn't go for the nice guy, who hid their dine-and-dash tendencies that, in her experience, unmistakably went hand and hand with a certain appendage.

She'd seen her friends find their person and fall in love and she was elated for them. But what were the odds of a third unicorn in their tiny state?

Sadly, there was a list of dine-and-dashers throughout her thirty-plus years, with her most recent breaking her heart and her bank—making her a six-time loser when it came to the game of love. But she wouldn't let that rob her of her deep and unwavering affair with all things romance and weddings, which was one of the reasons why she'd started Cake Goddess. The other was to stay current with the electric company.

Jillian was a special-occasions cake designer, who the Portland Tribune called one of the premiere pâtissiers in Portland. She specialized in classic, couture, and edible happily ever after. What had started as a small home business to supplement her income had turned into a cake company that sold decadent desserts all up and down the west coast. The demand was almost more than her kitchen could handle. Between being a single parent and a mompreneur, nights like tonight were a rarity. She loved her son, Sammy, but was desperate for some time to focus on herself.

Which was why, last week, after her birthday celebration, Jillian had signed up for *Hear Me Roar,* a podcast designed to help single women get their groove back. To resuscitate the bold, fun-loving, adventurous side that divorce and dating had annihilated. Tonight's session was titled, *Get it, Girl*, where she'd explore a series of resolutions that she'd painstakingly compiled, to help bring some much-needed fun back into her life. Between baking and being Sammy's whole world, Me Time was hard to come by, but since it was his dad's week, Jillian had a whole seven days to herself.

And she knew exactly where she wanted to start.

Grabbing a bottle of wine and a glass, and her TODAY YOU ARE AN EAGLE, AND YOUR WINGS ARE MADE OF AWESOME journal, Jillian headed next door to the main house for her skinny dipping date-of-one, middle-of-the-night adventure. With three years between her and her divorce, this was her way of shedding the past and arising from the water a new woman.

Jillian sinched the belt of her white, with kissy lips, silky robe and walked barefoot from her little cottage, where she and Sammy lived, to the main house she rented out as a vacation destination to help cover the cost of the two dwellings and six acres of property she'd inherited from her grandmother. Tomorrow, she was expecting a tenant who'd rented out the main house for the entire summer. He was a rather famous musician, and her best friend's brother-in-law, who needed a quiet place to unwind away from the spotlight of his impending divorce. But for tonight, the entire property was hers to enjoy.

She walked across the small bridge separating the two houses, scattered pine needles pressing into her feet. The June air was crisp and still, the sky so clear she could see a billion stars twinkling overhead. There couldn't have been a more perfect night to begin her journey into a sexy, single, and capable woman, who lived life to the fullest.

She'd decided to leave the pool and back lights off—she wasn't that bold—to camouflage her courageous first step from potential peepers. Enjoying the night surrounding her, and sipping her glass of wine, she sat on the edge of one of the padded loungers, pulled her small notebook and a pen from her pocket, and pressed play on the latest episode.

"Welcome back, you're listening to Hear Me Roar, *a psychological look into the world of dating and I'm your host, Dr. Claire.,"* the podcast began. *"Today starts your new journey and I'm here to tell you that Single Girl Anxiety is real. From check-one invitations to the single's table, and well-meaning family members who invite you to dinner and fail to mention the balding, middle-aged neighbor who works at the button factory and is waiting just for you. You can stop the crazy and take back your life.*

"I know what it's like to be that single girl in a sea of penguins. Being single in the city isn't always easy but it can be fun. But this isn't only a course in being single, it's a course about finding love. Self-love, familial love, and, yes, even the kind of love that comes when you find your person. But to find that forever love, first, you need to remember how to learn to love that scared, scarred girl deep inside who looks for validation over value."

Jillian had made that mistake once and vowed never to do it again, which was why her list was so important. Red flags, gut instincts, different ideals—these were things that would make up her manifesto.

After watching her friends find love, Jillian was starting to wonder if maybe she was missing out on something. She wasn't looking for her penguin, and after three generations of lemon pecker pickers, she didn't even believe in marriage, but a date here and there wouldn't be so bad. Neither would an orgasm. All she wanted was a small taste of that fancy-free, single-girl life she'd lost.

"You can be single and happy without suffering from Single Girl Anxiety by taking stock of your life and building a place where you get back in touch with you—that bright, confident woman who

reveled in her freedom, went to the movies alone without breaking out in a cold sweat, and flirted with strangers for flirt's sake.

"You can go back to the person, that Girl on Fire who isn't afraid to get a little burned because she knows that the safe path isn't always the fun path. Through this program, you'll learn you can still be Responsible You without silencing the Girl of Fire You."

Jillian's heart picked up, and an empowering flutter warmed her chest. That's what she wanted. To remember how to love herself. To fill up her passion cup so that she didn't start her day depleted. She was even open to some adult fun with no strings, but mainly she was on a search for her inner Girl on Fire.

"Now, I want you to pull out your Get it, Girl list. Look at it and let your brain absorb each and every resolution."

Jillian smoothed a hand down the paper a looked at her list. It had exactly twenty items. She's settled on twenty because it was an even number and divisible by two, five, and ten.

"Now, I want you to turn to a clean page and at the top of the page, under the first item, I want you to write.

1. Stop making lists. If it's important you'll remember it."

Jillian hit pause. "What kind of list asks you to abandon the list?" she asked the universe.

She could scarcely remember to put on underwear, let alone an entire list. It would be like going to the grocery store and saying, *Okay chips and powdered sugar doughnuts, come jump in my cart* and then forgetting the kale.

If Jillian was going to take the time to write a list, then everything on said list was important.

Hoping Dr. Claire was joking, she hit play.

"I know for most of you, that's a hard thing to wrap your brain around. But the only way you are going to get in touch with . . .

Fftt . . .

Fftt...
Fftt...

Jillian fast-forwarded to the next step.

"*I want you to go back a moment, to when I asked you to abandon your list. How did that make you feel?*"

"Like this is a stupid podcast and I'm wasting my time," Jillian said.

"*I often get words like empowered, alive, ready for anything that comes my way.*"

"Then they're liars," Jillian announced.

Fftt...
Fftt...
Fftt...

"*Now for number two. I want you to really think about what your second resolution would be. It can be one from your discarded list or one that stands out in your mind. Without peeking, I want you to write it down.*"

She quickly wrote down her next rule then read it back to herself. "Rename Resolutions to Recommendations, so that I can, at any time, ignore them without a trace of guilt."

And because she felt that was more of a guideline, and she made her own rules, she wrote down another resolution. A real make-change, show-what-you're-made-of kind of resolution that would take her from frazzled single-mom to sexy proud-to-be single woman.

Taking a fortifying-sized sip of wine, Jillian walked to the pool's edge and dipped her toe in—just one. Then, with her confidence boosted, she submerged her entire foot before stepping on the top step.

The pool was set to a balmy eighty-seven degrees, and she could see the steam rising off the surface. Feel the nerves floating up in her belly like helium balloons. Hear that Girl on Fire telling her to jump without a life preserver.

Closing her eyes, she undid her robe, let it slide down to her elbows, revealing her bikini, and jumped. Well, slid down to the next step and said to the stars above, loud and proud, putting her resolution out there, "Lose the negative whispers and lose that suit."

"While I'm in strong favor of both those statements, you might want to wait until I turn my back," a very low, very unexpected voice said from the abyss at the deep end of the pool.

Jillian squeaked. Panic rose and grabbed her by the throat, and every horror movie she'd ever watched came flooding back. She moved backward, her robe's belt catching between her legs, yanking the silky coverup and sending it into the water, where it slowly sank to the pool's bottom and leaving her in three scraps of material and teal strings.

Telling herself it was the wine, she closed her eyes and whispered, "Your imagination is working overtime, and you are dreaming."

"It bodes well for me that you imagine me in your dreams."

Recognition hit hard, and her eyes snapped open. It was not the wine. She was not even a little tipsy. She was stone-cold sober, and swimming over to her was an Easton, the youngest and sexiest of the brothers—and the only one Jillian let herself fantasize about because with their age difference *that* was never going to happen.

Clay, who lived in Seattle, was way too young and therefore had an expiration date—which was why she'd allowed her fascination morph into an embarrassing crush. So when he stood, arising from the now waist-deep water that sluiced down his body, her mouth went dry.

Like some Greek god, his hard chest glistened with moisture in the moonlight, and a thin patch of wet hair trailed down the plains of his flat stomach, disappearing beneath the water. His hair and lashes were spiked, and his lips were turned up into a grin that had her bathing suit nearly melting off her body.

"Clay?" she asked, squinting her eyes to ensure it was the Seahawks running back swimming in her pool. She gulped. There he was, in only the night's air and steaming water. "What are you doing here?"

"Waiting to hear what number three on your list is. Number two was a showstopper," he said, his gaze flickering with amusement and something a little more dangerous.

Interest. Even worse, it was clear that Clay of the chiseled abs and bulging biceps was teasing in a very flirty way.

"If you'd waited another minute, you would have seen the real showstopper," Jillian flirted back in that flirt for flirt's sake way Dr. Claire talked about.

Clay took another step toward her, revealing a pair of board shorts that hung indecently low on his hips and matched his cobalt blue eyes. "My loss."

A wave of single-girl anxiety washed over her, causing her to fold her arms across her body—at least concealing the top half of her bikini.

"Why are you here?" she asked.

"Going for a swim before I turn in," he said. "It seems you're doing the same."

"I was actually just—"

"About to lose your suit?"

"Not expecting Rhett until tomorrow," she finished, referring to his older brother who was her renter.

"I'm not expecting Rhett at all," he replied, amusement thick in his tone.

"I don't understand." Although, her gut understood perfectly. "You're my new tenant?"

With a dangerous grin, he walked toward the stairs, every step revealing more of his delicious body until he was within reaching distance and the water only hit his thighs. He reached out and she took a step back—up the stairs and out of the pool.

He froze, and that grin turned into a smile as he scooped up the robe and held it out to her. "Disappointed, Jillian?"

And that's when she saw it. The knowledge in those deep blue eyes. He knew about her little crush. A silly but very real school-girl crush that caused her to blush whenever he so much as looked her way. Heck, every time she was within the same square mile as him, she stumbled over her words or gawked.

Like she was now. And here, all this time, she assumed she'd played it cool. It was clear she had not.

"What? No." She was in trouble, that's what she was. She took the robe, which was dripping wet, and used it as a shield for her body. She shivered at the warm water on her chilled skin. Or at least that was the story she was sticking to. "Sorry, I'm just a little confused. You're Darcy's brother-in-law who rented my place?"

"Is that a problem?"

A gigantic one. "No, I'm still a little startled." She was also panicked and thrown and incredibly turned on. "When Darcy called last week, saying her brother-in-law needed a quiet place to decompress, I thought it was Rhett, because of all the craziness surrounding his separation. I didn't even look at the signature on the lease. I just assumed …"

He lifted himself out of the pool, water slicing down his body, and she forgot what she was talking about.

"You're probably one of a handful of women in the world who wouldn't check out the famous Rhett Easton's signature. The rest of us only share his last name."

She shrugged, then grabbed the towel she'd intended on using and held it out for him, quick to pull her hands back when he took it. "More of a country fan myself."

"I'll add that to the list of things I like about you." He towel-dried his hair in a way that was all things manly, then wrapped the towel around his waist. It didn't help, his chest was still bare, his shoulders glistening in the moonlight, but it was his smile. That genuine and warm smile that always made her nervous. Because smiles could be deceiving.

"We barely know each other, so it must be a shortlist," she said.

"It has more than three items. Yours?"

She ignored this. "You weren't supposed to come until the tenth. Today's only..." she silently counted off all the activities she had accomplished this week and grimaced. "It's the tenth. I am so sorry. I lost track of the days. Well not the days, because Sammy and I are practicing days and he wakes me up every morning to tell me what day it is, but we haven't reached actual dates yet, which is why I'm here dressed in this, interrupting your swim."

"You aren't interrupting. In fact, the pool's a bit lonely with just me and my thoughts," he said. "You're welcome to join."

"Oh, I couldn't." She pulled on the robe, tightening the belt and sending drops of water splashing on the concrete. "The pool is part of the rental. It's for you. For the summer." God, every time she was around Clay she came off as having an IQ equivalent to a pack of gum.

His eyes locked on hers and held. It was the kind of stare that told her he was making a conscious effort not to look down. The kind of stare that made her nervous. She shivered again—but for a whole other reason.

"Are you aware that the robe is sheer when wet? And, um, clingy?"

"Oh my God." Her robe was more than sheer; it made a wet t-shirt contest seem tame. She had almost shucked the suit altogether. At least she'd kept on a bikini—a teeny tiny bikini that she only wore when alone. The last thing she'd ever want was

Clay to compare her to the cleat chaser in triangles and dental floss he was usually seen with. Then again, a muffin top might be less embarrassing than being caught in a swim-dress her grandmother would have worn.

"Are you saying I can't invite friends?" he asked.

"Of course not. It's your place to do whatever you want with whoever you want and, wow." She closed her eyes. "I just said that."

"You did."

Great, now she was sweating in uncomfortable places. "I meant that the pool is all yours. I already talked to Sammy about how we aren't to bother you while you're here. And if my uncle hounds you to join his poker night, he's trying to fleece you."

He smiled at that. "I'm a pretty good player."

"He cheats. Sleight of hand, card counting, stacking the deck. He was a professional hustler in New York before moving here. Some people call him a crook."

"What do you call him?"

"Uncle Eddie." That earned her a smile. "He's at the back room at the senior center, likely cleaning house. He's been banned from the VFW hall. Six times."

"I'll keep that in mind." He sounded as if her warning amused him. "As for the pool, I'll only need it early morning and at night for PT. Doctor's orders."

"Darcy told me about your surgery. How are you feeling?" Last winter, Clay had torn his ACL, taking him out for the rest of the season.

"Better by the moment."

She swallowed. "Let me know if there's anything I can do to make your stay easier."

"That's the plan." He pointed to his lower leg, but her gaze stopped much higher. "Not sure what you're offering to help with, but the surgery was on my knee."

Realizing she was staring, Jillian jerked her gaze upward, and when she met his eyes, he winked. *Oh boy.*

"What time do you want to eat breakfast?" she asked.

"Is that an invitation?"

"No. A homecooked breakfast is part of the package. You just tell me what time you want it, and I will make sure it's ready."

He smiled at that.

Oh my god, everything she says sounded sexual. "Where do you want to eat? Patio? Kitchen?"

"Kitchen's fine."

Why was she so ridiculously ruffled? She was too old and too tired to experience tingles. But there they were, zinging north and south of the equator.

Her phone rang and she checked the screen. It was Dirk.

She'd bet a pile of dry, non-see-through towels, her ex was calling because of a problem with Sammy. "Excuse me, I have to take this." Clay walked over to the table to gather his things and turned away. "Is Sammy okay?"

"You need to come and get him right now!"

Continue Summer Affair

NEWSLETTER

Get the inside scoop on upcoming appearances, giveaways, book releases, and all things Marina Adair delivered right to your inbox!

Don't wait, sign up today and join the club!

Sign Me Up!

XOXO,
   Marina Adair

ABOUT THE AUTHOR

Marina Adair is a *New York Times* and #1 National best-selling author whose fun, flirty contemporary romcoms have sold over a million copies. In addition to the Easton series, she is the author of the When in Rome series, the Heroes of St. Helena series, the Sugar, Georgia series, and the St. Helena Vineyard series, which was the inspiration behind the original Hallmark Channel Vineyard movies: *Autumn in the Vineyard, Summer in the Vineyard,* and *Valentines in the Vineyard*. Raised in the San Francisco Bay Area, she holds an MFA from San Jose University and currently lives in Northern California with her husband, daughter, and two neurotic cats. Please visit her online at MarinaAdair.com and sign up for her newsletter at www.MarinaAdair.com/newsletter.

Made in United States
North Haven, CT
05 August 2023